I0676406

GHOSTLY MELODIES

GHOSTLY MELODIES

The Dancing Princesses

R. L. STEDMAN

This is a work of fiction. Names, characters, businesses, places, events, lyrics and incidents are either the products of the author's imagination or used in a fictitious manner.

The Lady of Shalott is an excerpt from *The Lady of Shalott* by Alfred, Lord Tennyson. Written in 1832, this work is now in the public domain.

Copyright © 2018 RL Stedman

First Published 2018

All rights reserved

ISBN 9780473456504

Waverley*Productions*

www.rlstedman.com

Cover Design: Novak Illustration

Illustration ornamental break: oxygen64, DepositPhotos

To my four sisters
Allie, Fliss, Janet and Viv

My brother Russ

And my father, mother and stepmother

Because, you know – families.

❧ I ❦

BEFORE

𖤐 I 𖤐

RICCARDO KING SELLS HIS SOUL

AT NIGHT the desert felt cold, but during the day it was like walking in an oven.

Aunt Carlotta's ghost scolded him. "Foolish boy! You should be like a wild animal. Hide from the sun. Night is the time for movement, not the day." She added sadly, "Unless you wish to end up dead, like me."

Carlotta's old, too frail frame had been unable to keep up the pace, so she lay down and never got up. Riccardo had felt guilty for leaving her, but what choice did he have? If he had stayed beside her, he also would have died. So he left her curled up as a corpse on the desert sand and continued on with the others.

Evidently, Carlotta had not appreciated this, because after she died, her ghost arose and followed. Now she trailed beside Riccardo as a small, scolding presence. Sometimes he was grateful for her company, but mostly he wished she'd be quiet. He needed his energy to keep moving one foot in front of the other.

"Is not as though I had a choice, Auntie," he said out loud.

Ernesto, in front of him in the line, paused. His hand flickered. *Silence!*

Riccardo shut his mouth but continued the argument in his head. *They walk so fast. If I don't keep up with them, I'll be left behind. Is that what you want, Auntie? For me to die too?*

Carlotta fell silent, and Riccardo smirked. Ha! He had bested her! Of all his family, he, Riccardo King, had finally won an argument with Aunt Carlotta. Of course, she was dead, but even so ...

The leader, a squat Mexican with a scarred face and a cast eye, held up a hand. *Stop!*

The convoy stopped immediately. Riccardo, standing in the baking sunlight, was suddenly aware of the sharp scent of crushed creosote leaves, the ugly smell of death (Carlotta hadn't been the only one taken by the desert) and the baking heat on his skin. And, in the distance, the deep thrum of a helicopter.

"Patrol!" yelled the Mexican. "Hide!" He dived under a thorn bush.

Ernesto and the others followed.

"They are fools!" scoffed Aunt Carlotta. "Look! That plant will not hide them."

Riccardo hesitated. His aunt had a point; the shrub gave little cover.

She tugged ineffectually on Riccardo's sleeve. "Nephew! Those patrol-men carry guns! You must hide!"

"Hey!" Ernesto waved at him urgently. The rotors grew louder.

Riccardo saw a shelf of red rock, half exposed in the sand, with a low overhang. Could he fit beneath it?

"Hurry, little sluggard!" Carlotta snapped.

Riccardo slipped under the overhang, sliding on the pleasantly cool sand, just as the helicopter passed overhead.

"This is a good place," said Carlotta approvingly, "but I wish–"

Her voice was drowned by the sharp *rat-tat* of an automatic rifle, firing at close range.

Cowering beneath the rock, Riccardo stuffed his fingers in his ears, closed his eyes tight. Above the dreadful din he thought he heard the Mexican shout and – was that Ernesto's voice, scream-ing? – but he didn't dare look. Instead, he burrowed into the shadow, like a snake, like a wild desert creature. He focused on his breathing. *In. Out. In. Out.*

"You should pray to Our Lady," Aunt Carlotta said. "She will protect you."

"How can you say that?" he shouted, loud above the guns. "She did nothing for you. Nothing!"

Carlotta did not reply, and Riccardo knew he was right. No sense in trusting to God, or praying to Our Lady; a man makes his own luck. He clenched his fists so hard that his fingernails drew blood from his palm.

One day, I will be powerful. I will be rich. And everyone will know my name.

Softly, he tried to hum small melodies of childhood; snatches of the songs his long-dead mother had once sung to him. Hands over his ears, he rocked slightly to and fro, like a babe in a cradle. But the roar of the guns intruded on those half-formed memories until finally he took his hands away and howled defiance at the sky:

> *"Running from the thunder*
> *What a way to die*
> *Resting in the sweet earth*
> *As lightning splits the sky."*

These words, where had they come from? Perhaps a teacher had read them to him as a poem, in the time before the soldiers burned the books.

The gunfire formed a fierce echo to the pounding of his heart. And, as the guns blazed; as his friends died. Riccardo shouted:

"Imprisoned in a barred cage
Clawing at the sky
Raging as the hunters pass –
'I don't want to die!'"

Faintly, he thought he heard Carlotta singing, and imagined she was beside him, stroking his hair, just as she'd done when he was a child. But her words brought little comfort.

"You might escape the thunder,
But you're not too young to die."

HOW LONG RICCARDO LAY THERE, he couldn't say. Gradually the noise, the spurts of hot dust, the twanging of bullets became distant, like something heard through glass. Slowly he relaxed, falling toward his future.

As he drifted into sleep, surrounded by the scent of death and gunpowder, Riccardo King realized this truth: music has great power. Music could take away fear. It could calm a troubled soul. Music could change the way the world was, and perhaps, it could change a man's heart. Whatever I do with my life, he thought, I will combine these things: music, and power.

"No!" whispered his aunt. "Music comes not from power! Music comes from love!"

But she was dead, so was not important, and Riccardo ignored her. Finally, he drifted off to sleep.

Riccardo never heard the helicopter leave. He didn't hear the groans of the dying or the Mexican's broken pleas for water. Instead, in his dreams he heard whispers of song, the strumming of a guitar and the roar of an adoring crowd.

He woke much later, when the sun was low.

"Hello," said a calm voice. A man stood above him, his figure silhouetted against the darkening sky. His golden eyes, slit horizontally like a cat's, reflected the setting sun.

Riccardo blinked up at him, too surprised to feel fear. Was this a ghost? A figment of his imagination?

The man smiled slightly and squatted beside him. "I heard your singing." He held out a hand. "We came to help you."

"We?" Riccardo asked. "Who is 'We'?"

The man glanced behind him. "Oh. My apologies, Riccardo King. I had forgotten you could not see us."

"You know my name?"

"Of course. And we long to hear your music."

The tall man turned and waved, and a crowd appeared behind him. Tall, slim people with skin as pale as ghosts. They stood motionless as statues, but their eyes – *ah their eyes!* – glowed golden.

"Come," the stranger said again. "Will you not join us?"

"No," Carlotta moaned. "Do not!"

But Riccardo ignored her and scrambled awkwardly from the hollow. His legs were stiff and cramped, so the stranger had to help him to his feet.

"Who are you?" Riccardo asked, rubbing his calves.

In the dim light, he could make out Ernesto. The man's open eyes stared up at the sky and behind him lay the Mexican's bloody body.

"My name is Evan. These are my people."

The desert still felt warm from the sun, but the wind was growing cold and Riccardo shivered.

"We seek music," Evan said, twirling in a circle. "Music of power; of mystery. Music of grace and blood."

"In the middle of a desert?"

"Wherever it may be found. You wish to get across the border, Riccardo King?"

Riccardo nodded slowly.

"Then I make with you a bargain. Sing for us. And we will see you safe across the border."

The flies buzzed about the dead. Riccardo shuddered.

"This is not a good bargain," Carlotta whispered. "Do not listen to them. They are *el demonio*!"

And I would make a bargain with the devil, Riccardo thought, if it took me out of here. "All you want is music?"

"All?" Evan smiled. His teeth were pointed and sharp, like a tiger's. He licked his lips: a hungry tiger. "Ah, not all. No. But we can speak about that later, you and I. But first, the music, Riccardo King." Above his head, the full moon shone brightly.

This is a dream, thought Riccardo. I am still asleep.

"Exactly," purred Evan. "This is all imagination. So," he stepped closer to Riccardo, "What's the harm in sharing? Just a little music ..." he sniffed, like a dog scenting water. "Just a. Very. Little."

"And you will see me safe into America?"

"Oh, Riccardo King," Evan clapped his hands, spun about excitedly. "That is not all we will do!"

"No!" Carlotta snapped. "Do not listen to them."

But she was dead and had no power. Riccardo ignored her.

Riccardo held up a finger. "One song."

"Agreed," said Evan, licking his lips.

Evan and his tribe squatted silently, motionless in the moonlight as Riccardo stood tall among the dead and sang:

> *Why have wings if you won't fly?*
> *Why stand staring at the sky?*
> *Lift your arms to soar up high*
> *Someday we'll be together, you and I.*

It was an old song, sung with a light, swaying beat. Sometimes Riccardo imagined how the melody would sound with a flute and drums. Flute and drums were not traditional, he knew, but whatever. Just like life, music must change and grow.

The strange people sat silent; only their fingers quivered in time to the music. When he finished, there was a long low sigh.

"Another," murmured the crowd. "Another."

Riccardo shook his head. "We made a bargain."

Inside, he heard Carlotta moan.

Evan rose gracefully to his feet. "That was beautiful, beautiful! You are a true musician, Riccardo King."

"You are a foolish, arrogant child!" said Carlotta viciously. "I wash my hands of you!"

"Do not listen to your aunt," said Evan. "She is old; she does not understand. You and I, we know that music is the key to power. Oh, Riccardo King, together we will make such music that the world will dance." Loudly, he sang: *"I'm sure we'll be together, by and by."*

"Nephew!" moaned Carlotta.

"Your aunt is dead," said Evan, "and what use is a dead woman? I, however," he added practically, "am very much alive and thus extremely useful. Also, I am extremely generous."

Aunt Carlotta, wavering and transparent, stared at Riccardo sadly. "You must not listen to him," she said. "He is evil."

"Tell her to go," whispered Evan. "And she will leave."

"I'm sorry," said Riccardo to his aunt, who had raised him as a boy and spent her savings and her life to bring him here, "but it is time for you to go."

Her ghost glared at Riccardo. "One day, nephew, you will regret this."

"You heard him," said Evan to the ghost. "Now, begone!" He waved his hand, and with an angry hiss, Aunt Carlotta vanished.

Evan held out a hand to Riccardo. "Come!"

Evan's slender fingers, tipped with long nails, looked like claws. But Riccardo clasped the hand anyway.

And, just like that, Riccardo King lost his soul.

2

ZOE BANKS DISCOVERS CELEBRITY

Excerpt: *The Daily Chronicle*, Crevasse Gap, NE:

Local Girl Wins State Competition

After learning she's reached the national competitions of Amazing Talent!, *Zoe Banks (21) is still in shock.*

When asked about the secret of her success, Zoe laughs. "My Mom. She's been fantastic!"

Amazing Talent!, *America's latest and greatest talent show, has taken the nation by storm. The show first involves performers battling it out on social media, until only one from each state remains. And then comes the hardest stage of the competition – the nationals.*

"The state comps were tough, but national? That's a whole new level," says Zoe.

This stage of the competition isn't judged by the public via social media. Instead, a discerning panel of judges will have the final say on which performers will go through to the next round.

The identities of the judges are a closely guarded secret, but this year, Riccardo King, the celebrated music producer, is rumored to be on the panel.

"*There are three rounds of competition,*" *Zoe says.* "*The quarter-finals, one semi-final and then the finals.*"

The competitions begin next summer in San Francisco, while the finals will be held in New York in the fall.

But Zoe isn't thinking that far ahead. "*Mom says: do your best. Everything else is up to God.*"

We're sure with God and her mom by her side, Zoe will go far.

𝄞

Excerpt: Television interview with Carole Healey, *Great American Music.*

Charley Banks shakes her head, and her bronze-tipped braids catch the light. "*Me? Teach Zoe to sing? Hell, no! Never needed to teach her nothing. Zoe, she was born singing! When she was small, we spent a lot of time on the road. I'd do gigs, and we'd travel about, you know? We sure did a lot of singing in that camper.*"

Carole Healey, the polished, shiny interviewer, raises perfect eyebrows. "*You lived in a camper?*"

"*Sure. Traveled all over, Memphis to Maine. But when Zoe got older, I rented us a house. Ain't good to be moving kids about much, too hard on their schooling. My dad was in the army. I sure wasn't about to do that to my own kid. School's where Zoe 'learned' music.*" *Charley makes air quotes.* "*Piano, violin, guitar: you name it, she can play it. Some folks have the gift of music, and others don't. Zoe, she has it.*"

Carole Healey turns to the camera. "*And don't we know it, folks? Zoe Banks, only twenty-one, will be competing in the quarter-finals for Amazing Talent! The competition rounds begin in only four months, and I, for one, can't wait!*"

"*Zoe will win,*" *Charley butts in, then coughs.* "*She's real determined, Zoe is.*"

Carole laughs. "And she's got a great supporter in her mom."

Charley's still coughing, but she nods.

Carole hands her a glass of water. "You okay, honey?"

Charley sips the water slowly and nods. "Sorry. Just wanted to say — been Zoe's number one fan since, well. Since forever."

❀ 3 ❀

JUBILEE JOHNSON MEETS A
DAMSEL IN DISTRESS

IN SPRING, Jubilee Johnson left the army and spent the summer traveling. At first, he'd planned to hitch, but standing on the side of the road with a thumb out wasn't as easy as the movies made it look; very few folks seemed willing to give him a lift. Eventually, he bought himself a Greyhound pass and climbed aboard. He planned to travel coast to coast: begin in NYC and end in LA. Seemed fitting somehow, sea to shining sea and all that.

On Sunday his bus pulled into a small town in Eastern California. In the early summer sunlight, the place looked strangely charming, with brightly painted wooden buildings surrounded by green forest. On a whim, he got off the bus to see the place. Half an hour later he wished he hadn't bothered. Everything was closed except for a gas station selling hotdogs. After wandering up and down Main Street, peering into store windows, he returned to the laundromat that doubled as the bus station.

"When's the next bus out?" he asked the clerk through a mouthful of tasteless dog.

"Where you want to go?"

"LA."

She peered at her computer screen. "Next bus to LA is at three o'clock."

"Three o'clock? But that's two hours away!"

"Sir? You want a ticket?"

"I guess."

The clerk glanced disapprovingly at his hotdog. "You'll have to eat that outside." She pointed at a sign on the wall, white capitals on a black background:

NO FOOD

NO BEGGING

NO PANHANDLING

NO SMOKING

"What's panhandling?" he asked, curious.

She shrugged.

"Okay. One ticket to LA," he said. "And yeah, I'll eat outside."

Jubilee finished his dog and returned to the waiting area. Through a grimy glass window, he could see into the laundromat. The place stank of diesel and washing powder, a strange mixture. Mostly, his fellow passengers appeared to be elderly women or down-on-their-luck families. Some played on their phones, a few chatted slowly, odd fragments of conversation that drifted over the drumming of the washing machines. Outside, thick clouds covered the sun. Perhaps it might rain.

What would it be like, living in this town? Seemed like the back of beyond. Jubilee yawned, pulled out his Lee Child and slouched back in the chair.

The room began to fill up slowly around him, but Jubilee barely noticed; he was caught up in adventure. Jack Reacher had been the inspiration for his road trip, and although life on the road had turned out to be nothing like the stories, Jubilee still enjoyed reading them.

A sound made him look up. A dark-skinned girl with a shock of black curly hair and a sweetly heart-shaped face was extracting a guitar from a battered case. As she began to tune it, other travelers lifted their heads. A couple of kids drifted over as the girl pushed the open case forward with a foot.

As she struck the first chords, the clouds parted and the sun came out. Golden rays struck the dirty windows and for the strangest moment, Jubilee felt as though he was sitting in a palace, while about him motes of golden dust twirled like tiny angels. He put down his book.

> *"On each side of the river lies,*
> *Long fields of barley and of rye,*
> *They clothe the wold and meet the sky;*
> *And through the field the road runs by*
> *To many-towered Camelot."*

Her clear voice caught the echoes, resounding through the tattered building. It was like listening to an angel sing, but he thought as he watched her that he'd never seen anyone so sad.

> *"And up and down the people go,*
> *Gazing where the lilies blow*
> *Round an island there below,*
> *The island of Shalott."*

The song told of magic and enchantment, rather like a fairy-tale come to life and Jubilee found himself fascinated by its melancholy and mystery. When it ended, the audience clapped enthusiastically. Some tossed coins into the music case. Jubilee strolled over, dropped in a fifty-dollar note.

Her eyes widened when she saw it. "Thank you," she said. "But that's too much." She picked it up, held it out to him.

He pushed her hand back. "Keep it."

She hesitated. "You sure?"

He nodded. "Definitely."

She smiled again, a gorgeous, heart-stopping smile, and for a moment the sorrow in her eyes lifted. "Thank you," she breathed, "*so* much."

"You're most welcome."

She tuned the guitar again, smiled at the people waiting. "Any requests?"

"You know any songs from *Moana*?" asked a tiny girl.

She smiled. "Sure."

As she launched into the song – the girl clapping and singing along with her, much to the enjoyment of the crowd – a burly security guard pushed his way through the door and stood in front of the singer, thumbs thrust through belt loops and his fat stomach level with her eyes. The tiny dancer twirled to a stop and the guitarist stopped playing.

"See that sign there, miss?" the guard asked, nodding at the white capital letters on the wall. "No begging."

"I'm not begging."

"Sure you are," he said. "Folk come up and give you money. I saw it. Makes it begging to me." He hitched up his belt.

"I'm playing. Busking. Street performing."

"Asking for money, ain't you? That's enough. So. Knock it off. And give the folks their money back."

"What?"

"You heard me."

"Hell no, sweetie," called a woman. "You keep that money. I done give it to you, and I say it's yours."

There was a low growl of agreement from the crowd. The room was filling up; a number of spectators drifted over. Jubilee wondered if the guard would back down.

A fat woman wagged a finger at the security guard. "That girl, she plays like an angel. An angel! And you're trying to shut her down!"

"Now, Ma'am, that's enough."

"Don't you 'Ma'am' me."

The guard put a hand on his sidearm. "I said, that's enough."

No, no, no, thought Jubilee. Don't go getting involved. But his legs weren't listening, for they were already walking him over to the guard.

"Officer," he said, in his best sergeant's tone, "is there a problem?"

The Voice, Whittaker had called it: snappy, authoritative, with a hint of concealed violence. The guard heard it and blinked.

Jubilee held out a hand. "Sergeant Johnson."

The security guard shook it blindly.

"You got a problem, son?" One hand, heavy and calming, on the man's shoulders. A solid, comforting weight. A weight that said *I am bigger and stronger than you, mess with me, I'll knock you into kingdom come.*

The guard swallowed. A CO had once said to Jubilee, "Built like the back of a barn, you are, son. Bet none of the boys give you any trouble."

"No sir, no trouble," he'd replied.

No trouble now, either, for the guard, tugging at his collar, seemed to deflate.

"Lady's breaking company rules," he said, then added, "Sir."

"I'm sure she didn't know," Jubilee said, glancing in the direction of the singer, hurriedly scooping up her change and notes from the guitar case.

The bus pulled up outside, and the guard had to shout above the noise of the engine. "But Sir, the money?"

"Let it go, soldier," said Jubilee softly. "It isn't much, and the folks seem happy for her to keep it."

The girl clicked the case shut.

"I dunno," said the guard. "Seems like begging to me."

"You tone deaf?" Jubilee asked. "It was nothing like begging."

"Never been much for music, that's true."

Jubilee grabbed the guard's limp hand and shook it vigorously. "That there's my bus. Thank you, son. You've done a good thing."

The guard, unconvinced, grunted. "Have a good trip, Sir."

Jubilee picked up his rucksack and book and climbed aboard.

"Wait!" The girl, her guitar case over her shoulder, ran up to him. "Thank you so much. What's your name?"

"Jubilee, Ma'am," he said, climbing the stairs.

She smiled her beautiful smile again, and said, "You going to LA?"

He nodded. "And you?"

"San Francisco," she said, waving a ticket. "Next bus. Thanks to you."

"You were singing to get the money for your *bus ticket*?"

"Sure. Yeah."

"Okay. Well. Have a good trip." He hesitated, wondering what she was doing in San Francisco.

"You too. And thanks. For the money and everything."

As the bus drew away from the station, the fat lady gave him a thumbs-up, and the girl ran alongside the bus, still waving. So, as the bus drew out into the traffic, the last view he had of that nameless, godforsaken town, was the most beautiful girl in the world, standing and smiling at him.

Jubilee felt a sudden, inexplicable joy, and settling back on the headrest, he closed his eyes, smiling. LA would be great. He knew it. Shame he hadn't got her name. But man, she sure could sing.

❧ 4 ❧
AMAZING TALENT!

EARLIER:

"You're entitled to a father, honey."

"I don't *want* a father."

Charley coughed. Zoe turned her face away. She couldn't bear to see her Mom like this.

"I don't get it," she said. "Why not just write to him?"

"What you think I've been doing?"

"What? Why didn't you tell me?"

"'Cos there weren't nothing to tell," Charley said. "I email – no answer. So, I write, old-fashioned like. My letters get returned unopened. I phone; they hang up. I see a lawyer, he say ain't no chance, not without a paternity test. 'How's that going to work,' I ask, 'when I can't never see the father?' Lawyer say, 'sue him.'" She snorted. "Like that's going to work – him with all his money. No, honey. This way is best." She stroked Zoe's hair with her thin, thin hand. "I got it all worked out. You gotta sing *Storm's Eye*, baby girl. I know he'll recognize it. He'll have to acknowledge you then."

Zoe sighed and plumped up Charley's pillows. "How do you even know he's on the judging panel?"

Charley tapped the side of her nose. "Little birdie done tell me. Oh, he's on it, all right. Strangest thing," she added reflectively. "Riccardo was real funny about music. Couldn't lie, not when there was a song involved. Like he was superstitious. Mind you, he got no trouble lying at other times. Okay, girl? You sing that song; he have to respond."

Zoe didn't care about her father, or his money or his fame. They were managing plenty well enough without him. "Mom. Why this? And why now?"

"Baby, he's rich. Connected. You want to be a singer? That man, he can help you."

Zoe shook her head. "I don't want his help."

Mom smiled. "Come a time, you might feel differently."

Zoe put her head on Mom's shoulder and felt her thin chest rise and fall. She wanted to stay there forever.

$$\oint$$

LATER:

Amazing Talent! A talent show like no other. Broadcast on network and cable, social, YouTube and app. Audience in the millions. To reach the nationals was huge.

Mom had acted like it was just a matter of time before Zoe made it this far, but Zoe had never really believed her. Sometimes, she still didn't believe it – these past five months seemed a dream.

First, the media hype, the excitement, and Mom's excited face glowing with pride. But then she'd fallen sick. Amazingly, Zoe had managed to keep Mom's short, vicious illness from the media. Probably, it helped that the candidates had been embargoed from giving interviews.

And after that, there had been a funeral to arrange and Mom's affairs to settle.

By the time the quarter-finals rolled around, Zoe had lost

interest in the competition. But what the hell, after all, Mom had wanted her to go. It was the thought that she might not be resting easy that spurred Zoe to pack a duffel and take the bus to San Fran. Perhaps she wouldn't make it in time, but that wouldn't be her fault, would it? But folks had been kind – one man had even given her a fifty-dollar note! So here Zoe was in San Francisco: backstage in a sequined dress with her hair all shiny-sleek and her stomach in knots.

A knock on the dressing room. "Last call!" called the stage-hand. "Zoe Banks. Last call!"

Taking a deep breath, Zoe opened the door.

"Okay. You ready?" asked the stagehand.

Zoe wiped a hand on her skirt. The sequins felt prickly against her palm. "I guess."

They walked to the wings. The stagehand's breath smelt of gum and cigarettes, and his eyes were fixed on the cue board. "Full house tonight."

A full house meant a thousand people. Plus the cameras. Meaning a million, give or take, would be watching.

Zoe swallowed back the stage fright. *Please don't let me be sick.* The cue light flashed red.

"You're on, sweetheart," he said. "Knock them dead!"

The stage was plain: white lights, white backdrop, a red stool and her acoustic on its stand. In the wings, the stagehand gave a thumbs-up sign; the audience applauded. The cameras moved like dancers, tracking smoothly around Zoe as she picked up the guitar.

Checking the tuning, she looked out at the sea of faces, but the lights were too dazzling to see much beyond the edge of the stage. She could just make out the judges' table because the white cloth reflected the light.

"Hello," asked a bored voice from the table. "What's your name, darling?"

"Z-Zoe." She clutched the neck of her guitar. "I'm Zoe."

"Pretend you're singing to me," Mom had said. *"You can do that, can't you?"*

But Mom hadn't said anything about the lights, or the audience, or the heat. And, worst of all, she'd left out the tiny detail that she wouldn't be watching from the audience. Still, Zoe heard her: *"Sing to me, then, baby girl."*

"Okay. Zoe. What are you going to sing?"

Was this a trick question? "Um, a song?"

Laughter rippled through the auditorium. Lifting her jaw, Zoe faced the lights. The judge probably saw her as just another talent desperate for a lucky break. She felt stupid and ugly; too tall and too awkward. Too brown.

His voice was patient. "And the name of this song?"

Taking a deep breath, Zoe said firmly: "'Storm's Eye.' My mom wrote it. With my father."

"And is your mom here today?" he asked, sounding interested now.

She straightened her spine and stared out at the faceless judges. "No. She couldn't come."

"Thank you, Zoe. You may begin."

She could feel herself shaking with nerves, but she managed to lift the guitar to her lap, and begin. Perhaps Mom was listening from heaven. The thought calmed her, and the note came true and clear.

> *"In the eye of the storm,*
> *A lone gull flies.*
> *Wings so bright,*
> *They burn the sky.*
> *Fly high bird, fly*
> *Fly, oh fly.*
> *The storm clouds roll,*

The waves rise high,
Your bright wings,
Will touch the sky."

Mom had told her about the writing of 'Storm's Eye.' Zoe's father had been on tour. Each week she'd posted him a verse and later she'd receive the next verse in the mail. But then the letters stopped; he'd met another woman. So Mom left him. On a Greyhound bus to nowhere she finished the lyrics, and much later, after Zoe was born, she set them to music.

The song ended on a long, sustained A. The crash of applause made her jump and she bowed awkwardly, still holding her guitar, before exiting the stage. Behind her, the applause continued.

The stagehand grabbed her shoulder and spun her around. "What are you doing? Go back on. Go on!"

Feeling foolish, Zoe staggered back on stage as the audience laughed and cheered, and she bowed again and wished she could disappear. But eventually the applause died, and she turned to leave for real.

From the judges' table came a shout. "Hey! Wait!"

More laughter.

Zoe exhaled slowly. Wished she could run from the stage, listen to the judging from the safety of the wings. Glancing out across the faces and the dazzling stage lights, she wondered again: what the hell I am doing here?

Zoe could see a silhouette against the lights. A judge was on his feet. "That song. You said it was written by your mother *and* your father? What did you mean?"

She cleared her throat. "The words were written alternately. I mean, Mom wrote one verse and my father wrote the other. He was touring," she added, "in a band."

"I thought you said your mother wasn't here?" said the judge. "So, where is she?"

A mutter from the audience and the heads of the other judges turned to each other, as though they couldn't see the point of this question.

"Sir, my mother is dead," Zoe whispered. "She passed three weeks ago."

The stage lights blurred into stars. *Great, and now I have the pity vote.* Angrily, she wiped the tears away. "But she taught me the song."

There was a crash from the judge's table, as though a chair had fallen over, and in the wings the stagehands were muttering into their microphones.

"Her name?" the judge asked. "What was her name?"

"Charley," Zoe shaded her eyes against the lights. "Charley Banks."

There was a gasp from the audience as the judge leaped around the table and ran up the stairs, onto the stage. Stagehands, fingers pressed to their headphones, shouted to each other. Standing this close, Zoe could see the fourth judge was, as Mom and the media had predicted, Riccardo King. Music producer, one-time songwriter, drummer, rock star. He was portly, black-eyed, black-haired. In Mom's photos he had looked younger. And thinner.

Riccardo grabbed her shoulders, peered into Zoe's eyes. "Who are you?"

"Your daughter. So I'm told. Mom was pregnant when she left you."

"Pregnant?" he said. In the strong stage-lights, Riccardo's face was pale and gleamed with sweat. He looked stunned. "But ... she never told me."

"She wrote you. Didn't you know?"

"No. I never–" He broke off, looked about at the cameras and the stunned faces of the audience. "Listen, you gotta see. This is kind of overwhelming. And you sure about this?"

"I'm sure."

He swallowed, then opened his arms. "Well, come on. Hug your old man." As he embraced her, the crowd clapped and cheered. "Later," he whispered in her ear. "We'll talk later."

"One thing you gotta understand, baby girl: don't you going trusting him. Whatever he says, no matter how kind – he is thinking of himself and how best to get what he wants. Never, ever forget that."

"Perhaps he's changed," Zoe had said.

Charley snorted. "Men like Riccardo don't change. They just get smarter. You listen to me, honey. Don't you trust him. Not for a moment."

Now, Zoe stood awkwardly in her father's embrace. What should she do? Should she show some family warmth and hug him back? Into her ear, he asked, "How old are you? Nineteen? Twenty?"

"Twenty-one," she said.

Riccardo tensed, then glanced over his shoulder at the cheering crowd. "The advertisers are going to love this. Listen, honey, I'm not admitting nothing, but we'd better play this out. Ladies and gentlemen," he shouted, adding to the stunned stage-hands, "Pass me a mike, won't you?" He thumbed it on, tapped it, and called: "Ladies and gentlemen! May I present – my long-lost daughter!" Covering the mike, he added "Your name, honey? What's your name again?"

"Zoe."

"Zoe," he shouted. Father and daughter embraced again.

The applause was deafening. The audience was on its feet; the concert-hall rang with cheers and screams.

Finally, going to the front of the stage, Zoe held up her hand. Eventually, the noise subsided. She turned to her new father, spoke clearly for the microphone. "You wrote this song?"

Riccardo smiled. "I did."

"Then," Zoe picked up her guitar. "You should sing it with me. Please?" She held out her hand. "Mom would have so loved that."

The audience cheered again.

As Zoe and her father sang together, Zoe thought: It went just like Mom planned.

Later, Zoe played the video clips. There were hundreds online, some from better vantage points than others. In all of them, despite his tears, and his professions of excitement, Riccardo did not look happy to meet her. If Zoe were to guess, she would say he was terrified.

II

DURING

5

THE AMAZEMENT OF JUBILEE JOHNSON

JUBILEE SLEPT the afternoon away on the bus, but by sunset he was sitting on a bench at Venice Beach, staring out at the shining Pacific Ocean. The sea itself didn't look that different to the Atlantic, but L.A was sure different to the East. Everyone here seemed to be exercising: rollerblading, bench-pressing, surfing. There were even folk out on the sand doing Tai Chi. He felt almost sinful sitting here. Then a bikinied rollerblader flashed by, and he smiled. There were worse places to be. He put his feet up on his rucksack and surveyed the beach with interest.

An old white woman with frizzy gray hair was tugging a shopping trolley with a faulty wheel along the sidewalk. She neared him, tipped her head uncertainly and asked, "Mind if I sit?"

She wore a shapeless blue dress under a plastic raincoat, slippers on her feet, and her trolley was full of rustling plastic bags. Her eyes, half-hidden behind enormous black glasses, looked tired.

Jubilee shuffled along the bench. "No problem, Ma'am."

"Thank you," she said, and sat down – plop – on the bench. With a grunt she poked about in her shopping bags. Extracting a piece of cardboard, she fluttered it about her face like a fan. He turned his face away from the smell.

"My, but it's a hot one," she said. "Heat bother you, honey?"

"No. I like it," said Jubilee.

"Ah, there's some as like the heat, and others that don't." Beads of sweat were trickling down her neck, and she sat with her knees wide apart, so he had an uncomfortable view of her thighs. "I'm Helen." She held out a hand. "Helen Mackenzie. What's your name, dear?"

Shaking Helen's damp hand, Jubilee replied: "Johnson. Jubilee Johnson, Ma'am."

"Nice to meet you, I'm sure."

They sat for a moment, Jubilee wondering where he would sleep that night. Whittaker had settled here, and Jubilee had thought of looking him up, but LA was a big city, might be hard to find him. Besides, the shabby streets of Venice made him twitchy – too much garbage lying about. Trash bags were always a potential bomb, but not here, not here. He hoped, anyway. But on his way from the bus station he'd walked along wide streets, just to be sure.

"Now, and since we're acquainted," said Helen, holding out a pink metal flask, "you wouldn't be so kind as to fill this for me? There's a fountain just over there."

He regarded the flask. It had flowers with thick pink petals on it. Her hand, the one holding the container, shook slightly.

"Not at all, Ma'am."

"You've got a good heart, Mr. Johnson. I can always tell these things." She handed him the flask, and he took it obediently to the fountain for her.

When he returned to the bench he stopped. "What the ...?"

Two more old ladies had settled themselves on either side of Helen. They smiled politely at him.

"Don't be angry, dear," Helen said. "These are my friends. This is Carlotta." She nudged the Latino woman on her left. Carlotta grinned a gap-toothed grin and waved a hand. "And this," she added, pointing to the woman on her other side, "is Inge. She's German."

"I am Austrian," said the long-nosed woman. She nodded unsmilingly at Jubilee.

Helen shrugged. "All the same. Oh, thank you dear." She held out her hand, and as though in a dream, Jubilee found himself passing her the cold, water-filled flask.

"It is *not*," snapped Inge. "Austria and Germany, they are different places."

Helen waved a hand at Jubilee. "Ladies? What do you think of the soldier?"

Carlotta, round as a berry and brown as a nut, winked at Jubilee. She had gold rings in her ears and a red and white head-scarf. "Maybe." She tipped her head, considering him. The gold hoops flashed in the setting sun. "Perhaps. I am not certain." Her voice was strongly Hispanic.

"What do you mean?" Inge asked. She was as thin as a rail, and her gray hair was the same color as her skin, her skirt, and her blouse. Even her eyes were gray. "He is perfect!" She considered Jubilee. "And how old are you?"

"Twenty-three, ma'am," he said. "No. Twenty-four."

Inge raised an eyebrow. "You do not know? How is it that you are not certain of your own age?"

"Well, um," Jubilee stammered.

"You're too hard on him, Inge," Helen said, smiling reassuringly at Jubilee. "The poor dear's just left the army. He's not used to thinking for himself."

Jubilee wanted to run, get far away from these crazies, but his feet seemed glued to the pavement. The noise of the people on the beach, the wind in the palms, even the waves, was weirdly muffled. As three pairs of eyes considered him, he felt like a soldier at a court-martial. The old women, the shopping trolley, the rustling plastic bags felt surreal. Like this was happening in a dream or something. He had a horrible vision of kidnapping, and an even more unlikely one of sex slavery.

Inge choked and Carlotta laughed.

"Oh dear," said Helen, wiping her eyes. "You poor thing! No, no. *That* is the last thing on our minds. Although," and she paused, "I daresay we could make an exception."

At that, the two other women broke into howls of laughter. Jubilee felt himself blushing.

Inge held up a hand. "Enough!" she said sternly, and abruptly the laughter stopped. "We apologize," she said to Jubilee. "We were, how do you say it? Teasing. Yes. We were teasing you."

"*Exactamente*," said Carlotta, wiping her eyes. "And we are very sorry. We were having fun."

"We are harmless," said Helen, inserting the container into the shopping trolley. She paused, then added, "Most of the time. So, ladies. What do you think? Has he met the criteria?"

"Criteria? What criteria?" Jubilee said.

"There was a test, dear."

"Test?"

Inge nodded. "*Ja*. He is ideal."

Jubilee stared at her.

"*Si*," Carlotta said. "'e is perfect."

"A soldier," said Helen, "and helpful. As we have seen." She indicated the dripping water flask.

"We have for you a gift," Helen said, rummaging through the plastic bags.

"I don't want a gift," Jubilee said, wishing he could just disappear. "I don't want anything."

Helen glanced at him, her strange eyes bright, and for a moment he felt himself falling, falling. Then she smiled and he was back in the evening sunlight. On the sidewalk beside him skateboarders raced past, and beyond the palms, ocean waves washed in and out.

"Here it is," said Helen, taking a long length of black cloth from a bag.

She held it up, and the sea breeze caught it, filling it like a flag. The fabric shimmered, shining like a night full of stars; like the desert just before the dawn.

Jubilee was transfixed. He'd never seen anything like this, ever. The way it gleamed and twisted, writhing like a living thing.

"What is it?" he asked.

Carlotta tssked. "There are instructions. Inge?"

"Ah, in here, somewhere," Inge said, and took the bag from Helen.

Helen handed Jubilee the length of fabric. It spilled over his arms, and he had to tug at it to stop it falling on the ground. It felt surprisingly heavy. But when he glanced at it, it was almost as though it wasn't there; as though his outstretched arms were empty. He blinked again, and there it was, darker than night, and filled with stars.

"What is it?" he asked again.

"Here we are," Carlotta said brightly, holding up a square of paper. "Instructions. And soldier, you can carry it in here." She produced a brightly colored carry bag. On the side was written: *A Present From Venice Beach.*

"A carry bag is not necessary," said Inge loftily. "Also, it is more effective if held close to the body. The piezo-electric effect ..."

"Oh pfft!" Carlotta held up her hands. "He cannot walk about LA carrying this thing. People will think he's *loco.*"

Helen nodded. "Jubilee, dear, keep it hidden."

Finally, Jubilee's voice returned. "Instructions to what?"

Helen glanced up at him mildly, "To the cloak, dear."

"Cloak? What cloak?" He could hear himself shouting.

A cop, half-hidden behind a palm tree, detached himself from its shade and walked toward them.

"Just put it in the bag," said Helen hurriedly. "Come on, dear."

Jubilee found himself shoving the dark mass into the carry bag. It moved sluggishly, slowly, like oil; not at all like fabric.

"Ma'am?" said the police officer. "This man bothering you?"

"Not at all," Helen said, squeezing Jubilee's wrist. "It's very hot here, officer," she added. "Why don't you go back to the nice shade?"

Her blue eyes glared at Jubilee from behind their heavy glasses. *Keep quiet!*

As instructed, the cop turned about and returned to the palm tree. The three women said nothing until he'd settled back into the shadow.

Helen smiled at Jubilee. "Now, dear. You'll keep it safe, won't you?"

"I guess so, ma'am," said Jubilee, still feeling dazed. He stood, for a moment, clutching the bag and barely able to speak, let alone think, while three pairs of eyes considered him.

"You are looking for work, are you not?" Inge asked, after a long pause.

"Not really, no."

Inge frowned, wrapped her cardigan about her scrawny chest. "You have just left the army, yes?"

He nodded.

"You were in it for, what, five years?"

"Yes, Ma'am."

"I know what it is like for men who leave the army. They drift. They grow fat. They become bored. This is true, yes?"

He was about to say not true at all, no. I like being a civilian. But something stopped him, and he sighed. "All true, Ma'am." And it was. He was bored.

"He's not fat," said Carlotta indignantly.

"Not yet," Inge said. "But you are already heavier than you were. Your waist, it grows wider, yes?"

Jubilee shrugged. It was true. He'd tried to tell himself it didn't matter, it happened to everyone, but still. He'd been proud of his condition, but then, he'd never had to make himself exercise, or watch what he ate; the army took care of all that. Now, he had to motivate himself all the time. Mostly, it was easier just to sit and look at screens than to make decisions. That was partly why he'd decided to travel. To give himself something to do.

Helen nodded. "Exactly. You need a job."

"Nearby is an office," added Carlotta. "Inside is a man. He is looking for someone like you. You go to him."

"What? Now?"

"*Si.* Now."

"Where is this office?"

"Not far. Down Washington." She waved at the road behind them. "Then second left. Is a side street. Very small. You see a cream-and-blue office. Called Arbor. You go in there, and say you're here about the job."

"After you take the job," Helen said, "you must be careful."

"Careful? How? *What* fucking job?"

There was an awkward pause.

"Sorry," he added sheepishly. "I didn't mean to – I shouldn't have cursed. I'm sorry."

"That is all right," Inge said. "We understand."

"You are good man," said Carlotta. "You have done some ugly things, but basically you are decent person. Listen to Inge. She is the cleverest of us."

He stared at her. *Who are you women, that I should do what you say?*

"Repeat your instructions," Inge demanded.

"I go down Washington," Jubilee muttered. "Second left. Cream-and-blue office called Arbor. I'm here about the job."

"Good. Very good."

When Inge beamed at him, Jubilee felt surprisingly proud.

"The sun is about to set," Helen announced. Stiffly, the old women rose to their feet. "You have the cloak," Helen said. "Use it wisely. And–"

"And do not trust him," said Carlotta quickly. "Not for a second. He has sold his soul."

Abruptly, almost unexpectedly, the sun dipped below the horizon. The golden hoops in Carlotta's ears flashed again, blinding him, and he blinked. When he looked again, the three women had disappeared. Only the shopping trolley, still full of its rustling plastic bags, remained. The water flask had vanished.

"Did you see that?" The cop stood beside him, staring at the shopping trolley. He shook his head. "Weirdest thing ever."

"That's for sure," agreed Jubilee. The bag in his right hand rustled as he heaved his rucksack onto his shoulders. "Say, can you direct me to Washington?"

"State or street?"

"Street," he said, although he wasn't sure. "Got a job interview."

The cop pointed south, down the beach. "Okay. Three, four blocks down. Washington Boulevard. Can't miss it. Chicken wing restaurant on the corner. This a cooking job?"

"Don't know," said Jubilee, walking away. "Don't rightly know what kind of job it is."

"Good luck then," called the cop.

Jubilee waved the bag of oily black fabric in reply.

❧ 6 ❧

JUBILEE MEETS AN OLD FRIEND

Jubilee found the side street without difficulty. The blacktop was cracked and ugly, and rubbish collection must be nearly due; the place was littered with trash bags. He eyed them nervously. Above, the sky was growing dark. Ping, ping, the streetlights flickered on. When he was a kid he'd loved to watch the lights turn on. Used to be a magical moment of the day. Not anymore. Now, the lights just made shadows. Shadows made him uneasy. Could find bad things, in the shadows.

His footsteps echoed from the concrete walls and his rucksack cut into his shoulder. Why would anyone set up a business here? But there was the sign, just as the old ladies had said: *Arbor Consulting*; cheap cream plastic hanging askew from a blue wall.

The door was made of frosted glass, with *PUSH* in large white letters. The frame stuck, so he shoved it open with his shoulder. A bell beeped a warning.

The office was painted in dingy yellow and the battered desk and chair were both a faded smoky-blue. Cream and blue, just as the old ladies had said. A dusty pot plant and last year's wall calendar. A humming copier. That was it: that was Arbor Consulting. Oh, and a laptop open on the desk.

"Just a second," a voice called from the back.

Jubilee set the plastic bag down beside the dying plant, and stepped quietly around the desk to the laptop. The screen was on, showing a dancing screen saver, but when he moved the mouse a password window opened. He sighed. Well, it would have been too convenient, wouldn't it?

At the back of the store a toilet flushed, and he stepped away from the desk and turned to the wall calendar. The Bahamas, he thought, taking in the photo. The calendar was from a trucking firm. Could this be a tax agent's office? Not a very successful one, then.

"Can I help you?" a voice said.

Startled, Jubilee spun about. "Holy hell!" he said, staring.

"Johnson!" said the man at the same time, and the next second they were pounding each other's backs in the manner of men long separated, and cursing in the style of army friendship.

Finally, Whittaker stepped back and looked Jubilee up and down. "Johnson!" He shook his head. "Just look at you! Look at you, man!" He grabbed Johnson by the shoulders. "What are you doing here?"

"Point of fact, don't rightly know."

"Heard you'd gone off the grid." Whittaker shook his head again. "All sorts of rumors. Some said you'd moved to the Caribbean. Someone said you'd gone to Australia."

"Australia? Why would I go there?"

"That's what I said. This calls for a drink. You want a beer?"

"Sure," Jubilee said, and indicated his rucksack. "Mind if I ...?"

"Oh yeah, of course, just set it down," Whittaker said, then disappeared out through the back door, returning a minute later with two bottles, water beads forming on their brown glass. He handed one to Jubilee. It was cold in his hand, slippery with condensation. He clinked it against Whittaker's, popped the cap and took a deep swallow.

"Sit, sit," Whittaker said, waving Jubilee toward the chair, as he perched on the edge of his desk.

Jubilee sat. Darn it, the chair was low. His knees were almost up about his ears. He grinned up at his old colleague. "What you doing here, Whittaker?"

"Got a business," Whittaker said proudly.

"No way! Doing what?"

"Protection."

Jubilee, about to take a sip, nearly choked. "You? Personal protection?" They'd hated the private security guys in Iran. Some, ex-army, had been all right, but most were just cowboys, treating the place like their personal Wild West. "You're kidding," he said.

Whittaker said defensively, "A man's got to eat, right?"

"True. I get it," said Jubilee, and took a drink of his beer. Cold.

"What you been up to then?" Whittaker asked.

"Nothing much. Wandering, mostly."

"So you just walked down this street – and bang, here you are?"

"Something like that."

"Another beer?"

Jubilee shrugged, a gesture that must have meant acceptance, for off Whittaker went, heading for the fridge at the back of the lock-up. Of course there was a fridge; of course it contained beer. Men like Whittaker didn't change. When his old comrade returned with his beer, Jubilee thought – they just get fatter.

As Staff Sergeant, Whittaker had been tough, and full of that wiry energy that some small men have. Well, that was then. Now, his buddy was still short, but no longer wiry. Jubilee finished the first bottle, accepted the second, and wondered what Whittaker thought about him. They'd both changed, that was certain.

"What brings you here?" Whittaker asked.

Jubilee told his friend about the long bus journey across the US, traveling West for no reason, except he'd never done it before. How he'd finally made it to the City of Angels, only to meet three old women. Who had sent him here.

"So here you are," Whittaker said. He hesitated, as though about to say something, then clapped his hand on his thighs. "So! You want to get something to eat?"

"Don't you have to be getting home?"

Whittaker shook his head. "Teena," he said heavily, "we separated. Last week."

"Shit! Oh man." Teena, Whittaker's wife, had been a kind, friendly person. "I'm sorry."

"Ah well," said Whittaker, but his voice was sad. "For the best, probably." He held out his hand to take Jubilee's beer bottle. "So. You want to get a bite?"

"Where are you staying?"

Whittaker jerked his thumb at the roof. "Upstairs. There's an apartment."

"I'm sorry about Teena."

"Not your fault," Whittaker said, the hurt naked in his eyes. "Just the army, you know."

Army divorces were almost a cliché. It was all down to the training, Jubilee thought. Aggression might be a useful trait in a soldier, but not so great in a relationship. He squeezed his old comrade's shoulder. "Yeah man. I know."

Whittaker took a deep breath. "Okay. Let's get some food."

"Sure. Yeah." Jubilee put the plastic bag onto the desk, where he'd be sure to see it again when he came in.

Whittaker jumped to his feet and ushered Jubilee from the office. Pulled down the roller door, locked it. "So," he said, dusting his fingers. "Where you want to eat, then?"

Jubilee shrugged. "I don't mind."

"Actually," Whittaker said, as they walked to his jeep, parked nearby, "I'm getting a better office."

"Where?"

"Different part of town." Paper blew about their legs, scrunched under their feet. "This is just temporary. Until I sort out the finances."

"Much demand for protection work in LA?"

Whittaker stared at him. "Is there much *demand*? This is L-frigging-A, man. Of course there's a demand."

"You do celebrities? Movie stars?"

"Some." Whittaker eyed Jubilee. "Actually – you looking for a job?"

"Protection work?" Jubilee shook his head.

He will offer you a job, Inge's voice whispered. Jubilee shivered.

Whittaker thumped him on the shoulder. "Well, think about it. You feel like Mexican?"

Later, seated at a table beside the ocean, Jubilee had to admit that LA wasn't all bad. Actually, he thought, as a group of Latino girls passed by, there were parts of it that were pretty okay.

"What are your plans, Johnson?" Whittaker asked.

"Don't rightly know." Jubilee took a swig of beer – the fifth bottle of the night. Five was all right. Just. Nice mellow glow, feeling good, feeling happy. Six beers, not so much. Eight, and he'd be throwing up into the sand. Better stop now. He signaled the waiter. "I'll have a coffee, thanks."

Whittaker glanced at the server, tapped his beer bottle. "Another. So?" He leaned blearily on the table and blinked at Jubilee. "Plans, my man? Got to have plans."

"Not me. No plans."

"What? You're not – homeless?"

Jubilee paused. Technically, he probably was.

The waiter placed a cup of coffee on the table, and Jubilee stirred it slowly. "In a way," he said. "I guess I am."

Funny, he'd never thought of it before. He'd just told himself he was traveling. But what if he never stopped traveling? What was it like, to not ever have a home? All those refugees, trundling about with their belongings in bags – oh, he'd seen them, lines and lines of them. Was he like that?

Whittaker tilted his head. "So. Not homeless, just not settled yet?"

The hot coffee burned his tongue. He blew on it gently. "I guess."

"Interested in working for me?"

"I don't know."

Whittaker blinked owlishly at him. "Don't you *like* me?"

"Yeah, sure. I like you."

"Great!" Whittaker pushed away from the table. "Come on, then. Gotta job for you. I'll show you." He counted notes onto the table. "Come."

"I'll drive," said Jubilee quickly.

As they walked back to the jeep, Whittaker didn't seem to notice the trash bags, the shadows, but Jubilee kept an eye out. Old habits. He wanted to ask Whittaker how he could act so casual, but the man was talking so fast he could barely get a word in.

"Weirdest damn shit I ever saw," Whittaker said. "And I gotta tell you, Johnson, LA is full of weird shit." They reached the office; he slid the roller door up and unlocked the door. "I'll show you–" He froze, and Jubilee saw the soldier inside the drunk: the held breath, the tension, the readiness for sudden, violent movement. He pointed at the plastic bag, set atop the desk. "Where did *that* come from?"

"I left it there. Sorry. Didn't mean to upset you."

Whittaker's shoulders relaxed, and he turned on the light as Jubilee picked up the bag.

The plastic rustled as Jubilee moved it and the black fabric spilled onto the carpet like an oil stain. Jubilee stuffed it back into the bag.

"Johnson? What's that you've got?" Whittaker asked.

Jubilee tugged out a corner of the fabric. It gleamed wetly in the bright light. "I don't rightly know. Those old ladies I told you about? They gave it to me."

"An old lady gave *that* to you?" Whittaker said, his voice unsteady. "What bullshit is this? Johnson, you know what it is?"

"A plastic bag."

"Not the bag, idiot. The stuff inside it."

Jubilee pulled the length of fabric out, held it up like a curtain. "What about it? It's just some material. Probably they picked it out of a dumpster. Liked the shine or something."

Whittaker opened his mouth, closed it again. "Some material?!" He shut his eyes. "Johnson. What you're holding? That's CAMO."

Jubilee's hand trembled, just a little, and the fabric seemed to dance with iridescence. But he shook his head. "No way. This ain't invisibility shit. Can't be."

C – A – M – O: Change, Acquisition and Modification Object. Long words to describe the indescribable. Even the scientists didn't know how it worked. Oh, they tried to explain it with long words like 'interdimensional' and 'probabilistic determination'. Some said it sent you elsewhere; others said it bent light.

The official report described Camo as emerging from military research, but Jubilee had heard other rumors: *Alien technology. Nano-tech. Gene-Mod.* Strands of Camo could be twisted into long threads and woven into fabric. But the platoon tasked with trialing it had called it 'the invisibility cloak' and that name had stuck.

It was a good description. When worn, Camo turned a soldier invisible. Not just hard to see – wear Camo and *nothing* could find you. Not radar, not infrared, not even good old-fashioned eyesight. A soldier wearing Camo totally disappeared. Field trials had begun, somewhere out in the Nevada desert: rumor had it an entire platoon had marched out in invisibility cloaks.

Jubilee had never seen Camo, but he'd heard the stories. Everyone had. It was an army legend – The Platoon That Disappeared.

Whittaker nodded slowly. "It is. That's Camo all right." He whistled. "Never thought I'd see it again."

"*Again?* You mean the stories are real?"

"Oh yeah." Whittaker nodded. "Yeah. It's real all right."

"Shit!" Jubilee said, and dropped the fabric. It lay in a black heap on the ground, like a stain. Or, he thought, like a hole.

The platoon had never returned. Army had sent out robots, tracker dogs. Satellites flew over the desert, drones orbited, they'd done 3D scans. They found some interesting archeological remains and a few unknown cave systems. Some sites used by drug dealers and a mighty concerning mass grave, at least twenty years old. But no soldiers. Not even footprints.

Turned out, the problem with Camo was that it *couldn't* be tracked. Were the poor squaddies dead, or just very far away? The scientists couldn't say; a soldier killed in Camo disappeared for good. Eventually, even the army had grown tired of waiting.

"They sent letters," said Whittaker. "You know?"

Jubilee nodded. He knew. *An unfortunate accident. We're very sorry, and here's your life insurance payout.*

"Mate of mine, his girlfriend was in that platoon," Whittaker said. "I thought the project was shut down." He shook his head, staring at the blackness on the floor. "I don't understand."

❦ 7 ❦

ZOE FINDS A PLACE TO STAY

ZOE NEVER MADE it to the semi-finals, simply because Riccardo, overcome with emotion, forgot to vote. So that was it, the publicists said. We're very sorry, but rules are rules. She was free to return home. But she mustn't give interviews about the competitions, nor talk about her competitors, not in any form whatsoever, not without the explicit consent of *Amazing Talent!*, such consent to be in writing. Sign here, Ms. Banks. All the best and you have a great day.

It all felt unreal. Go home, they had said, but where? Technically, she had no home, the lease having ended when Mom died. She thought about going back and packing up her and Mom's stuff (the landlord had pestered her to do so) but somehow she couldn't face it, not just yet. All Mom's clothes, her albums – no.

On the stage, after they'd sung together, Riccardo (too early to call him Dad) had told her he'd be in touch. Actually, he'd said, "I'll get my people to call you." As though he came with a crowd.

But his people never called. Although perhaps they couldn't get through – journalists, begging for interviews, left message after message on her phone, until Zoe turned the thing off. She left a note with the publicist, telling Riccardo she was going to LA and would meet him there.

So now she stood outside a high metal gate in a Beverly Hills street. The hot sun cast her sharply outlined shadow onto the concrete sidewalk. Above, palm trees rustled.

Zoe pushed the button on the speaker. "Um. Hello?"

"Yes? Can I help you?" The accent was British, the voice crisp and efficient.

"Um, it's Zoe Banks. For Riccardo."

"Is he expecting you?"

"Not exactly, no. I'm Riccardo's … um … daughter. You know, from the TV show?"

A pause. Then: "Look, I'm Riccardo's assistant. Valerie. I need to talk with Riccardo before I let you in. Where can I reach you?"

"I don't have a phone. The journalists."

"Well, I'm very sorry," said Valerie, not sounding a bit sorry. "But I do need to have instructions from Riccardo."

"He said he'd get his people to call me."

"He did? How very odd," Valerine said. There was another, longer pause, as though she was thinking. "I tell you what. Why don't you get another phone, and text me your number? Riccardo's away at the moment, but I'll talk to him, and as soon as I've heard from him I'll be in touch." The intercom crackled, then: "I'm afraid Riccardo is very strict about security."

A limousine drove past, its occupants turning their heads to stare at Zoe. She felt her face flushing because, with a guitar on one shoulder and a duffel slung over the other, she probably looked like a beggar.

"Hello?" Valerie asked.

Zoe just wanted to get away. "Okay, yeah. That's fine." She turned to go.

"Don't forget my number. You have a pen?"

"Oh," said Zoe, feeling stupid. "Hang on a minute." She fished in the rucksack pocket, pulled out a pen, and when the intercom told her the series of numbers, wrote them on her wrist.

"Where are you going now?"

Zoe shrugged. "Don't know. Find somewhere to stay, I guess."

"Venice," said Valerie.

"Sorry?"

"The beach. It's nice. And the hostels there are good value."

Zoe flushed. She was used to being poor, but it hurt that other people might recognize it through a speaker.

"I'm really most terribly sorry about this," Valerie said poshly. "But don't worry, I'll call in a day or two."

"Sure," said Zoe, wanting to punch the grill. "Well, bye."

IT WAS late afternoon by the time the bus reached Venice Beach. Zoe sat on a bench with her guitar on her lap. Listening to the waves breaking, she felt her soul relax. Absently, she began plucking the strings, Hawaiian-style double strumming, and just like that, from nowhere, came a melody.

A bare-footed woman hauling an enormous bag passed by. At the sound of Zoe's guitar, she paused. "Very nice." She looked to be in her seventies, and she smiled at Zoe from a mouth of broken teeth. "Hey *querida*, you new to town, *si*?"

Zoe nodded, and hoped she didn't look too obviously out of place.

"I know everyone on this beach," said the woman with simple pride. She wore a bright red bandana dotted with small white pineapples, and golden hoops in her ears. "You got a place to stay, no? Is not good, to have nowhere to rest the head."

"I thought I'd look for a hostel."

"Hostel not good," said the woman decisively. "Not safe. Many rough people." She hitched her bag higher. Her bare feet were deeply engrained with dirt, and even from this distance, Zoe could smell her rich scent of spice and cooking oil. "But don't worry," the woman said. "I help."

"Um, thanks, I guess."

"See the building down there? With the sun on it?"

Along the strip lay a narrow lo-rise, a boarded-up storefront at its base and blank black windows on its upper floors.

"I tell you secret," whispered the woman, looking about furtively, as though there might be eavesdroppers behind the palms. She dropped her voice lower. "Is empty."

"Oh," said Zoe uncertainly.

"*Si*. Very safe, very clean," said the woman proudly. "I have key." Fishing down her ample cleavage, she pulled out a small, shiny key. "See? You like?"

"I do. Yes. Absolutely." Zoe began packing up her guitar. "I have to go now, sorry."

The woman swung the key like a pendulum, and for a moment, watching it, Zoe felt dizzy.

"Take it. Is for you."

"Excuse me?"

The woman picked up Zoe's hand, pressed the key into it. The metal felt surprisingly cold. "For you."

"I can't ..."

"*Si*," said the woman. "You can." Still holding Zoe's hand, she reviewed her palm with an expert eye. "You have good heart."

"Do I? Oh, good."

"The hand never lies." She folded Zoe's fingers about the key. "You stay in my place." She nodded at the building. "Will keep you safe."

Zoe was tempted. Free lodging sounded nice, and if this woman was telling the truth it was safe enough. But was she really about to take a key from a strange, bare-footed woman? Yet something about her seemed familiar, and safe, and yes, trustworthy.

You got a good instinct for people, baby girl, Mom had said. Trust your instinct.

"What's your name?" Zoe asked.

"Me? I am Carlotta," said the woman, picking up her bag with a grunt.

"Can I help you with that?"

The woman grinned at her. "What do I say? Carlotta knows the heart. No, *carino*, I am fine." She walked off along the strip, leaving Zoe standing, still with the key clutched in her hand. Then she stopped. "Hey, girl. Cat okay?"

"Sorry?"

"In house is cat. Okay?"

"Yeah. A cat is fine."

"Name Helen. Very bossy."

The low sun laid strips of shadow across the bright pavement, and for a moment Carlotta seemed to almost disappear into the shade.

"Hey! Wait!" Zoe called, dangling the key on its string. "How do I get this back to you?"

Carlotta turned, holding her bag in both hands "Just leave in house. I find. Time to go now."

"Okay. Nice to meet you. And, thank you."

"Riccardo. You see him, you say hello. *Si*?"

The sense of unreality deepened. "Riccardo? You know him?"

Carlotta twisted her mouth, like she'd eaten something sour. "You see him, you be sure say Carlotta says Hi."

It was like this whole conversation was happening to someone else; another place, another time.

"All right," said Zoe. "I'll tell him. Thank you."

"*De nada*," Carlotta said, just as the sun slid below the horizon.

Zoe put up her hand, shading her eyes, and when she glanced

at the old lady, there was no sign of her. It was as though she had vanished into the golden rays. In Zoe's hand the metal of the key was growing warmer. Shouldering her duffel and guitar, Zoe set off along the beach. She wondered what it would be like, to have a cat named Helen.

❦ 8 ❦

JUBILEE TAKES A JOB

WHITTAKER LOOKED at the cloak in Jubilee's hand, and shuddered. "I don't know where you got that from, don't want to know. But you shouldn't have it. Keep it out of sight."

Jubilee stuffed it back in the bag. The thick fabric felt silky smooth under his fingers, cool to the touch, and curiously slippery.

"I don't get it," he said. "It doesn't turn me invisible." He wiggled his fingers; they looked as normal as ever.

"Needs contact with skin."

"I'm touching it, right here, look."

"A lot of skin."

"What, like the whole body?"

"So I was told."

"You mean, you got to be *naked* to wear this shit?"

Whittaker half-smiled. "Johnson, you getting prudish?"

"No, but–"

Whittaker yawned. "Too tired to think about it now. Secure that shit, we'll deal with it in the morning."

"Got somewhere safe?"

"Sure. There's a gun locker out the back. Come. I'll show you." They went into the back room, behind the office. It was small and crowded with filing cabinets, and behind was an equally tiny kitchen. Whittaker slid a door open. "Toilet," he said, snapping on a light. "Case you need the head."

"Thanks."

Another door led to a tight staircase. "That's where I sleep," Whittaker said, pointing. "And here," he tugged the bunch of keys from his pocket, unlocked the gray gun locker. "Put it here."

Jubilee swung the plastic bag into the locker. Looked kind of weird, sitting next to the rifles. "I swear, man," he said, compressing the bag smaller, "I had no idea what that was."

With the Camo locked away, Whittaker seemed to relax. "Well, I'm for bed." He hesitated. "You okay to sleep on the floor?"

"Yeah. Sure. No problem. I've got a sleeping pad."

Privately, Jubilee wasn't sure Whittaker had it right about the cloak. The man was full of booze, probably wasn't even clear on what day it was, let alone top-secret military tech. Besides, how likely was it that three old biddies would have access? But, glancing up at Whittaker's frown, he sighed. Talk about it tomorrow. Yeah, that was best. Tomorrow.

Whittaker clapped him on the back. "Tomorrow," he said, in a strange echo, "I'll tell you about that job."

"Job?" Jubilee said blankly.

"Got a job, just right for you."

"Hey, I don't know."

Whittaker shook his head. "Tomorrow."

NEXT MORNING, Jubilee blinked up at a dirty ceiling and tried to remember where he was.

"You're awake," said Whittaker, stating the obvious. "Good." He held an electric razor to his face; its gentle drone reminded Jubilee of a wasp. Pretty big wasp, he thought, as he struggled from his sleeping bag.

He yawned. "What time is it?"

"Time to get up. Nearly eight o'clock."

Jubilee lay back with a groan. "So early!"

"You," observed Whittaker, "definitely need a job."

Jubilee threw a cushion at him. "Go away!"

Whittaker chuckled and withdrew. "Breakfast stuff is out back," he yelled. "By the sink."

Later, shaved and coffeed, Jubilee felt partly human. "This job?" he asked, as they ate their breakfast in the office. "What is it?"

"Security, mostly."

"Who for?"

"You interested now?"

Jubilee shrugged. "Maybe. I guess."

Whittaker pushed his plate away. "Why?"

"I thought you were right, what you said, about having no direction."

Whittaker considered him. "That's a first."

"What's wrong? I thought you'd be pleased."

"Nothing's wrong. No. Sorry." Whittaker picked up the plates. "I'll get the files. Easier to show you."

Out in the tiny kitchen, he began rattling crockery into the dishwasher. "You heard of King?" he called above the noise. "Riccardo King?"

"Something to do with music?"

"Yeah," called Whittaker. "Hang on." A filing cabinet banged open and shut, and then, through the wall, Jubilee heard Whittaker talking on the phone.

"Eleven o'clock," he said, coming back into the office. He threw a folder on the table. "Riccardo King."

"What?"

"Snotty chick, name of Valerie. We're expected."

"You were just getting me a folder. Not an interview."

"Now I got you both." Whittaker went to the door. "Take a look at it. Let me know what you think."

"I don't know," said Jubilee doubtfully.

"Take a look at the file. Then we talk."

RICCARDO KING, possibly Guatemalan, possibly Mexican, had arrived in the States by means unknown. Quickly rose to prominence in the music industry, first as a recording artist (guitar, drums and vocals) and, on falling out with his label, started his own label, King Records. One newspaper clip caught Jubilee's eye:

King With the Midas Touch?

Riccardo King (37), famed music producer, goes from strength to strength. The powerful executive, once a penniless refugee, is the sole owner and manager of an international recording franchise. One of the first producers to foresee the rise of online music, he quickly branched out to develop his platform: King Dance. Thanks to King's connections, Dance was able to access new and emerging artists, and is now the third-largest music channel in the world.

But despite all his good fortune, King is no stranger to tragedy. His first daughter, Alice, disappeared when only three days old. Although Alice's body was never found, his estranged partner Amy La Fontaine was convicted of her daughter's murder. La Fontaine remains in custody in East Louisiana State Hospital.

King is reportedly paranoid about the security of his surviving daughters, Belinda (20) and Chrissie (18). He calls them his Princesses, and like the princesses of old, they're kept behind walls and rarely seen in public.

Riccardo's tragedy further mirrors the Midas legend: the king with

*the golden touch, who turned his own daughter into gold, and lost her
forever.*

"What do you think?" asked Whittaker.

"Why does he need us?"

"Man, don't you read the news?"

"Sometimes."

"You don't, do you?" Whittaker sighed. "You're like a frigging
hermit, Johnson. No wife, no kids, traveling about on a bus." He
knocked his knuckles, hard, on Jubilee's head. "Wake up, man! It's
the twenty-first century." When Jubilee pushed his hand away, he
laughed and added, "He's got a new girl. King has. New daughter, I
mean."

When Jubilee just stared at him, Whittaker sighed. "Seriously,
man. You need to be a little bit connected. Look. Come here." Sat
down at his desk, pulled up Google and typed in *Amazing Talent*.

"What's that?"

"Stupid talent show. You know. Go around the small towns, say
we'll make you famous to all these guitar-playing kids, come
along, get on national TV. Win for the networks, 'cos they have the
audience; win for the kids, maybe, who knows? Perhaps they get
famous, get a record deal or something. Couple of weeks back,
King was judging this one. Bit of a coup for the organizers, getting
someone like King. Anyway ..." his voice tailed off as he pulled up
the video. "Look. Watch. It's amazing, really, this girl starts playing,
and King recognizes her."

Johnson frowned at the image of the girl in the sequined skirt.
Coffee-colored skin, hint of Latino about the eyes. Sad face, beautiful smile. "That girl. I think know her."

Whittaker stared. "You do? How?"

"Ran into her at a laundromat."

"Laundromat?"

"Also a bus depot. You know. Laundromat slash bus depot."

"They do that?"

"Yeah. Course."

"I never knew," said Whittaker, shaking his head. "Laundry and bus services. Weird."

"She was going to San Francisco."

"That's where the competition was held," said Whittaker. "I don't get it – you really met her?"

The video showed the sad-eyed girl singing in that same beautiful, clear voice. Jubilee thought he preferred the song she'd sung at the bus station.

"Watch," Whittaker said, pointing at the screen, as an overweight man with a too-hairy chest leaped onto the stage. "That's King."

The burly man put his arms about the singer, and they stood there together, crying. General pandemonium in the theatre. Then the man turned to the audience, waved for quiet, and the two began singing.

Whittaker sniffed and wiped his eyes. "Gets me every time. That's his long-lost daughter."

"Alice? The one who was kidnapped?"

"No. Another one. That's what I was telling you. King never knew about her. This girl – Zoe's her name – well, apparently her mom ran off. Never told Riccardo she was pregnant."

"How do they know she's legit, then?"

Whittaker glared at Jubilee, apparently unhappy that Jubilee was questioning the happy-ever-after story. "DNA tests. She's the real deal, man."

The camera panned onto King's face. He didn't look happy. Jubilee knew that look: he'd seen it in the field. Sometimes, if a bomb robot didn't work, a soldier had to diffuse the charge manually. The expressions they'd worn then, he saw now on King's face, on that video. The man was packing himself.

"I don't get it," said Jubilee, after Whittaker had finished wiping his eyes. "Why this? How is this even relevant?"

"King's looking for a special security detail. You read the article, right? He's paranoid about security. He's got two other girls and now it looks like he's got an extra daughter; he's suddenly real nervous that she'll disappear just like the first one did. What was the first one's name? The one that disappeared?"

"Alice. Her mom murdered her."

"Yeah. Alice. Weird about their names, don't you think?"

"How you mean?"

"Alice, Belinda," Jubilee glanced at the clipping, "Chrissie. A, B, C. The first letters of their names. And now this girl. Zoe. Z."

Whittaker stared. "Sometimes, Johnson, you are one weird son of a bitch."

"It's true, though."

"Whatever. Coincidence, that's what it is," said Whittaker, getting to his feet. "Come on."

"Where we going?"

"King's house."

"We're meeting *King*?"

Whittaker shook his head. "His assistant. Name of Valerie. She's British."

❧ 9 ❧

RICCARDO KING PACES THE
STUDIO AT NIGHT

WHEN RICCARDO PACES his studio floor at night, he tells himself that he'd fufilled his part of the bargain. Hadn't he given up his first-born? When Alice went, a tiny bundle wrapped in a white woolen shawl, he couldn't even bear to look at her. Yes, most certainly he'd complied. But the reason for this insomnia is, he knows, the unexpected arrival of Zoe. Charley's daughter, born three months before Alice and verified as his. DNA confirms it: Zoe is Riccardo's first-born child.

Riccardo calls his daughters his princesses. The gossip columns laugh about it, but hey, if he's a King, why shouldn't his daughters be princesses? He has three princesses – four, if you count the long-gone Alice – Chrissie, Belinda, and the newly discovered Zoe.

Chrissie, dark-haired and sweetly pretty, has inherited her Austrian mother's complexion. Chrissie is Riccardo's favorite. He's disappointed she has no talent for music, but hey, perhaps she'll turn out to be good at something else. Plenty of time. She's only eighteen.

Belinda, the second daughter, is like her mother, Felicia, who disappeared long ago into the Australian outback. Belinda's deformity is a disappointment. Perhaps that's why she and Riccardo don't get on. But Belinda's temperament is, Riccardo wryly admits, the same as his: she is stormy, rebellious. Sometimes she disappears, for a day, a week; occasionally longer. He tried to give her bodyguards, but she ran away from them, too (or worse, slept with them). Finally, using a spy company, he put a bug on her phone and in her shoes, and installed spyware on her computer.

Turns out Belinda was running with a street gang – tagging, or graffiti, or something. Riccardo had wondered if she could get him some interesting music, because the streets were the cutting edge, but he wasn't sure how to approach the subject without giving away his actions. Somehow he didn't think the sulky cow would take it well.

The spy company sent photos of her graffiti, and he could tell from their emails they had been quietly impressed at her talent; they called it art. This had surprised Riccardo, because stuff on a wall is freaking graffiti, whatever Banksy said. He didn't really care for her stuff, either, all strange lines and darkness. If only she'd been good at music, now that might have been useful. But she's rubbish at music. Wouldn't touch a guitar or a piano, even when he'd paid her to take lessons.

The appearance of this new girl, Zoe, has changed everything. What will Evan do now?

Riccardo unlatches the doors, stares up at the stars, so far away. He hadn't known about Zoe, so surely Evan would understand. Riccardo pours himself a whisky, throws it back. As the liquid burns the back of his throat, he shudders. Riccardo knows that Evan is a creature of exactitude in all things, and especially promises. Evan has little patience with oath-breakers. Likely, he'll demand another daughter, and this time it will be a daughter of Evan's choosing.

Riccardo sighs, swallows back the amber liquid. If Evan

chooses Belinda it won't be the end of the world. But if Evan should take Chrissie, then Riccardo thinks he might die. She is his favorite, after all. Setting down his glass, he smiles grimly at his reflection in the window. If Evan were to take Zoe, Riccardo would *not* be devastated. Well, he's only just met her; it's not like they're close. Yes, Zoe is the best solution. Riccardo rubs his forehead. Evan will appear, he knows it: there's a feeling in the air, a sense of being watched, like a bug through a microscope.

After Alice disappeared there had been hard-eyed cops. Fortunately, Amy had been high most of the time (okay, so he'd helped that along, a good move that had been) and she made an easy scapegoat. But if Zoe disappears? Riccardo shakes his head. One daughter being kidnapped is bad luck, but two – well, that's a pattern. If another daughter vanished, the cops might look harder. And then they might find other things too, and then they'd never let him go.

He needs a scapegoat, someone to take the blame when his daughter disappears. But who? Seated in his high-backed desk chair, Riccardo considers his options. Juan? No. They go far back, he and Juan, and the little man knows things that Riccardo would rather not have shared. No, he needs a stranger, someone who knows nothing about his unusual, peculiar world.

Riccardo broods, thinking of this and that, wondering if Belinda might be a suitable offering, but the girl is too erratic, her guards could never keep track of her ...

Guards.

A bodyguard is charged with care. But if something should happen and the girl in his charge disappeared? Then where would suspicion fall?

He sighs. First, he needs to have the new daughter, Zoe, close. She should be staying in this house. Otherwise Evan might still take Belinda, or, God forbid, Chrissie. Yes. He'll invite Zoe here, and get a bodyguard for her. Someone with experience, but not someone who knows him. And then, when his pieces are on the board, he'll make his play and call Evan.

"He'll come," Riccardo whispers. "Oh yes. He'll come."

He knows how to call Evan.

Music.

Riccardo smiles, rubs his palms together. *I'll offer Zoe a recording deal. And with the right session musicians ... Yes, oh yes, definitely, Evan will come. And once he hears her voice, he won't be able to resist; he'll take her.* Riccardo smiles. *And Chrissie will be safe.*

Riccardo strides from his studio. First thing in the morning, he'll get Val to ring the security firm. Yes. He needs to get this underway, because soon it will be the full moon.

❧ 10 ❧

DISTURBED BY A CAT

THE APARTMENT WAS JUST as the old lady had promised. Sure, it was plainly furnished, but it had everything Zoe needed: chair, table, and a mattress on the floor. There was even a roof terrace to sit out on and watch the waves. She couldn't figure why the place was vacant, until she remembered the winter floods, when the waves had almost washed into the buildings. She guessed some folk had moved out and not returned.

Zoe spent hours up on the terrace, staring out at the sea, fingering chords on the guitar. In the early morning she ran on the beach, in the evening she walked, and slowly, over the next week, felt her soul returning.

She wasn't going to buy a phone, wasn't going to call Riccardo. Why should she? Her father had done nothing for her. Let him and posh Valerie disappear from her life, like some barely remembered dream.

Mom's memory whispered to her: *Gotta face your future, baby girl. Can't hide away forever.*

Zoe ignored it. It felt healing to have no pressure, nothing to do except play music and watch the waves. Sometimes she imagined living in this sun-soaked seaside bliss permanently. But it was just a dream; she needed money. The apartment might be rent-free, but she still had to eat. And so, of course, did Helen. Helen was most insistent about food.

HELEN HAD MADE herself known on day three. Zoe wasn't sure where she had been up until then: probably spying on her from a distance. Early in the morning there was a dull scratch on the door, and an insistent *Meow!*

Groaning, Zoe rolled from the mattress, hit the floor with a thump, and staggered to the door. Unbolted it and peered down at a silver-gray cat.

"Meow," said the cat insistently, and darted into the apartment.

"Hey!" called Zoe, but the animal had already curled up on the mattress and was eyeing her with interest. "What you doing? That's my bed."

The cat purred in reply.

Zoe sighed, closed the door and bolted it again. Squatting on the mattress, she rubbed the cat's neck. "Hello. Are you Helen?" The animal butted her hand in reply, and purred louder. "I guess so."

Helen was of medium size, with silver-gray fur. She had a black marking on her face, like a side-on figure eight, that rimmed her green eyes and gave her the appearance of wearing eyeglasses.

Bored, the cat leaped lightly from the mattress and darted to the fridge (empty save for an apple and a half-empty carton of milk). She meowed inquisitively.

Zoe sighed, got to her feet. "Hungry, are you?"

She poured a bowl of milk. Helen lapped it eagerly, then when it was empty, meowed again.

"Tough. I'm going back to bed."

Later, she realized she should have given way, because Helen was insistent, prowling and growling and generally whining, until Zoe caved. "Okay. Fine." Pulling on a pair of jeans, she glared at the cat. "Satisfied?" Opening the door, she added, "And I hope you're not fussy. 'Cos I don't have a lot of money."

Helen yawned.

It was still early. Already the joggers and the Tai Chi people were out, but the store on the corner was closed. Zoe hesitated. Where was the nearest place for cat food?

"Meh," said a small voice by her ankles.

"Hey there," said Zoe, bending to stroke the soft gray fur. "How did you get out?" She had definitely bolted the door behind her.

Helen, ignoring her, darted down the sidewalk then dashed across a side street, fortunately free of traffic. She pattered over folded cardboard boxes, sniffed at plastic trash bags then turned right, disappearing into a narrow alleyway. Zoe followed her, then stopped. Angry growling was coming from the end of the alley. It sounded like a huge dog.

"Hey!" Zoe called.

The alley opened into a courtyard filled with pots of flowers, their bright colors cheerful against the drab concrete. On a stoop sat Helen, licking her paws and looking superior. From behind a wall of trash cans came a whining sound.

Zoe, hands on hips, glared at the cat. "What have you done?"

Helen dashed between her legs, up the steps, and like a gray shadow, slid through an open door. Above the door was a gold sign with black writing: *Scheherazade Dreaming*.

"Hey!" a surprised voice called, then a girl in a headscarf peered around the door. "Is she with you?" She spoke with a European accent, soft and strangely exotic.

That headscarf meant the girl was Muslim, and for a moment Zoe felt nervous. But when the girl smiled, her apprehension vanished.

"I'm sorry," Zoe said. "She's hungry, I think. Say, you know where I might find cat food?"

"There's a store two blocks down," said the girl doubtfully. "But I don't know if it's open." She hesitated. "Actually, I do have some spare. You're welcome to take some."

"Won't your cat mind?"

The girl laughed. "Not if I don't tell her. Have you not owned a cat before?"

"I'm not sure I own one now," said Zoe ruefully.

The girl nodded. "I get it. You feel like that the cat owns you?"

"Something like that," Zoe acknowledged, and grinned.

The girl held out her hand. "Fatima."

Zoe shook it. "Zoe."

"Nice to meet you. So, you want this food?"

"Meow," said a tiny, bossy voice.

Zoe grinned. "Yeah. Guess I do. If it's not too much trouble."

"No trouble. Come in, please." She gestured at the door, and Zoe followed her inside. "I'll be just a moment," said Fatima, disappearing behind a curtain.

"Sure," said Zoe, staring at the room.

An empty leather chair was set beside a fireplace. Was this a bookstore? There were shelves filled with books, more volumes in scattered piles and a laptop open on a counter. The place had an ambience of mystery and musk, and made Zoe think of a song ...

> Mystery, musk and an unknown regard,
> Magic and music and long-ago nights,
> And a place where dreams are for sale.

The lines came so easily; now she was thinking of chord changes: A, D minor, C, or should it be B flat? Zoe's fingers itched. She wanted her guitar.

Fatima reappeared, holding a glass jar. "Here you are. This

should be enough."

"Thank you," said Zoe gratefully.

"Not a problem. Nice to meet you."

"Helen," Zoe called, and as though in answer the cat darted through the curtain. "We're going now." Zoe hesitated on the doorstep, glanced over at Fatima, who was seating herself at the laptop. "Excuse me, is this a store?"

Fatima nodded.

"What do you sell?"

Fatima smiled. "Dreams."

A butterfly fluttered from the screen of the computer, landed on the countertop, and opened wings of iridescent blue.

"Oh," Zoe said, uncertainly. "Right."

With Helen following, Zoe left the alley. Turning into the sidewalk, she nearly tripped over a young man carrying a brown bag of groceries in each hand.

"Excuse me," he said, as he narrowly avoided her. Then he stared at the cat. "Helen?"

But the animal darted away.

"Hey!" called Zoe after her.

"Don't bother," said the man, smiling. "You'll never catch her."

"You know her?"

He shook his head strangely. "Sometimes, I really don't."

From along the road came a shout, and out from the corner store (now open) tumbled a man carrying a broom. He swiped angrily at the silver-gray cat. "You! Out!" But the cat darted between his legs, and through the open doorway. The man howled, raced inside after her.

Zoe ran up the road, but at the store she paused, because the angry Chinese owner was kneeling on the floor, and poking under a bench with a broom. "No cats!" he hissed angrily. "No cats! You go! Get out!" Glancing up, he saw Zoe and said, "This your cat? You get her. Now!"

"Sorry," said Zoe. Feeling ridiculous, she knelt on the floor. "Hey, Helen. Come on!"

But Helen wasn't moving.

"She go!" said the man angrily.

"Yeah, yeah. I heard you. Helen, look. Cat food!" She undid the screw top on the jar, held it out. Helen blinked, considered it, then retreated back.

"Oh for goodness sake!" said Zoe, and shook the jar. "Come on, yum yum!" She bit back a laugh.

"You want cat food?" asked the store owner.

Zoe got to her feet. "Yeah. You got some?"

"Sure, sure, pet food. Come, come." The man, still holding his broom, trailed to the rear of the store and indicated a shelf containing cans of cat food, batteries, lighters, and cheap cellphones. A dying fly buzzed on its back on the windowsill as Zoe considered the dietary options.

"Meh," said a small voice at her feet.

Helen hopped up onto the shelf, and butted her head against a can of cat food. The most expensive one. Of course.

"No way. That costs too much."

"Meow."

"You take her. She go."

"All right!" Zoe said, and whispered to Helen. "You hear that? You gotta go."

The cat ignored her, walked along the shelf on silent feet, batted the trembling fly with a paw, and knocked over a phone. Zoe grabbed at it just in time.

"You break, you pay," called the man.

"Okay, come on," said Zoe.

The phone was cheaper than the cat food. With a sigh, she scooped up Helen, settled her into the crook of her elbow, picked up the cat food in one hand and the phone in the other. Perhaps it was time to call Valerie. Let them know where she was.

In her arms, the cat struggled to be let down.

"Very bossy," observed the clerk.

"Yeah," said Zoe bitterly. "You got that right. You have any SIMs? For the phone?"

"That one come with SIM."

Helen, tail upright as a flagstaff, led the way back to the apartment. Zoe served her up a generous helping of cat food, and went to get her guitar. She had a phone now, so she could get in touch with Valerie. But first, she wanted to think a little more about the song.

A world of magic and sorrow
Glimpse of a new tomorrow ...

Zoe clambered up the ladder to the roof terrace and stared out at the waves. She could feel the melody slowly growing, but as to how it might eventually emerge? She didn't yet know. Gently, she plucked the guitar strings. Some songs were like that.

The cat put her head through the trapdoor entrance. How had she climbed up the ladder?

"You like it?" Zoe asked. "Well then, you can stay and listen. As long as you're quiet."

That was what Charley had told her, when she was a child. And Zoe had always done her best, because she loved listening to her mother sing. But Helen wasn't obedient; she prowled about the terrace, sniffing at corners. Once, she jumped on the balustrade. "Girl, will you get down?"

When Helen finally disappeared down the trapdoor, Zoe gave a sigh of relief. Until downstairs, the cat began meowing. Finally, Zoe clambered down the ladder. Helen was pacing up and down, pushing at the phone with her head.

"Meh," she said insistently. Her food was untouched.

"I missed a call?" Zoe asked, and checked the screen. It was blank.

The cat wailed again, and pushed the phone with her foot, as though trying to pass it to her. Zoe took it, stared at the cat. "You want me to call someone? Who?"

Helen nodded.

"You're weird," said Zoe.

Helen just stared at her. With a sigh Zoe sent a text. *Here is my number. Zoe.*

Half an hour later, Valerie called. Riccardo was eager to meet. Would she like to come and stay? Just for a couple of weeks?

"Perhaps," said Zoe.

Helen, who had finally tucked into her food, looked up.

"I've got a cat," said Zoe quickly, then bit her lip.

"You want to bring a cat with you?"

"Yeah."

Helen sniffed.

Zoe made a face at the animal. "If it's okay with you, I mean."

"Well," said Valerie, doubtfully, "I will have to check."

"I wasn't talking to you," said Zoe.

"Oh," said Val, and paused. "Okay. Well, then. Yes. I'm sure we can manage."

Now Helen seemed to be smiling.

THAT NIGHT ZOE lies asleep on her mattress, dreaming. In her dream, the silver moonlight touches her face, and she wakes.

Yawning, she stands to face the full moon, and realizes without surprise that she wears a ballgown. It shimmers, white-gold in the moonlight. Her feet are bare. She stands, staring up at the full moon for the longest time, while about her a melody whispers, trying to be heard.

She hears a man say: "Come to me, come to me," and for a moment sees a room of dancers, moving, bending, swaying, to the half-heard melody. They are reflected in long mirrors, and so the room seems to go on forever.

Zoe steps forward, into the music, into the moonlight, and now the song is louder. The ballroom is lit with milk-white globes that hang like radiant pearls. Music tumbles from a terrace and look, there is a girl with a violin. The musician turns to face the light: it's Fatima, the girl from the store. And behind the girl stands a tall woman, with thick-framed glasses and a curiously familiar face. The music swoops and plays, and the violinist bends and sways with it, like a dancer, like a ghost, and all unseen, Zoe stands in silence, watching, watching.

Then: "Join us, my dear," and a tall man with eyes of orange-gold holds out his hand. A butterfly, purple and blue, flutters past, and for a moment Zoe pauses, caught in the strangeness of the moment: the colors, the music, the dancers and the strange man with his gloved hands held out to her in greeting.

She is about to take his hands and join the dance, when the woman with the glasses moves, and seems to leap toward her and there is a sudden throbbing and something hits her, bang! Like a freight train—

AND ZOE WOKE. She had rolled from the mattress onto the floor. Above her stood Helen, purring. She blinked at the cat – the dream had been so real – and stroked the soft fur gently. Really, the black fur about the animal's eyes did look like glasses.

"Hey there," she said softly. "You were in my dream."

The cat yawned, and began to lick her paws. From the window came a gentle tapping. Glancing over, Zoe saw a moth fluttering against the glass. It must be trying to get to the bright, nearly full moon. Yawning, she went to the window. The moth's outspread wings were blue and black. It wasn't a moth – it was a butterfly.

How did it get inside?

As she opened the catch, the thing flew into the night and was gone.

✣ 11 ✣

ZOE RIDES IN A SPORTS CAR
CLICHÉ

THE WHITE CONVERTIBLE with a clichéd red leather interior drew up at the sidewalk and its driver glanced up at her. "Zoe? I'm Valerie."

Conscious of her ancient denim shorts and lack of luggage, Zoe felt a moment of embarrassment. All she had with her was her duffel, her acoustic in its battered case, and a cardboard box containing an irritated cat. But when she nodded, Valerie smiled and popped the trunk.

Valerie was as white and glossy as her car: blonde hair topped with sunglasses, white linen shorts and white stilettos. Her nails, though, were as red as the car's upholstery.

Zoe stuffed her battered rucksack inside. But the guitar case wouldn't fit, so with some difficulty she managed to lay it along the rear seats. Valerie watched without comment, and without offering to help, so Zoe took some pleasure in scraping the guitar along the leather. She held Helen's box on her lap. The cat glared through a narrow slit in the cardboard, and now and again emitted a plaintive wail.

"Okay?" Valerie asked, gunning the engine.

"Yeah. I think."

The tires squealed as Valerie pulled into the traffic. Without warning she turned left at the lights, heading toward the freeway. Car horns sounded in her wake, as Zoe tried to balance the swaying cat box.

Valerie dropped her sunglasses over her eyes. "I was so relieved when you called," she confided. "Riccardo couldn't *believe* I hadn't let you in. I thought I might be fired."

Abruptly she changed lanes, and roared onto the freeway ramp. The whole thing felt bizarre; like stepping into a fairytale: a convertible, the LA sun, the wind in her hair. I feel a song coming on, Zoe thought, and tried not to giggle at the strangeness of the moment.

Valerie was still talking. "The others can't wait to meet you."

"Others?"

Valerie glanced at her. Zoe wished she wouldn't. At this speed, the woman should be focusing on the road. "You know. Your sisters."

Sisters! Rapidly, Zoe's hilarity subsided. Mom had shown her the news clippings – of course, she had sisters. Alice, Belinda, Chrissie. A, B, C – how they'd laughed over that. One of them, Belinda, was in a wheelchair, and Alice, the oldest had died long ago. A tragedy, Mom had said, like Zoe should be sad, but these girls with the alphabet names had felt unreal, like something from a story. Now Zoe realized: her half-sisters weren't a piece of fiction. They were real.

"They're at the house?"

"Of course. Where else would they be?"

"I thought ..." Zoe swallowed. "I don't know. I guess I thought they lived with their mothers."

"Chrissie's mother passed away when Chrissie was a baby. Belinda doesn't get on with her mom." Valerie laughed, a brittle, hard sound that made her look older. "Belinda can be awfully difficult. Not," she added quickly, "that you'll have a problem, of course."

"Of course."

"No. I'm sure you'll be just fine."

They drove the rest of the way in silence, broken only by the wails from the cardboard box.

Finally, Valerie left the freeway and drove into a quietly expensive neighborhood of tall trees, high fences and barred gates. The road wound up the hill, Helen's moans growing more and more insistent, until Valerie drew up at the high white gate.

"Here we are," Valerie said brightly, and touched a button on the dash. The gate rumbled open, and she drove inside. "So, welcome."

12

JUBILEE MEETS A MILLIONAIRE

THE DOOR OPENED. "Johnson, isn't it?"

Jubilee jumped to his feet. "Sir!"

Riccardo King was dark-skinned, wide-shouldered, barrel-chested. White shirt, chest hair visible, a hint of gold chain. There were plenty of rumors about the man: *music producer? No, it's a front. Really he's a drug importer. An arms dealer. Trafficker.* Variously Guatemalan, Mexican, Brazilian. All three, perhaps. King had first appeared on the celebrity circuit over twenty years ago, when he took up with a famously unstable singer before rapidly dating a whole host of blonde, long-legged creatures. Most of whom, Jubilee remembered from the photos, had been taller than King.

King waved a hand at the chair. "Sit, sit."

Jubilee sat. Been years since he'd had a job interview; he hoped he wouldn't screw it up. He coughed nervously.

"Val thought I should meet you," Riccardo said. "She seemed impressed with you. Said you were quiet. Discreet. Is she right?"

The British girl had been snotty, withdrawn at first, but by the end of the interview she'd been like butter in Whittaker's hand. He'd used words like: *special forces, highly trained, discreet.* And then

Whittaker, damn him, had offered to leave Johnson with her. Let him meet King, see what they thought. No obligation.

Like Jubilee was a piece of furniture.

"You know why you're here?"

"Assumed you wanted a protection service."

"Yeah," said King. "Well." He opened the wooden box on his desk, picked out a cigar. Waved it at Jubilee. "Cigar?"

"No thanks."

King grunted, took out a cutter. "You mind?"

"Not at all."

King grunted again, beheaded the cigar efficiently, then sat back and exhaled a cloud of richly scented smoke. "I need confidentially."

"Of course."

King nodded slowly. "Val. My assistant. What did you think of her?"

Jubilee shrugged. "She seemed ... nice."

"She's efficient, all right," said King, knocking ash onto the floor. "Nice ass. Good organizer. But," he leaned across the polished desk, "fucking frigid. Cold as the fucking North Pole. Don't bother trying to get in her pants."

"Okay. Sure, I'll keep that in mind."

"Good man. Good man. Like your style." King stood quickly. "Want a drink?"

"No, thanks."

King was itchy as a cat. Perhaps he had something to hide? A youthful indiscretion perhaps, or a shameful vice. Perhaps both. If Jubilee had to bet, he'd say a vice. King looked the type.

"What's the date?" said King abruptly.

"Um, third of October."

"And the next full moon?"

Jubilee blinked. "I couldn't say."

Riccardo stood at the window and puffed out smoke. "I need

someone to live in. Twenty-four seven." The view was eye-catching: from here you could see LA, spread out below like an enormous carpet. "For a couple of months, maybe."

Whittaker had seemed to think the free living quarters were a bonus. Jubilee wasn't so sure, because living at the job felt uncomfortably like being tied down. Although, he had to admit, the money would be nice.

Riccardo sank back into his chair, glanced at the resume on the desk. Whittaker had typed it up, and made it look something professional. Privately, Jubilee felt strangely proud, to see his history in print. Made him feel real, or something. Sergeant Jubilee Johnson: four years' service. Deployed to Afghanistan and Syria. Anti-terrorism specialist. Weapons training, hand-to-hand combat, licensed to carry concealed weapons.

Riccardo tapped the resume with one finger, paused, then said abruptly: "I've a guest house. Usually used for singers, musicians. You okay with living there?"

"Um, sure."

"It's on site. I mean, inside the walls. I need you to keep an eye on her for me."

"Her?"

"Zoe. My daughter. My long-lost daughter," he said, with a grimace.

"The one on the news?"

Riccardo nodded. "Need to know where she's going, who she's staying with. Anywhere she goes, I want you to follow." He waved a hand. "Discreetly, of course."

"You think something might happen to her?"

"It happened once," said Riccardo heavily.

Jubilee frowned, and wished Whittaker hadn't dropped him in this mess. Sounded like a job for a nursemaid, not an ex-soldier. "You mentioned the full moon? Why?"

Riccardo paused. "Did I?"

"You did, yes."

Riccardo turned his chair so he could keep looking out the window. "She disappeared in a full moon. My daughter. Alice."

"Does your new daughter – Zoe – know about Alice?"

"Maybe. It was a big story at the time, I guess Charley – her mother – might have told her something."

"And she's never asked you?"

"We've never talked about it," Riccardo said, and got to his feet. "Okay. You start tomorrow."

Jubilee stood, too. "Yes, Sir. Thank you, Sir."

"Don't 'Sir' me," grunted Riccardo. "Not in the army now. All right. Val will talk you through the job. Just remember what I say: You follow Zoe. Find out where she's going, what she's doing, who speaks to her. She might be my daughter, but I know stuff-all about her. And at full moon, you be extra watchful." He went to the door, yelled down the corridor: "Val!"

A brisk click-clack of heels, and Val appeared. She smiled brightly at Jubilee. "Is he staying?"

"Yeah, he'll stay," said Riccardo. "And he'll be watching."

"How lovely," said Val, and held out her hand. Jubilee shook it solemnly. "Welcome to the family, Mr. Johnson."

"Just Jubilee." He hesitated. "Do your other daughters know? About me?"

"Of course. Don't be scared, Mr. Johnson," said Val. "I'm sure the girls will *love* you."

"They'd better not," said Riccardo, wreathed in smoke.

13

CHARLEY AND THE MERCEDES

For the longest time, Zoe hadn't known who her father was. This didn't bother her; she and her mom formed a tight unit. Her father was everywhere; he was nowhere. Sometimes she imagined him as a handsome knight, a mysterious prince, perhaps a millionaire. She saw him in every unattached male, from the bus driver to the gas station attendant. Being fatherless was both a curse and strangely liberating.

Zoe knew that her mom had been going steady with her dad; that they had holidayed together, and planned to get an apartment. They even took a holiday to Europe. They couldn't afford it, but, "*We went anyway. Gotta make the most of life, baby girl.*"

Charley had been a backing singer, a good one, in demand, and in her own way, famous. Her stage name had been Charley C. She'd loved her job: the lifestyle, the stars, the excitement of being on stage. But mostly, she'd loved the music.

It was after they'd returned from Europe that the split happened. Riccardo had returned to touring and when his letters stopped, Mom flew out to him and caught him in bed with another backing singer. She threw a hairbrush at him and stormed out. She often told Zoe that the only thing she regretted was the hairbrush. "Men come and go," she said, "but girl, it ain't easy to replace a good hairbrush."

All her life, until cancer took her voice, Charley sang. Zoe had files of her voice. When the ache grew overwhelming she put Charley's songs on shuffle. In those moments, she could close her eyes, and her mother was almost there, beside her.

Zoe was fifteen when Charley told her about her father. At first Zoe didn't believe her. Riccardo King! He was famous! Charley brought out old photos and things that he had given her. There was a t-shirt, a band poster, and for some reason, a bus ticket.

"What language is that?" asked Zoe, staring at the strange letters.

"Greek," Charley said, turning it over in her fingers. "We went to Mykonos for my birthday. Riccardo bought me the ticket. I got him one too, just to keep it even. That way neither of us owed the other anything."

Mykonos was an island in the Aegean Sea, full of white houses and blue roofs. It looked like something out of a tourist brochure. Zoe had tried to imagine her mother sunbathing on the beach, riding a donkey, visiting ruins.

Charley had made a face. "It was so hot. All I could think was, when can I get in the water? I swam topless." She smiled at the faded ticket. "Riccardo liked that."

Zoe had looked up her father on Wikipedia. She learned about the houses, the ex-wives, the ex-girlfriends, and her alphabet sisters. And Alice. The nanny had put baby Alice in her crib, and then the baby disappeared. Alice's mother, the very same Amy that Mom had once thrown a hairbrush at, had been charged with her murder, but the gossip columns were full of rumors: Alice had been abducted by the nanny or kidnapped by someone with a grudge against Riccardo. It was terrorists, or even the Russians. Wacko sites blamed aliens, and someone reported strange lights in the sky. Whatever the truth, Alice's body was never found. Alice would have been nearly twenty-one now, three months younger than Zoe: almost a twin. Sometimes, Zoe wondered what Alice might have looked like, if she was still alive.

Wikipedia had some blurb about the albums Riccardo had produced, the artists he'd managed, adding, 'A seminal influence on modern music, Riccardo King was inducted into the Hall of Fame in 2016.' Zoe hadn't cared so much about that. A producer doesn't create music; a producer packages it, makes it sell. It was music she loved, not how much money it made.

Mom had warned her about Riccardo: You have to use him. Make sure you put him to work. Otherwise he'll destroy your life, if he can.

Like he destroyed yours?

Charley's hand touched her hair. *Not exactly, no. I wouldn't put it that way.*

Zoe had expected Riccardo's house to be a glitzy mansion, like something in a magazine, all gold and fountains. But as the gate slid open she couldn't see any buildings – the place was smothered in green: palms, tall conifers, and a dark hedge to her left.

Slowly, as the car crunched along the white gravel drive, the house emerged from the undergrowth. It was reassuringly unostentatious: a low, sprawling, white plaster building with a terracotta roof. The double-storied central portion had dark, deep-set windows and there were two single-storied wings, one to either side of the main house. To her left was that view of LA, and on the right, the pine-covered hills. It was a gorgeous spot.

As the car slowed to a stop, a small Latino man stepped from the shade of the porch.

"That's Juan," said Val. "The gardener."

She stopped the car, and Juan opened the door for her. "Thank you, Juan."

Then the house door was flung open, and Riccardo bounded down the steps. "Zoe!" he said, beaming, as she climbed from the car, still carrying the cat box. "Great to see you." He hugged her.

It felt weird; like he was someone she should feel close to, instead of this stranger. She wasn't sure whether she should hug him back, so she put the cat box on the car roof.

Riccardo handed her an envelope. "For you," he said proudly.

She weighed it in her hand. It contained something small and heavy. "What is it?"

"Open it," he said, grinning.

Behind her, Val loudly instructed Juan. "The bag and guitar go in the guest suite. I'll take the box."

When Val seized the cat box Helen meowed loudly.

"Shouldn't I help?" Zoe asked.

"Don't worry. Val and Juan have it under control." Riccardo indicated the envelope. "Open it."

Inside was a car remote with a Mercedes emblem on one side. Feeling strangely breathless, Zoe stared at it, trying to process what this meant.

"You like it?" he asked.

"I don't know," she said, tipping the remote into her palm. It felt heavy. It was real, not a plastic toy. "What is it?"

"What do you think?" he asked, beaming.

She stared at him. "It's not ..." She swallowed. "A car?"

"I wouldn't give you a key," he said, "if I didn't have something for it to fit in. Come," he said, and seized her hand.

His palm felt uncomfortably sweaty and she resisted the urge to retrieve her hand.

"Where are we going?"

"The garage," he said, tugging her along the drive.

"How far is it?"

"Not far," he said, pointing.

"*This* is a garage?"

This two-storied building was larger than her house. A wide dark window above the hanger-like vehicle door stared out at them like an eye.

"Sure," he said, and laughed.

"It's so big," she said.

He laughed again, and she bit her lip, feeling like a country hick.

"Not that large. Plenty of my friends have ridiculous collections. We've only got seven, eight cars."

"*Seven?*" she asked, in a high, strained voice. How many cars did one family need? "Sure. Not many."

"I want to see your face, when you see it," he said, gesturing her to the garage. "Come on."

He took a remote from his pocket, pressed the button, and the enormous door slid up and out of sight. It looked like something out of *Thunderbirds*.

"Well?" he asked, gesturing expansively, "What do you think of it, eh?"

Zoe gasped, hands to her mouth. She couldn't breathe. There, at the very front of the garage, was a convertible: red, Mercedes, and utterly, utterly gorgeous.

"It, it's ..." Zoe stammered, couldn't find the words.

This was unreal! She'd heard about the wealth in Hollywood – private jets and limos and mansions – but that was the movies, not something that happened in actual life. Yet, here was wealth casually displayed, like it was just nothing. She wanted to laugh at the insanity of it. *Here, have this crazy-expensive car, that you totally don't deserve and haven't done anything for.*

He put his hand on her shoulder. "You all right?"

She was feeling dizzy. "I'm ... I'm fine."

"So," he said, smiling like a kid at Christmas. "You like this? Is it okay?"

"It's amazing!" Zoe said.

She shut her eyes, half-hoping the car might disappear, but – no. Still there.

She touched the car's hood gently. The thing was stunning in its shiny sleekness. She wondered how much chemo it might have bought.

Riccardo smiled. "I thought it would be useful. You need a car in LA."

Zoe nodded numbly, like yeah, a Mercedes convertible was *essential*.

They walked slowly back to the house, feet crunching through the gravel. The white house walls reflected the sunlight. The patio was white, even the gravel was white; Zoe was starting to get a headache from all the dazzle.

"You know," he said seriously, "you have a great voice. The way you sang that song? I felt," he thumped his chest, "Magic."

"You think so?" Zoe knew he was flattering her, but what the hell, still nice to be praised.

He nodded seriously. "You and your mother both have it. Had it, I mean," he said, pausing respectfully. "I have some old recordings of Charley. You want to hear them?"

Zoe blinked rapidly – *I'm not going to cry, I'm not* – and nodded.

"I'd love to record you too. Say, do you have more of Charley's songs?"

"Some," she admitted.

His eyes opened wide, like he was really excited. "You do? Great!"

It felt awkward, trying to make conversation with this stranger-father. She gestured at the house. "How long have you lived here?"

"A long time," he said vaguely, and indicated the south wing of the house. "That's my studio."

"You have a recording studio *in your house*?"

He raised his eyebrows. "Of course."

Of course.

Juan, the small Latino man, stood on the threshold, watching them.

"Juan," called Riccardo. "Come here!"

He put a heavy arm across Zoe's shoulders. She felt an uncomfortable urge to shrug it off. But gritting her teeth, she said nothing as Juan came over.

"This is Zoe. My daughter."

Juan's head only came up to her shoulder. Thin as a rake, the man wore a dark gray singlet, full of holes; old leather sandals, and a wide-brimmed straw hat. He gazed at her solemnly from dark eyes. "Miss."

To Zoe's relief, Riccardo took his arm from her shoulder and put it about Juan's. The gardener did not move.

"Juan is a miracle man," said Riccardo, and gestured at the low hedges, the palms and brightly colored flowers. "When we came here, there was nothing. Juan did all this."

"Amazing," Zoe said. She knew nothing about gardens. "How big is this property?"

"The place goes down for a long way. How far is it, Juan?"

"He is twenty-five, maybe twenty-six acres." His soft voice sang with a thick Spanish accent. "Go down the hill, here." He indicated the dark green trees beyond the flower garden. "You can follow path all the way down to river."

"Juan is one of my oldest friends. How long have I known you, Juan?"

"A ver' long time, Senor."

Zoe wondered if the two men were lovers, they were standing so close.

Riccardo slapped Juan on the shoulder. "Juan knows all my

secrets. You want to know anything about this house, you ask Juan, you hear?"

"She should not have come," the gardener said abruptly.

Riccardo laughed. "Listen to him! Always the joker."

Juan shrugged his shoulders, and Riccardo's arm fell away. "I not joke."

"You kidding? But I wanted to meet my new daughter. Introduce her to her sisters," said Riccardo petulantly.

"Is mistake. Big mistake." In a low voice, he added, "*He* will come. You know this, yes?"

"Who will come?" Zoe asked, and they swung toward her, like they'd forgotten she was there.

"No-one," said Riccardo quickly. "No-one's coming. Don't listen to him."

Juan's eyes were black and unblinking. "Miss. Is not safe for you here. You should go."

Despite the sun on her shoulders, Zoe felt suddenly cold, and glanced uncertainly at her father.

"Ignore him," said Riccardo. Taking Zoe by the shoulder, he marched her away. "He's being stupid."

"Miss," Juan called. "You should leave."

"Tell you what, why don't you go into the house? Meet the girls." Riccardo sounded embarrassed. "Honey, I'm real sorry about this. Juan's getting old, doesn't always know what he's saying."

"That's okay. It's not a problem, really."

He smiled ruefully. "Still. You go. I'll handle it." He walked back to Juan, crunch, crunch through the gravel. Behind her, she heard the two men talking in low voices.

"Hey," she called. "Thanks." Riccardo stared at her, until she added, "For the car, I mean."

He nodded, grinned perfunctorily, and turned back to Juan.

For a moment the two men, so physically dissimilar, appeared alike. It was the expression on their faces, she thought, and frowned. They had both looked afraid. No, more than afraid – they looked terrified.

Riccardo's gifts come with expiry dates, Mom had said. But cash ain't never going to expire. He ever give you anything? You sell it.

Zoe made a note to herself: *Sell the Mercedes.* But for some reason, the idea hurt.

✹ 14 ✹

THREE SISTERS

"Hello?" Zoe called, into the house.

"There you are," said Val, coming forward out of the gloom. "I was wondering where you were. Did Riccardo show it to you?" There was envy in her voice.

"The car! Oh yes. Of course. It's ... great."

"He's ever so generous, you know. Come in, do."

As Zoe stepped into the lobby, the coolness of the interior washed over her skin, and she shivered.

"I want you to meet the girls," Val said, taking her arm.

Zoe stopped. "What? You mean – they're *here*?"

"Of course. They're simply dying to meet you. Come on."

She ushered Zoe through a collection of silent shiny rooms: kitchen, dining room, movie room, sitting room. Through tall windows lay a shimmering turquoise pool and, half-hidden by haze, were the distant streets of LA.

"The girls' bedrooms are in the north wing," said Val, pushing open a cream door. Immediately, heavy drum and bass music filled the air. "Oh, my!" She pressed her fingers to her ears. "That's Belinda," she whispered. "So sorry."

Zoe inhaled the pounding music with relief; here was something she could relate to.

To the right, windows gave a view of the drive. White curtains stirred as Zoe passed, so for an uneasy moment it looked like there was a ghost beside her. Then a door on the left opened, and the grunge rock simply *powered* into the hallway.

Val covered her ears. "Belinda! Please! Will you turn that down?"

Belinda had a tiny, elfin face, with heavily kohled eyes and a nose stud. Her long hair was a brilliant improbable red, shaved high at her temples, and she was seated in a jet-black wheelchair, speckled with stickers.

She glared at Val. "Don't like it? Then leave."

"And here's your sister," said Val sourly. "Belinda."

Belinda stuck out her hand. "Half-sister. Hey."

Zoe shook her hand. "Hey."

They stood, surveying each other, as the bass pounded like an echoing heartbeat. Belinda had splatters of paint across her black t-shirt and wore a pair of fingerless gloves, leather with suede palms, like weightlifter gloves, and steel-studded leather bands at her cuffs. Wikipedia had said she was twenty, but she looked younger.

"Juan said you have a cat?" Belinda asked suddenly.

"Yeah," said Zoe, "Helen."

When Belinda grinned, she looked even younger. "We always wanted a cat. Can I see her?"

"Sure."

"Juan put her in Zoe's room," Val said, adding brightly, "Well, I'll leave you girls to it. Dinner's at seven-thirty. Don't forget."

Belinda made a face at Val's retreating back. "Whatever."

The girl smelled of greasepaint and sweat. Seated in the chair, her head only reached Zoe's shoulders, but Zoe felt weirdly comfortable with this unfamiliar sister. Belinda felt a lot more real than shiny-white Val.

"I'll show you your room," said Belinda, wheeling into the passage. She used the suede grip of the gloves to push the wheelchair, hands on the tires, pushing forward in an easy smooth motion. Zoe couldn't remember why she was in the wheelchair. Something about her spine? Had she had an accident? Or was it a birth defect? Belinda wore heavy black boots, and her ankles, the way they sat on the footplates ... Zoe realized she was staring, and glanced away.

Belinda stopped at the end of the corridor and indicated the door to her left. "Here's your room." She turned the handle, pushed it open.

"Wow!" said Zoe.

"Do you like it?"

The room was all white: white coverlet on a four-poster bed, white muslin curtains, white walls. A white sofa sat opposite white French doors. It felt like an asylum. Her duffel lay on her bed, looking weirdly out of place, and her guitar in its ancient case was propped in the corner. Helen's cardboard box sat squarely in the center of the white carpet.

Zoe closed her mouth. She didn't *dislike* the room. "Um, it's very clean."

Belinda laughed. "Val only likes white. Says it goes with everything." She made a face, wheeled herself into the room. "So. Cat."

As though in answer, there came a meow from the box in the center of the floor.

Belinda spun her chair toward the box, then hesitated. "Is it okay? Can I open it?"

"Sure," Zoe said.

Quickly, Belinda tugged the box open. "Oh, she's gorgeous!" She picked up Helen, cradling her in her arms like a baby. Helen purred smugly. Belinda banged on the wall. "Chrissie! Chrissie!"

"Go away!" came a shout through the wall.

"There's a cat!"

"A cat? Where?"

"Here, dumbass," Belinda shouted. "Come and see!"

A door banged open, and there in the doorway stood Chrissie, her dark curly hair tied back with a red bandana. She wore gold hoops in her ears, and a red polka-dot dress. Like a 50s fashion-plate crossed with a gypsy. Zoe felt acutely aware of her own lack of style.

"See?" said Belinda, pointing to the cat in her lap. "She's called Helen."

Chrissie tickled Helen under the chin, then glanced at Zoe. "I'm Chrissie."

"Zoe."

Chrissie nodded. "We know." A sideways glance at Belinda, still fussing over Helen. "We're jealous. Have you met him yet?"

"Met who?"

"Your security."

"Security?" Zoe stared. "What security?"

"She doesn't know," said Belinda.

Helen leaped from Belinda's arms, and scooted into Chrissie's room. Belinda raced her wheelchair after her.

"Hey! You're not allowed in my room," shouted Chrissie and ran after her. Zoe followed.

Chrissie's room was strewn with piles of half-made clothes. A sewing machine was set up on a long table, and in the opposite corner stood a dressmaker's dummy, swathed in bright colors. Zoe was impressed; Chrissie was clearly seriously into fashion.

"Did you make that dress?" she asked. "The one you're wearing?"

Chrissie nodded.

"Wow! You're really talented."

"Thank you," said Chrissie. "But I'm not that great, not really."

"Are you kidding?" Zoe inspected the sewing machine closely. "I never met anyone who made their own clothes before. You're amazing!"

Being so enthusiastic felt weird, but hey, beginnings are important and you only got one chance to do them right.

Chrissie blushed. "Thank you."

Belinda was peering under the bed at the reluctant Helen. "How do we get her out?"

Zoe shrugged. "Food usually works okay."

"You got any?"

"In my bag."

"Come on out, Helen," cooed Belinda.

"I'll go get the food," Zoe said.

Sure enough, at the sight of a meal, Helen crept out from under the bed and the three sisters watched the cat eat.

"I love her face," sighed Chrissie. "Those markings – it's like she's wearing glasses."

Belinda nodded. "They are cool." She pulled a phone from her pocket, took some photos of the busily eating Helen. "Where did you find her?"

"I was staying in this house," said Zoe. "And Helen was there. When I left, she wanted to come with me."

"She wanted to come? How could you tell?"

"I don't know. I just did." It was true, although she couldn't say why. Then she remembered something. "Security. You said something about security?"

"Riccardo's paranoid," said Belinda.

"Although," Chrissie glanced sideways at Belinda, "you seem to have scored yourself one luscious bodyguard."

Zoe sat up straight. "What do you mean?"

"Comes tomorrow."

"A bodyguard? Is this normal? I mean, do you guys have them?"

"We used to," Belinda said. "To get to school and stuff."

Chrissie made a face. "They smelt."

"Some did," Belinda agreed. "Not all of them." She smiled slowly. "Actually, a couple were mighty tasty."

Chrissie put a finger in her mouth, like she was trying to be sick.

"Hey, I was just checking out the help."

"You're a slut," said Chrissie.

"Better a slut than a prude."

"I'm not a prude," said Chrissie angrily.

"Sure you are."

Zoe, still processing, wasn't really listening to the argument. "I've got a bodyguard?"

The girls turned to her. "From tomorrow, yeah."

"Jubilee something. Cool name, don't you think?" Chrissie said. "Hey, don't worry. It's nothing. Lots of people have them."

"I don't." Zoe felt panicked at the thought of some slab of a stranger being with her, wherever she went, watching whatever she did.

"Don't worry. We know how to charm them," said Belinda. "Riccardo hates it."

"How do you mean, he hates it?" Zoe asked. "And why do you call him Riccardo?"

"Well, because that's his name," said Chrissie.

"Sure, but I thought you'd call him Dad or something."

Belinda and Chrissie glanced at each other.

"One thing you should understand about our dear father," said Belinda

Chrissie snorted.

"Don't trust him." Belinda's dark eyes were deeply serious.

"Remember Alice?" Chrissie whispered.

"Dinner!" shouted Val loudly, "Dinner! Girls! Come on!"

Belinda made a face. "Later," she said. "After dinner."

15

FAMILIAR STRANGERS

DURING THE MEAL Val took call after call, arranging Riccardo's schedule. There seemed to be no end of people wanting to meet with him. Riccardo, though, was absent – apparently, he ate in his studio when working.

"I thought I'd show Zoe around the place," said Belinda, after they'd finished. "Chrissie? You want to come?"

"Sure."

The sky was turning pink as Belinda pushed her chair along the driveway. She moved the wheelchair quickly. The gravel surface would probably make it hard, though, and Zoe wondered if she should offer to assist, but Chrissie, catching her eye, shook her head. Beside them, the pine-scented hedge reached above their heads. The only sound was the crunching of gravel and the distant hum of traffic.

Soon they reached an opening where the hedge had been cut to form a narrow archway.

"Through here," said Belinda.

Spiky branches pricked at Zoe's skin as she squeezed through. They went down a winding path, Belinda cruising easily.

"Wow," Zoe said.

In front of her lay a wide terrace that overlooked a low valley, filled with trees and birdsong. In front of them the lights of LA shimmered like a magic carpet. The sunset-sky glowed salmon pink.

"The golden hour," said Chrissie happily. "My favorite time."

Belinda snorted. "Me, I like the night." Nodding at a sloping pathway, she added, "Down here." She led the way, coasting easily on the paved surface, pushing the wheels in long, easy strokes. "So, Zoe," she said over her shoulder. "Tell us about you. What do you like doing, huh? Do you have a job?"

"I used to waitress," Zoe said.

"I thought you were a musician."

Zoe shrugged. "I sing, I play the guitar. But it's hard to make enough to live on, playing music. So, yeah, waitressing."

Chrissie seemed surprised. "I thought musicians made heaps of money. I mean, look at Riccardo."

Zoe laughed. "Yeah, well. Not everyone is Riccardo King."

"Good thing too," said Belinda.

Trees surrounded them, blotting out the sky. A myriad small rustlings filled the night, and the scent of pine and fir blew on the faint breeze.

"What kind of music do you do?" Chrissie asked.

"R&B mostly. And rock. Hard rock."

"You write your own songs?"

"Mostly. I play covers too. What about you?"

"She's a painter," said Chrissie, from behind.

"I'm not a *painter*," said Belinda. "I'm an artist."

They reached a clearing, where the grass grew thick around the stump of an old tree. Belinda stopped. "Although, some days, I don't feel very artistic."

Zoe could relate. Some days, she didn't feel much of a musician. "What kind of art?"

"Street art," Belinda said. "On walls. Done outside. For free, as a public good."

Chrissie rolled her eyes and sat on the tree stump. "Graffiti."

"Ignore Chrissie, she doesn't understand the concept."

"Her studio's above the garage," Chrissie said. "You should check out her work."

"But," Zoe pointed to the wheelchair. "How do you–"

"This? Oh, I have an elevator," said Belinda. "A studio's okay, I guess, but I like urban walls, with cracks and history and shit. That's what I need. Just, Riccardo–"

"– keeps us prisoner," Chrissie finished.

Belinda snapped on her brakes then eased herself forward in her seat. Arms braced, she slowly lowered herself onto the grass, and settled back against the chair. Zoe hesitated, then sat beside her. The moon filled the clearing with a pearl-like light, and the breeze had stilled, so the night was calm and warm, fragrant with the scent of pine and crushed grass.

Zoe knew she'd always remember this first evening with her new sisters. Perhaps it was the way they could hear each other, yet their faces were only pale blurs in the moonlight, so each sister became a stranger, telling stories in the dark. Or maybe it was their shared genes. But no matter the reason, Zoe felt strangely relaxed. Whatever she thought she'd discover when she found her father, it was not this; these familiar strangers.

"What was it like, not knowing about your father?" Chrissie asked.

How to answer such a massive question? "He was the great mystery," Zoe said. "It was like having a hole at the center of my life. Not that I felt like I was missing out on anything – I had Mom, right? I guess it was just the not knowing."

Inwardly, she was amazed that she might share so much.

"And now?" Belinda asked softly.

"I don't know. It's kind of overwhelming."

"What did your mother say about him?"

Zoe hesitated. "Honestly? She told me not to trust him."

Chrissie and Belinda glanced at each other.

"What about you?" Zoe asked them. "Do you have anything to do with your mothers?"

"My mother died when I was two," said Chrissie. "I get emails sometimes from my cousins in Austria."

"My mother lives in Australia," said Belinda. "On a sheep station. In the middle of nowhere. I haven't seen her since I was a kid. If I did meet her, I don't know what I'd say." Flopping onto her stomach, she plucked at a blade of grass. "You know about Alice?"

"That she disappeared? Yeah."

"Your mom tell you what happened?"

"She had newspaper clippings about it."

"And ... did she think Alice's mother had actually done it? Did she know her, or anything?"

"Amy? Mom knew her, yeah. I don't think she liked her much." Zoe told them of the hairbrush.

They laughed. Then Belinda said, "I visited Amy once."

"You did?" Chrissie asked. "When?"

"Couple of years ago."

"You never told me. What was she like?"

Belinda paused. "Sad. Alice would be about your age, Zoe, wouldn't she? If she was alive, I mean."

"I guess. She was a couple of months younger than me."

"So, she'd be like what, twenty-one? Anyway, Amy kept talking about her darling baby, and saying how she longed to hold her in her arms again. She kept saying, '*She's still alive.*'"

"Delusion?" Chrissie asked.

"Probably. I'm not a shrink. Just, I kept thinking, if Amy hadn't killed her, then *who had*?" Belinda rolled onto her back, stared up at the stars. "I sometimes wonder – could Alice be still alive?"

Chrissie cleared her throat. "He's been really weird, since he found you."

"Who?"

"Riccardo."

"Something's bothering him," Belinda said. "All those phone calls? You heard Val, didn't you?"

"At dinner? Sure."

"Never used to be like that. I bet half of those calls, she's got no idea who they are. She's his assistant, and she's setting up appointments for whoever."

"And some of the people he meets?" Chrissie shuddered. "They're seriously freaky."

"We wanted to warn you," Belinda said, and in the moonlight her eyes glittered.

The grass was soft and damp with evening dew, and in the trees an owl hooted softly. A moth fluttered past on ghost-white wings as the full moon broke free from the clouds.

"He's like Teflon," said Belinda. "Nothing sticks." She held up her hands, framed the moon with her fingers.

"He looks after you, doesn't he?" Zoe said, fairly, thinking of the house, the convertible.

"He won't let us go," said Belinda.

"But you're adults," Zoe said. "He can't keep you here against your will."

"Easy for you to say," said Belinda. "You're independent. Got money, a job. Friends."

"But you've got money," Zoe said.

Belinda shook her head. "Trust funds."

"Until we're thirty-five," said Chrissie.

Zoe blinked. "Thirty-five?"

Belinda nodded. "And if we leave before then–"

"We get nothing."

Zoe wanted to say: so leave. Money isn't that important. But, biting her lip, she kept silent. How would these wealthy princesses, accustomed to so much, cope if they had nothing?

"Three little maids," said a soft voice. Out from the bushes stepped a slim figure, face half-hidden by the shadows.

Chrissie started to her feet; Belinda sat up. "Who are you?"

"I heard you talking, and thought I could offer sympathy. And perhaps – a solution. Unhappy, are you, my doves? Discontented with your lot? You are right to feel thus. Your father does not care for you as he should."

"This is private property," said Belinda.

The man laughed. "You people, and your property! As though land can be broken up into little pieces and sold. Don't be afraid, my dears. I come to offer you a gift."

"Who are you?" Belinda asked.

"An old friend. A very old friend. My name," he said, bowing, "is Evan."

Evan squatted down beside Zoe. His breath felt warm on her cheek, and his gold eyes glowed. Their pupils were wrong: like a cat's eyes, or a lizard's. Caught motionless in that golden gaze, she stared up at him, unable to move, unable barely to think.

"Look at you," he said softly. "The oldest. The unknown mystery." Gently, he put a finger under her chin, tilted her face to the moonlight. She closed her eyes, and tried not to breathe. Finally, he let her go.

"Sir," Zoe said, hating the way her voice quivered, "What do you want?"

"I have come to offer you a gift." Evan seated himself on the tree stump and regarded them with interest. "I heard your conversation. You are discontented with your lot; you feel you are trapped here, by a father who does not understand you, yes? I say: a fig for your father's commands! You are young. Healthy –," he glanced at Belinda's wheelchair, "– well, almost healthy. And you have a right to be independent. So I have come to offer you an escape, a solution to your troubles." He got to his feet. "Tomorrow night, I host a ball; a magnificent occasion, full of dancing and music. And I," he spun gracefully, "am extending an invitation to you!"

"Sir?" Zoe asked.

"Isn't it brilliant? Your father will never know, and you – you get to go out! Leave this place. Dance, have a little fun. Some food, some wine, sparkling conversation ..." He stared at them. "So? Girls? What do you say?"

The sisters glanced at each other and Zoe wished this strange, uncanny figure would let them be.

Evan's smile faded. "I try to be nice. Invite you to a ball, yet you just – do nothing. Look at you, sitting like stuffed puddings. Girls!" He clapped his hands. "I'm talking about a party! For you! Who's in?"

Chrissie glanced at Belinda; Belinda glanced at Zoe. Slowly, Chrissie raised her hand.

"Good. Very good. And you two," he said, his strange eyes glittering at Belinda and Zoe, "like it or not – you're coming. Midnight tomorrow. Here."

Abruptly, he vanished. Like someone had thrown a switch, or closed a door: he was there, and then not. Chrissie reached toward where he had stood; her hand brushed empty air.

"Who," she said, her voice shaking, "was that?"

16

JUBILEE TRIES OUT CAMO

An old Latino woman sat on the sidewalk beside Riccardo King's gate. She wore a grimy bandana and was surrounded by carry bags. She hummed to herself, rocking to and fro, apparently oblivious to the cars passing by. Her feet were in the gutter.

Jubilee skirted past her, and went to push the bell at the gate.

"Soldier," she called, and waved at him. "Ho, soldier!"

"You talking to me, Ma'am?"

"Sure I'm talking to you," she called, and pulled a grubby handkerchief from her sleeve. "See this, soldier? Watch." She rolled the square of fabric into a sausage shape, gave a complicated twist and a tug with her finger. "Watch closely, soldier boy. You watching?"

"Yes Ma'am, I'm watching."

She waved a hand and the handkerchief – vanished.

He stared. "What the hell?"

"Ha!" she said. "And now he's wanting to talk. Ain't he?" She nudged the air beside her, then frowned at Jubilee. "She's ignoring me. She always ignores me."

"I'm not ignoring you," said Jubilee, stabbing at the gate buzzer.

"Not you," she mumbled. "Her." And as she spoke her face began to change, moving like putty – until there she sat, the old woman from the beach, one of the three that had given him the cloak. Carlotta.

She laughed at him. "Your face, soldier," she said. "Your face! Look at you, like you've seen a ghost."

Beside her, the air shimmered, like the air above a hot road. Jubilee rubbed his eyes, wondering. Finally, the disturbance settled; the air calmed, and there stood another of the women. The Austrian, Inge: tall, angular, with short gray hair and reading glasses about her neck. For some reason she reminded him of a kindergarten teacher, and he felt himself shifting from foot to foot, like a child in trouble.

"You have tried it, yes?" she asked him.

"Um, tried what?" he said, darting anxious glances at the gate. *Open, won't you?*

The woman in the bandana heaved herself to her feet. Her legs were stippled with an angry rash. "Soldier," she said firmly. "You must wear it."

"I will, Ma'am, I promise."

"Tonight," said Inge. "You wear it tonight."

Behind him, the gate clicked, and began to open.

"Soldier – remember what we say. *Si?*" said Carlotta. "You remember?"

"Yes, yes," said Jubilee, and backed his way through the gate. "I remember."

"Very good," she said, and nodded. "Very good. I check on you later. We talk again."

"Ma'am," he said, and pulled the gate to with relief, "I look forward to it."

. . .

LATER, in the chauffer's lodge, Jubilee unpacked his belongings. He distributed them about in a way that he hoped wouldn't make the room look too empty, when Val put her head around the door.

"Settling in all right?"

"Yeah fine, thanks."

The place was so white: white walls, white curtains that drifted disconcertingly in the breeze. Even the sofas were white. The most impractical color ever; he wondered if he was expected to keep the place clean. Best he never sat down, then.

Val glanced about with a satisfied air. "It's looking quite homely."

He was tempted to say that this was because of the designer, not him, but instead he smiled and nodded: *Yes I'm settling in just fine, look at me with all my things.*

"When you've finished," Val said, "come to the house. I need to introduce you to the girls." She gave a last look around, then left.

He heard her brisk footsteps marching through the gravel path and turned back to his bag. When he was sure she wasn't coming back, he pulled down the shades, and tugged out the cloak. Spread it wide on the bed, where it pooled like an ink stain. Rubbing his neck, Jubilee considered it carefully, and tried to remember what Whittaker had told him.

"What I heard," Whittaker had said, "each suit is different. They're custom-make. Tech's acoustic resonance."

"What's that?"

"Way I understand it, a wearer gives off an acoustic resonance. Sound, or something. Anyway, Camo does the opposite. Like noise-canceling headphones, maybe." He looked sharply at Jubilee. "Looks like an ordinary wetsuit, kind of, but it ain't. It's smart tech. No-one else can wear it, except the soldier it's made for. So that thing you've got (if it even is Camo, which I highly doubt), is probably no use to you."

"What happens if you wear a suit made for someone else?" Jubilee asked, having visions of going up in flames.

He felt relieved when Whittaker shrugged. "Nothing. Except you'll look like a total pervert." Whittaker smirked. "They're freakin' ugly, man. Like some sort of weirdo S&M bondage."

"So, I wear this thing, worst case is – nothing happens?"

"That's what I said."

Jubilee didn't know why he felt so intrigued by the suit. Perhaps it was the idea of new tech, or maybe it was just the bizarreness of the thing. Either way, he was itching to give it a try. As long as the tech didn't kill him, of course. He wasn't *that* interested.

Now, in the small chauffeur's lodge, Jubilee saw, as Whittaker had described, that the suit was actually two layers; separate garments connected at the shoulders and across the upper back. He laughed, because it reminded him of a bat suit. The outer layer was iridescent, kind of like oil, with faint rainbow marbling that flickered across its dull black surface. When he touched it, the marbling seemed to flow toward his finger.

"PV fabric," Whittaker had told him. "Photovoltaic. Smart tech. Think of it as a flexible solar panel."

Underneath the outer layer was the wetsuit-like inner layer. This part was smoothly rubbery to the touch, kind of a cross between latex and Lycra. There was black mesh at the backs of the knees, the inside of the elbows and the underarms: probably, this was to help keep the wearer cool.

He'd looked up Camo on the web after Whittaker's explanation. He'd had to go to a local library, Whittaker being crazy paranoid about the NSA tracking his searches. There wasn't much out there. Some conspiracy websites; creepy-pasta type blogs with weird references to Slender Man, or reports of disturbances near to supposed Camo test sites. Surprisingly, there had been some information on extreme sports sites: BASE jumpers and freedivers had discussed the suits. Now, seeing the garment spread out before him, he understood why X-Sports freaks might be interested.

"You know what the real problem with Camo was?" Whittaker had said. "Overconfidence. See, it might keep a soldier invisible, but it won't stop bullets. Camo's dangerous that way. Makes you complacent."

Jubilee nodded slowly. In enemy territory, a complacent soldier was heading for a body bag.

Whittaker said, voice low, "Say, how does the army find a dead man? An invisible dead man?"

Jubilee shook his head.

"Exactly. It doesn't. Unless another soldier trips over the corpse, I guess. Or the smell."

"Okay, I get it. I get it."

"They think that's what happened to them, the missing platoon. They died."

"How?"

"Who knows? Perhaps just dumb things. Maybe they walked in front of a train. Snakebite. Perhaps they just got lost. They were in the desert, man. All kinds of things can happen to you there. You wear Camo, you better stay alert. 'Cos if you get injured, you're on your own."

As Whittaker had instructed, Jubilee stripped and sprayed himself with conducting gel. It was slippery and cold and gave him goosebumps, but Whittaker had been clear; the thing needed a coupling agent. Once finished, he stepped into the suit. It had no fastening, not that he could see, so he just had to hope it would fit.

It went over his legs easily enough, rolling on like leggings, but as he tugged it up over his hips, his cock feeling uncomfortably slimy, the material seemed to *flow*. Jubilee paused for a moment, because it felt mighty uncanny and shoved his arms into the sleeves, then, like putting on a wetsuit, he shrugged it up and over his shoulders. He tried not to think of the strangeness of it: a wetsuit had a zip, but this garment just stretched.

There was a mesh attachment on the neck that presumably went over his head. He tugged it up and over his eyes, wondering in passing if this was what it felt like to wear a burqa, and feeling studs at the side of his neck, closed the fastenings.

The whole suit tightened abruptly across his shoulders and chest and neck, and for a panicked moment he thought he was about to be suffocated. But no, when the suit felt snug, the squeezing stopped.

Standing up, he saw, reflected in the mirror, a dark, faceless figure with a weird cape hanging from his shoulders. He flung the cape about, feeling like a bullfighter, or a performer, and saw immediately its purpose: the lines of the cape broke up the man-shaped silhouette. Even without the smart-tech, this would be useful for camouflage. Kneeling, he could settle beneath the cape's ink-black folds, and merge into the night. He tried high stepping, lunging, and almost laughed. Despite the weirdness of the mesh across his face, the garment was amazingly easy to move in.

Running his fingers down his legs he discovered pockets, half-concealed. Jubilee turned about, regarding himself in the mirror. The real tech lay below the surface, Whittaker had said. Arching his back, he felt a rigidity along his spine, some sort of flexible plastic, perhaps. And there, at the base, was the depression with its central nub: the on/off switch. Awkwardly placed, so it couldn't be set off by accident. Taking a deep breath, he pressed the nub.

"Aargh!" he groaned. It was like being zapped with electriciy.

His body quivered like a trapped bug. His spine tingled, then arched in agony. He opened his mouth to shout but the words died in his throat, because there, in the mirror – his reflection! He could see himself, rigid, trembling. The current poured across his skin, growing in intensity, sharper and sharper, like a million needles. Then, as it seemed the agony could grow no further, the room darkened, shifted. And in the mirror, his reflection trembled, the outline breaking up; fragmenting like a patch of fog, like a sand-castle when the tide comes in. As he watched, the reflected image of Jubilee Johnson crumbled into nothing and disappeared.

Abruptly, the needles stopped their attack. He bent over, trying to catch his breath. Finally, he looked up. Reflected in the mirror was the bedroom, its white walls, white-covered bed unchanged. But something was missing: the room was empty. He, Jubilee Johnson, had vanished.

17

ZOE DREAMS OF MUSIC

THAT NIGHT, Zoe heard chords played softly on a steel-string, and a man's voice, singing:

Someone else's dreams
Someone else's things
But you're my beautiful girl
My beautiful girl.

She stirred, tried to slide back into sleep, but the song was too catchy. The chord progression was nothing amazing, just your standard I-V-vi-IV, but the strum rhythm was really cool. Also, those lyrics. Could do a lot with those words: *things – rings – kings – strings*. She sighed, sat up and blinked at the unfamiliar room.

The song teased at the edge of her memory, darting and tumbling until ... it was no good. She couldn't sleep. Turning on her bedside lamp, Zoe staggered to the bathroom. In her head, the music still played, and she wondered if she'd heard it before, somewhere.

Coming back with a glass of water, she stopped. Across the

back of her chair lay a red-gold organza ballgown, studded with sequins. Where had that come from? Surely it hadn't been there earlier? As though in a dream, she touched the fabric gently. *Soft.*

The song grew louder, more inviting, and she lifted the dress up, placed it against her. Would it fit? The fine fabric drifted, and almost without thought, she pulled it over her shoulders, its straps and bodice fitting perfectly. It looked like something an actress might wear on the red carpet.

When she twirled in a circle, the skirt of the dress fanned out about her legs. She glanced in the mirror. Was that reflection actually her, Zoe Banks of Nebraska? This must be a dream. She smiled. She could live with this dream.

As though in reply, the music returned, so now she could hear it clearly:

> *Leave your bed you sleepy head,*
> *Join me, be free,*
> *Be wild, be free.*
> *For why must you dream of other things?*
> *When together, we can live as kings*
> *'Cos you're my beautiful girl*
> *Oh, you're my beautiful girl.*

There was a knock on the door. Zoe tugged it open, and there stood Chrissie, resplendent in green silk.

"Wow!" said Zoe.

Chrissie's shoulders were bare and an upturned collar framed her face, its color exactly matching her eyes.

"What do you think?" said Chrissie. "Isn't it gorgeous? So retro!"

"It's amazing!"

Chrissie spun and the heavy skirt, green as a new-formed leaf, flared out above her ankles.

"You look like a tree," called Belinda, wheeling down the corridor toward them.

"And you look like you're from *The Addams Family*," said Chrissie.

"I know," said Belinda happily. Gray lace, delicate as spider silk, formed a choker about her neck. On her hands were black leather driving gloves and her dress was of shimmering gray. "Are you ready?" she said impatiently. "Let's go!"

"Go where?" Zoe asked. Was she awake or asleep? She could still hear that distant music.

Belinda grinned. "Out."

"Come on," said Chrissie, and took Zoe's hand, and together they followed Belinda through the sleeping house.

At the front door, Zoe stopped. The music was louder. "Do you hear that?"

"Hear what?" Belinda whispered, unlocking the door. She tugged the safety chains free. "Come on. Before Val wakes up."

Chrissie and Belinda headed down the driveway. Zoe, still feeling half-asleep, followed. The stones pricked her bare feet, but she couldn't stop, because she could not pull against the beat. This *must* be a dream, Zoe thought, and felt a strange relief.

When they reached the gap in the hedge, Chrissie waved back at her. "Come on!"

Belinda pushed her chair through the archway, and disappeared. Chrissie grabbed Zoe's hand and tugged her through. Giggling, they followed Belinda down the path, and into the clearing. Above, the full moon gave enough light to see clearly. The grass, thick with dew, felt damp, and Zoe regretted that she had no shoes. Then all thought vanished as the fascinating stranger, Evan, appeared. He smiled, eyes half-hidden in shadows, and beckoned to them.

"Follow me," he whispered. "Follow the music."

The music grew louder until, roaring and thundering, it

churned like a torrent that picked at Zoe's heart and pulled her forward. She followed him. They all did. They had no choice.

The world faded into black.

$\flat$

NEXT THING SHE KNEW, she was standing beside a lake. The moon had set, and the night sky was filled with stars. Lamps, bobbing on the dark water, cast rippling reflections. Beside them was a tall house, windows dark and empty.

"Where are we?" Chrissie asked.

The house lights flared gold; its wide door flew open. Music tumbled out across the lawn, palpable as a wind. It seized them, whirled them about, and they danced like bright-colored butter-flies across the grass. Belinda laughed with delight as her wheel-chair spun into the air and hovered above the steps. Chrissie, leaf-like in her green dress, flew into the house, and Zoe followed. Turning in wide circles, Belinda pirouetted in midair, then tumbled through the door.

They were in a ballroom, bright with candlelight. Tall mirrors, reflecting the candles, made the room appear larger. The place was crowded with people in glorious, beautiful masks. Each mask was different, each splendid. Some were topped with crystals, while others were bedecked in feathers and jewels, and painted so they almost appeared alive.

"May I have this dance?" asked a tall man in brown velvet.

His mask was shaped like a cat and his long, curly hair was brown. He bowed over Zoe's hands. The music paused as Zoe curtsied.

"A dance, a dance!" called the crowd.

The music grew louder as Zoe and her partner began sashaying about the floor like competitors in a dance show. Zoe felt like she was flying. Chrissie danced with a stranger in red silk, and Belinda, spinning about the floor in her chair, danced too.

The girls passed from one partner to another, the music barely pausing as the rhythm changed from tango to waltz to foxtrot. Once, Zoe danced rock and roll to a half-familiar melody, and her partner, hands tight about her waist, lifted her high in the air. His eyes glinted through the slits in his mask as he tumbled her across his shoulders. When finally he set her on her feet, she laughed in exhilaration.

Throughout the evening, she never felt tired, or thirsty, or short of breath. Occasionally she glimpsed the musicians, but their reflections moved dizzily in the mirrors, so to look at them too closely made her nauseous. Once, she was sure she saw a string orchestra, replete with violins. Another time, it was a jazz band with saxophones and muted trumpets. Yet the music, pounding with percussion and bass, sounded like rock.

She thought she saw Fatima too, the headscarfed girl from Venice Beach. Their eyes met in the mirror; a look of sheer astonishment crossed Fatima's face. Stretching out a hand to Zoe, she seemed about to speak. But Zoe's partner laughed, and whirled her away, and Fatima's reflection fragmented. As she disappeared, the wild melody returned, and Zoe continued with the dance.

Finally, the music stopped, and Zoe stood, panting and sweating. Her feet throbbed. The crowd shuffled aside, creating an aisle along the center of the huge ballroom. A bell rang: once, twice, thrice. Its shining, silvery tone reverberated around the chamber as down the aisle came a man and woman in delicate crowns. The woman's mask was fashioned into a shining butterfly, but the man's mask was plain, and through the eye slits his eyes gleamed golden.

The crowd bowed. Zoe's partner pulled her at her hand, until she bowed too. As the couple passed, Zoe saw the woman's feet were bare.

At the end of the room, two chairs had been set on a golden dais. The couple seated themselves, glanced about the room, and the company stood.

"Begin," said the man.

Chrissie jerked, as though someone had prodded her. Awkwardly, moving like a puppet, or a sleepwalker, she stepped forward. The butterfly-faced girl turned toward her.

"Sing," commanded the man in the crown.

"Sing," murmured the crowd, like an echo, then loudly, they began to chant: "Sing! Sing! Sing!"

And Chrissie sang:

> *Jack and Jill*
> *swallowed a pill*
> *As wide as a cartwheel*
> *Jill lay down and Jack he frowned*
> *He said, my dear, how do you feel?*
> *Oh brother Jack*
> *his sister cried*
> *I am feeling ill*
> *And I might die*
> *Unless you try*
> *For water on yonder hill*

Chrissie nodded to the crowd and in unison they sang:

> *Off Jack went*
> *and climbed the hill,*
> *that day he climbed the hill*
> *But coming down*
> *He broke his crown*
> *The fool!*
> *Yes, a fool he was, a fool.*

Belinda glanced at Zoe and smiled. Zoe grinned back, feeling ridiculously proud of Chrissie. Her voice was okay, nothing to write home about, but what a song! Totally crazy!

Clapping, she cheered: "Woo-hoo! You go, girl!"

"Yeah!" Belinda shouted. "You got it, girl!"

Chrissie stepped back into the crowd. She pressed her hands to her face, blew out, then grinned perkily at her sisters.

The queen got to her feet. It was impossible to gauge what she was thinking, because her mask covered her face, but somehow Zoe was sure she was laughing. A small harp appeared in her hand; the audience murmured in anticipation. Carefully, she tuned the instrument, and the crowd grew still. Zoe wished she could be closer to the dais, so she could see how such an instrument might be played. Then the girl, cradling the harp close, began to sing.

Ah, but her voice! It was like summer and wind and the grass in the field. Standing in this strange room, in the midst of a strange crowd, Zoe forgot herself, forgot her surroundings. All she had was the music.

> *Sweet dreams,*
> *Together midst the flowers*
> *Resting there for hours*
> *Just we two*
> *Sweet dreams*
> *The two of us together*
> *No matter what the weather*
> *Just we two.*

When the song ended, the crowd cheered, stamped. The queen glanced at Chrissie. Zoe knew that look: this had been a contest, and the queen had won. Chrissie dipped her head. Evidently she agreed with the outcome.

"We have a winner!" said the king. He took the queen's hand, still holding the harp, and held it high.

She smiled, and through the slits in her mask her eyes gleamed.

"The next tournament," called the king, "Is at next full moon."

"The full moon!" the crowd cried, in voices of anticipation. "Full moon!"

They tossed ribbons, flowers, even gems into the air; they clapped their hands and whirled about. It was like standing in a glittering, multi-colored storm.

The queen's voice cut through the chaos:

Sweet dreams
Sweet dreams
Enjoy your sweet dreams
Sweet dreams
Sweet dreams
Dreaming here together
Just we two

A sudden gust of wind blew into the ballroom, lifting the jewels and the flowers high into the air.

"Wait!" Belinda said, struggling to hold her wheelchair still. "What do you mean, a tournament?"

"At the full moon," called the king.

The queen smiled at them, as they stood in the middle of the multi-colored tangle of ribbons and lace and swirling dancers. "Don't worry, girls. I'll win. I always win."

She picked up the king's hand, and whirled him away. The room spun and turned, as the crowd lifted, disappearing like a dream.

𝄞

ZOE WOKE with the song fresh in her mind: A major, A minor, B flat major. *Together midst the flowers ...*

She hummed the melody. It was beautiful, happy and carefree. She had to take this song and make it work before she could properly wake. Otherwise the music would disappear. She staggered to her desk to write out the melody.

When she was done, Zoe set down her pen and looked at the scribbled score. She felt happy and scared at the same time. This song, with its quirky lilting melody, was totally not her style. What had her dream showed her?

She had been dully aware of the pain in her feet, but at first, caught up in the music, she'd barely noticed. But now – *ow!* She clutched at the desk for support. Her feet felt as though they'd been cut by glass. Holding her breath, she limped to the bed and sat down heavily. Lifting up her right foot, she winced. There was fresh blood on the floor tiles, and parts of the soles of her feet were almost raw.

Beside her, a mirror reflected a tired-looking girl wearing ... With a sense of disbelief, Zoe fingered the red-gold organza. The fabric was torn and the sequins had been ripped away. She looked like a beggar.

Zoe flopped onto her back. Her head ached. *What happened?* Surely, it had all been a dream. But, her mind whispered, a dream won't leave you in a ripped ballgown. It won't leave you with bloody feet and a pounding headache.

She thought she might be sick. *Where have I been? What happened to me?*

✴ 18 ✴

ZOE HAS SORE FEET

THERE WAS a knock at the door.

"Come in," Zoe called shakily.

Val put her head around the door. "Good, you're awake," she said briskly. "Riccardo wanted ..." She gazed around the room, taking in the torn dress and the bloodstained floor tiles. "What on earth?" She came into the room and shut the door.

Zoe tried to stand up. "Aargh!"

Picking up the dress, Val stiffened. "What is it? What's wrong?"

"My feet," said Zoe, and bit her lip.

"Let me see," said Val, squatting beside the bed. When Zoe showed her the damage, she winced. "Goodness! How on earth did you do that?"

Zoe shook her head. "I don't know."

"Does it hurt?" Val asked, poking at Zoe's right heel.

"Yes! Ow!"

"You'd better stay there," said Val briskly. "I'll call the doctor." She straightened and narrowed her eyes at Zoe. "You sure you don't want to tell me anything?"

"I told you, I don't know! I don't remember."

"Okay, look. You don't have to say anything to me, I get that. But Riccardo wants to see you. So you'd better have a good reason for him."

"I can't go now," Zoe said, and to her horror, her eyes filled with tears. "Please? Can't you say I'm sick?"

"I can tell him you're not well. But I can't promise anything. If he wants you, best you're available."

"Hey! Val!" It was Belinda, shouting down the hallway. "Help! I need you!"

Val sighed. "It is going to be one of those days." She glared at Zoe. "Okay. Stay there. Don't move. I'll call the doctor."

THE DOCTOR GAVE Zoe a shot of antibiotics and arranged for an irritatingly cheerful Australian nurse to come and clean the wounds. They gave Zoe painkillers first, but still the picking out of all those tiny stones hurt like hell. As the nurse left, Val returned. Opening the French doors to let in the fresh air, she indicated the bedraggled dress over the back of the sofa.

"Where did this come from?"

"I don't know," Zoe mumbled groggily. She still felt limp and shaky from the drugs and the memory of pain. "I saw it on the chair, and tried it on." She frowned. "Least, I think I did."

She'd thought it had been a dream. But there were her feet, and this torn dress, so no, that couldn't be right, could it?

"Zoe? Are you okay?"

"Me? Sure." Well, she amended to herself, I *think* I'm okay.

Val inspected the dress. "It's actually rather pretty," she said. "Shame about these tears. Did you drag it through brambles?"

"I don't remember."

"Look," Val said, coming over to the bed. "Listen. This is Beverly Hills. It's not ... wherever you're from. Nevada."

"Nebraska."

"Whatever. The thing is, you've got to be careful. Whatever drugs you've used in the past, well – I'm just saying, they're a whole lot stronger here."

Zoe struggled upright on her pillows. "I don't do drugs."

"I'm serious. You've simply no idea how powerful they can be, here."

"I didn't take anything. Really."

Val looked skeptical. "Okay, right. If you say so. You want something to eat?"

"I can't," said Zoe. "I feel sick."

"You'd better have something. Riccardo still wants you. I did what you asked – I told him you weren't well. But he's adamant; says there's something he wants to talk to you about." She shrugged. "Apparently it can't wait."

Zoe couldn't deal with Riccardo, not now. "I can't!" She thought she might cry. The painkillers were wearing off, and now her feet were throbbing worse than ever.

"I told him you couldn't walk. So he'll come to you." When Zoe began to protest, Val held up a hand. "Don't! You can't begin to imagine the morning I've had. What with you and Chrissie, I've hardly got anything done. You want to go out all night – fine. But don't expect me to cover for you."

"Chrissie?" asked Zoe. "She's sick, too?"

Val shrugged. "Sick, hungover, whatever. She's got what you've got."

"Her feet? Like mine?"

"Cut open too. The nurse is just finishing with her."

"Can you leave my door open?" Zoe asked. "I want to talk with her."

"It's like you've been walking all night on gravel," said Val. "I can't work it out. Surely you'd have thought to wear shoes?"

❦ 19 ❦

JUBILEE MEETS A GARDENER

RICCARDO WAS FURIOUS. He shouted into Jubilee's face, drops of spittle flying. "You're supposed to be the freakin' *bodyguard*, for Christ's sake! And what happens? The girls are abducted. *Abducted!* From my house. MY HOUSE! I should bloody well fire your sorry ass," Riccardo said, breathing heavily. "And I might yet, too."

Taking a deep breath, Jubilee tried not to say anything he might regret. "Mr. King, Sir. I'm truly sorry for your trouble. But the girls weren't abducted. They're okay. Well, except for their feet."

"You think they *planned* this? Don't be ridiculous!" Riccardo stabbed a thick finger at Jubilee. "I want you to find out who did this to them. And then I want you to make the son of a bitch pay."

Jubilee wanted to say: I'm not a cop. I don't investigate. But he said nothing, just nodded tightly. "That all, Sir?"

"Yeah. Go," said Riccardo heavily.

Jubilee wondered if he should call the police. King had been adamantly against it, because with the cops came the media. So instead he went looking for Val. Perhaps she'd seen something.

Val was in the kitchen. "Herbal," she said, indicating her steaming teacup. "Ginger. You want some?"

Jubilee shook his head. "How are they?"

"The girls? Resting."

"You see anything? Last night?"

She shook her head, and sipped her tea. "Nothing at all. Sorry."

"What about Juan? The gardener?"

"I don't know. You could ask him."

"Where is he?"

"In the garden, I guess, or his house, maybe."

"His house? Where's that?"

"It's a cottage really. He lives on site. Behind the garage. But I don't know if he'll be of much assistance."

"Why not?"

She shrugged. "This is Beverly Hills, Mr. Johnson. The girls could have taken anything."

"Drugs," he said slowly. "You think – drugs?"

Val dropped her eyes, said nothing.

"I'll talk to Juan," he said, hoping she was wrong.

HALF-HIDDEN BY TALL TREES, Juan's wooden cottage looked more a shack than a house. Jubilee approached quietly. He was wearing Camo beneath his clothes, because he figured that was the safest place to keep it. Don't want the help finding top-secret military tech. But the looked like today was going to be hot, and already he was sweating like a pig.

He felt exposed here, without back up, without his rifle. *Old habits*, he thought wryly. Stupid, really. This wasn't enemy territory; this was a private house, for chrissakes. Yet, pushing back the undergrowth, Jubilee had the creeping feeling he was being watched. It was as though he'd never left the battle-ground. Perhaps, in his head, he never had.

The paint on the wooden door to Juan's cottage was peeling, but the lock looked new. Jubilee knocked loudly. Silence, so he knocked again. This time he heard a shuffling sound within. The bolts were slid back and slowly the door opened, Juan's face appearing in the crack.

Seeing Jubilee, he pulled a gap-toothed grin. "Soldier. *Hola.*"

"Got some questions. About yesterday."

"*Si*, of course," he said, and opened the door wide. "Come, come."

Juan ushered him down a narrow corridor and into a room at the rear where bulbs hung drying from rafters and tools stood on shelves. In the corner of the room were two old, ripped chairs, half covered with newspaper. The place smelt of garlic, earth and growing things. It looked kind of like something out of a fairytale, only dirtier. And earthier, as though the magic here was from seed and soil.

"Sit, sit," said Juan, waving at an ancient easy chair. "Senor, you like coffee?"

"Yeah. Thanks."

The coffee was black as oil and bitter as sin. Coffee grounds floated on its surface; Jubilee tried not to make a face as he sipped.

"Coffee good, no?" Juan said. "Is special import."

"Where from?"

Juan smiled proudly and gappily. "Honduras."

"That where you're from?" Jubilee asked.

"*Si, si.* Long time ago."

"How long you been here?"

Juan counted on his fingers: *uno, dos, tres* ... "I think," he said slowly. "Oh, twenty-four, -five year. Maybe."

"You came from Honduras with Mr. King, didn't you?"

Juan shook his head. "Mr. King, he came much later."

"I thought you arrived in LA together?"

"LA? *Si*, we together then. But first in US was me. *Si, si*. I was first. I found him. Senor King."

"You *found* him? Where?"

"Desert. He was in the desert."

Hondurans, desert ... Jubilee stared at him. The newspaper had called King a refugee. "Hang on – what, you're telling me you and King, you were *illegals*?"

Juan glanced away, said nothing.

"Oh-kay," said Jubilee. Hardly relevant to the girls going missing last night, was it? Unless there was someone with a grudge against King, perhaps. "So, King. Where was he, when you found him?"

"Under a rock, Senor."

"What, as in *buried*?"

Juan smiled. "No. Senor King, he was hiding. Under a rock."

"Hiding from what? The border patrol?"

Juan nodded slowly, eyes sliding away from Jubilee's.

"Okay," said Jubilee eventually. It was hardly his problem, was it? "So, how did you end up in LA?"

"Senor King, he said we must go to here."

"And what? You just went with him?"

"*Si*," said Juan, surprised.

It was like being back in Afghanistan, trying to gain the locals' trust. "All right, and so you've been with King ever since? In this house?"

Juan nodded.

Seemed a mighty unlikely twist of fate, to go from nowhere to superstar. "You're telling me, King went from illegal to *this*?" He gestured toward the estate.

Juan smiled. "Senor King, he is very smart."

Yeah, right. "And you've been the gardener here all this time?"

"Senor King, he travel a lot, he ask me to stay, do garden, keep house safe. When girls born, I watch them, too. Keep them safe."

Jubilee thought about Alice, the baby who had disappeared, and wondered how effective a guardian Juan was. "Can you tell me about the gardens?" he asked.

"What do you want to know, Senor?"

"Are they ... I don't know, is there a wall around the property?"

"*Si*, all around."

"Is it hard to climb?"

"*Si.*"

"So, whoever took the girls could be inside the property?"

Juan snapped his cup onto the table so hard that the porcelain cracked. His eyes blazed. "You think I let someone in? You think I want to hurt the girls? No! I never hurt them, never! They are like my own children."

Jubilee raised his hands. "Hey, man. Chill. I meant, could someone be hiding in the grounds?"

Juan was breathing heavily. He glared at Jubilee.

"I'm sorry, okay?" Jubilee said. He sure was great at putting his foot in it. "Really. I just meant, is there a place on the grounds someone could hide?"

Juan's shoulders relaxed. "I am sorry, Senor. I did not understand."

"No, that's okay. My fault. Hey ..." A thought struck Jubilee. "You got any plans?"

"Plan, Senor?"

"Maps, drawings of the garden?"

"Oh." Juan nodded. "*Si*. I do." He hesitated. "I, sorry. For being angry, Senor."

"It's fine," said Jubilee. "Really."

"Maps, I have, but not sure where. I find for you."

"Thanks. When you locate them, can you leave them with Val?"

Juan nodded, just as the phone rang. "Excuse me, Senor." He spoke a torrent of Spanish into its receiver. Jubilee could pick out the odd word or two, but his Spanish wasn't good enough to translate. "*Si*," Juan said finally, and glanced at Jubilee. "I tell him." He set down the receiver. "Miss Belinda, she want to talk to you."

Belinda, the daughter in the wheelchair who, like many children of celebrities, described herself as an 'artist'.

"Belinda? Where is she? In her room?"

"Her studio. Above the garage, Senor. There is elevator."

"Okay, well," Jubilee said, getting to his feet. "Thanks for the coffee."

"*De nada*, Senor."

Was it his imagination, or did Juan give a sigh of relief as the door closed? Jubilee scratched at his stubble. *Should have shaved this morning, Johnson.* Whittaker was right, he was starting to go to seed.

Crossing under the cool shade of the trees, Jubilee turned. Through the grimy windows of the gardener's shack he could just make out Juan, talking into the receiver. The man was clearly agitated, gesticulating wildly with his free hand. As Jubilee watched, Juan shouted loudly, then punched his fist into the wall.

❧ 20 ❧

JUBILEE SEES A MONSTER

JUBILEE PUSHED the buzzer on the glass-paneled door at the rear of the garage. A girl's voice said: "Yeah?"

He looked up into the camera. "Jubilee. To see Belinda."

"Sure. Hi. Come in." The door popped.

He stepped into the tiny glass box of the elevator, pressed the small red button. The mechanism hummed softly as the floor receded.

The light-filled studio took up the entire loft of the garage, and smelt strongly of paint. The view from the south window was amazing; below, the city blocks of LA were dimly visible through gray smog, and far in the distance lay the blue line of the ocean. Huge canvases, vibrant with color, hung from boards. They had an angry energy: the two half-finished paintings on display were vibrant red and stark yellow, stippled with black lines. Standing close, like this, it was hard to make out the subject of the work, but stepping back, Jubilee could see the lines of a hand, closing like a great fist about a distorted figure.

A woman in a wheelchair appeared from behind the canvas. This must be Belinda.

"What do you think?" she asked, nodding at the painting.

"It's ..." Jubilee said, searching for the right word, "powerful."

Belinda smiled tightly. "I want to show you something."

She wheeled the chair neatly through the light-filled space, navigating around shelves and half-finished canvases with ease, but her wrists and hands were bound with crepe bandages, and she took good care not to touch the heel of her hand to the wheels, almost as though she'd hurt herself not long ago. Jubilee was just about to ask her what had happened, when Belinda thrust a sketch pad at him. "Here."

He blinked at the drawing of an elongated figure, shouting into a microphone. Its face was distorted, darkly shadowed, but the eyes, smudged with golden pastel, seemed to glow. There was an air of menace, and a vaguely sexual attraction.

"What do you think?" she asked.

"It's good," he said slowly. "Is it Bowie?"

She tipped her head sideways, considered the image. "There is a Bowie vibe, isn't there?"

Belinda's paint-splattered jeans were black, as was her t-shirt. But the canvases on the wall were full of color. A strange mix.

"Kind of," he said, staring at the image. "But those eyes ..."

"Pastel," she said, pointing at the golden haze of the eyes. "Has a depth of color that you don't get with paint, I think."

"I guess. I don't know much about art."

She wheeled over to a low sink, peeled off her gloves and set them on the bench. "You know why I'm in this chair?" she asked, speaking over her shoulder.

"Spina bifida," he said.

She paused. "Which means?"

"Bifid spine."

She turned, raised eyebrows at him – *go on*, so he added: "The arch of your backbone didn't fully fuse in utero. So when you were born, your spinal cord was exterior to the body, not encased in bone. Like mine is."

She clapped slowly. "Very good. You did your research, Mr. Johnson. I'm impressed."

"Just Jubilee."

"Well, Just Jubilee, most folk don't have any idea about my disability. I've been asked if I was in a car accident, or if I had a disease. But you actually know the name of my condition, so I'd say you're ahead." She nodded at the drawing in his hands. "What do you think? Would you recognize him again?"

"Bowie?"

"Oh, that's not Bowie," she said. "No, definitely not. He's alive, for one thing. And kicking. Very much kicking."

"I don't get it," he said. "Why are you showing this to me?"

She turned her bandaged palms out to him. "Because he is the man who took us. Last night. The others don't remember. I do. He did something to their memory. Don't ask me what, I don't understand it."

"What happened to your palms?"

"I was pushing the chair. All night."

"You were – what?"

"Like this," she said, demonstrating: the base of her palm on the chair's wheel, her arms propelling the chair forward. She shrugged ruefully, checked her hands again. "I guess I got carried away."

"Why were you wheeling your chair for so long?"

"Because, unlike my sisters, I can't walk. So I dance in my chair." She paused. "Actually, I guess I was lucky." She touched a bandage gently. "Hands heal faster than feet, don't they?"

He stared at her. "You're telling me your sisters cut their feet? Because they were *dancing*?"

"Yeah." She nodded at the Bowie-like image. "That's what he can do, Mr. Johnson."

"Jubilee," he said, absently, staring at the compelling figure on the sketchpad. He took a deep breath. "I think you better start again. From the beginning. Exactly *what* happened?"

She put up a hand. "Hang on. Wait." Her gaze was fixed on the window behind him.

He turned, following her eyes. "What is it?"

"Shh!" Slowly, she rolled her chair toward the north window, where the pines blew softly in the breeze. Jubilee, looking over her hair could see into the gray-green of the sparsely set branches. On one tree, a gray bird wiped its beak against a branch.

Slowly, slowly, Belinda moved closer to the window. "Can you see it?" she murmured, low.

"See what?"

"Beside the trunk. The crooked branch, to the right. Look."

He stared out the window, narrowed his eyes. The trunk was patterned gray, green, brown. On the branch, the bird chirruped anxiously, and then ...

He blinked. Surely, he was imagining it.

"You saw it, didn't you?" she said, in a fierce whisper.

He didn't answer, he was watching the tree, where, just a moment ago, a figure had appeared. Its skin had blended with the rough bark, so it was almost perfectly camouflaged. It had claws, long teeth. Bright, gold eyes. A mountain lion, perhaps? No, too large for a cat, even a big one. And the way it crouched, one hand on the trunk; the way it had been looking at them, like it was *interested*. Whatever it was, it was clearly intelligent.

The bird scraped its beak again along the branch and the thing *pounced*. A cloud of feathers drifted past. Belinda covered her mouth with her hands. The creature glanced her way and grinned, mouth dripping blood and feathers. Then abruptly it disappeared. Like magic. Leaving only a gnarled pine tree, needles rustling in the wind and a few feathers, wafting past.

"What. Was. That?" she asked.

"Shh," he murmured. "Let's see if it comes back."

Obediently, she froze. Standing behind her, Jubilee stood motionless, counting out his heartbeats – oh, he'd waited before like this, sitting beside well-worn jungle trails or on cold mountains, rifle at the ready. He was good at waiting. What the hell had he just seen? The camo was slick with sweat beneath his clothes, but despite its heat he shivered.

Finally, Belinda took a deep breath. "I think it's gone."

Jubilee said nothing. He wasn't sure – somehow, he could feel the creature watching him. And its gaze did not feel friendly. Slowly, he reached up and closed the louvers.

The doorbell rang, breaking the tension.

"Hello?" A girl's voice.

Two young women stood at the studio door. One had dark hair, wrapped in a bandana. And the other must be Zoe. Jubilee grinned. He'd wanted to see her again, and now she was just outside.

"What do they want?" Belinda muttered.

Jubilee's breath caught. What if that creature was still there, crouched on that branch? What if it was still hungry? That thing had fangs and claws. If it leaped on the girls, they wouldn't even see it coming.

❧ 21 ❧

THE JEALOUSY OF SISTERS

CHRISSIE AND ZOE lay on their respective beds in their own rooms, talking to one another through their open doors. It felt kind of nice, Zoe thought. Sisterly, and it distracted her from the throbbing in her feet.

"Last night," Zoe said, slowly. "I felt like ... I thought I was in a dream, you know? What do you think happened?"

Silence, then Chrissie said: "All I remember is just ... I don't know, music."

"Yes," said Zoe softly. "Music. That's what I remember."

"So," asked Chrissie brightly, "what are you doing today? Any plans?"

She was changing the subject. Fair enough. "Nothing planned. Oh, yeah, that's right." Zoe made a face. "Val said Riccardo wanted to see me. Guess he'll be here soon." She wished her room wasn't so messy.

"He was talking about an album," said Chrissie flatly.

An album with Riccardo King was a Big Deal. Zoe should be excited, but right now the pain in her feet was making her queasy.

Also, something in Chrissie's voice worried her. "Chrissie? Are you annoyed?"

There was silence, then: "It's just – he's never wanted to do anything like that with me. Or Belinda."

Zoe flopped onto her back, stared up at the ceiling. Chrissie was jealous. *Great. I've only just met my sisters, and already they hate me.*

"It's not your fault," Chrissie added, but Zoe wasn't sure she meant it.

They lay for a moment in silence.

"Screw this," said Zoe, angrily, and heaved herself off the bed.

"What are you doing?"

"Getting up."

"We're supposed to be resting."

"I'll survive," Zoe said grimly, and put her feet on the floor.

"Hey," Chrissie said, sounding alarmed, "Is this because of what I said? Because you shouldn't walk about."

Zoe found that with the padding on her feet, she could stand. Sure, it was uncomfortable, but she could hobble. Feeling like an old lady, she shuffled her way to Chrissie's room, and put her head around the door. "Hey."

Chrissie looked relieved when Zoe appeared. "I thought I'd upset you."

"Last night," Zoe said, sitting on the bed beside her half-sister, "You know I said it felt like a dream?"

"Yeah."

"Thing is – you were in this dream, too," Zoe said.

Chrissie propped herself onto an elbow. "What?"

"Also Belinda. Hey, where is Belinda?"

"In her studio," Chrissie said, struggling upright. She swung her legs over the edge of the bed and rested a moment, a look of concentration on her face, then asked, "hand me my jeans, will you? They're on the floor behind you."

Most of Chrissie's clothes were on the floor. Zoe located the jeans in the pile and passed them over. "What are you doing?"

Carefully, Chrissie pushed her feet into her jeans. "I'm going to talk to Belinda."

"What? Why?"

"Because," said Chrissie grimly, "She was in my dream. And so were you. So obviously, it wasn't a dream at all. And, since B never answers her phone ..." Taking a deep breath, Chrissie straightened slowly upright. "Not so bad. Zoe? You coming?"

"I guess," said Zoe. "Only, can I lean on you?"

Chrissie smiled. "Yeah, sure. Of course."

22

JUBILEE IN AN ART STUDIO

BELINDA DEPRESSED THE BUTTON, and the lock clicked open as Jubilee ran downstairs into the lobby just as Chrissie and Zoe, struggled through the doorway. Jubilee tugged Zoe inside, then slammed the door closed. He turned the lock, and for good measure rammed the security bolt home.

Zoe leaned against the lobby wall, eyes closed and breathing heavily. Her face was pale and her feet were wrapped in two white pads.

"Are you all right?" Jubilee asked.

"I'm okay," she said, softly, keeping her eyes shut. "It's just–"

"Our feet hurt," said Chrissie, by way of explanation. She too rested against the wall. "We can't move fast."

Zoe's eyes opened. Glancing at Jubilee, she froze. "You!"

Jubilee smiled.

"The bus depot, right?"

Jubilee grinned. "You remember?"

"Remember? Of course! How could I not? It's great to see you."

Chrissie groaned. "Don't tell me you know him?"

"We've met," Zoe said.

"Hate to interrupt," called Belinda from above, "but are you guys coming up?"

Jubilee pushed the button for the elevator. "Let me help, okay?" He slipped an arm under Zoe's shoulder, helped her cross to the elevator.

"What about me?" Chrissie asked. "I need a hand too."

"I'm coming back," he said, depositing Zoe in the elevator. She was breathing heavily. "You okay?"

She swallowed, nodded. "Thanks."

"You're welcome," he said, and returned to Chrissie. Installing her in the elevator beside her sister, he followed them in, then pushed the button and watched the floor recede.

"What are you doing here?" Zoe asked Jubilee as they exited.

Belinda wheeled over. "You two obviously know each other. How come?"

Jubilee parted the louvres, stared out at the tree. Nothing.

"He helped me out," said Zoe, and glanced at Jubilee. "What are you doing?"

"Well, and aren't you lucky?" said Belinda. "What happened?"

"I was busking," said Zoe.

"Busking?" asked Chrissie.

"Street performing, duh," Belinda said. "Okay, yeah, so?"

"A sheriff or something wanted to arrest me. This guy here," she turned to Jubilee with a smile, "rescued me."

Involuntarily, Jubilee glanced away from the window and smiled at Zoe. Meeting her eyes made him feel warm.

Chrissie sighed. "How romantic."

"But I don't understand. How come you're here?" Zoe asked.

"Don't you know?" Chrissie asked. "Jubilee's the new body-guard. You remember? We told you." She groaned. "Oh man, I have to sit." She perched herself on a high stool and looked at Belinda. "What happened to your hands?"

"I was dancing."

"Dancing?" Zoe asked, confused.

"That's from the wheels?" Chrissie said. "You were propelling the chair? Like, all night?"

Belinda nodded.

Chrissie glanced at Zoe. "So yeah. I guess it wasn't just a dream, then."

As the girls talked, Jubilee kept a wary eye on the pine tree. It seemed empty: just gray-brown bark and pine needles quivering in the wind. Camouflage, he thought, wondering again about the creature's ability to hide itself. *If only I had my rifle, and my scopes.* But they were in the gatehouse, along with his other stuff.

He had something else, though, didn't he? The Camo. If he turned the suit on he could retrieve his weapons without being seen. And who knew, possibly in Camo he might be able to identify the thing that had been spying on them. Knowing that thing, that whatever-it-was, might still be out there left him profoundly uneasy.

"Jubilee? Why do you keep staring out the window?" Zoe asked.

"We saw something, earlier," said Belinda. "Before you arrived. Some sort of an animal, I think. We saw it eat a bird."

"A mountain lion?" Chrissie asked.

"I don't think it was a lion," Jubilee said. "Actually, I don't rightly know what it was."

"But it sure didn't seem friendly," Belinda said.

"Is that why you pulled us inside?" Zoe asked.

"Something like that, yeah."

"It was grayish brown. Had weird eyes. And claws," said Belinda. "Teeth." She was rifling through her pencils.

"What are you doing?" Zoe asked.

"Drawing it," she said, grabbing a sketch pad.

"Hey," Chrissie said.

At the intensity in her voice, Jubilee turned. "What? What is it?"

The girls were staring at the drawing of the David Bowie-like figure.

"It's that man," Chrissie said, "from the other night. Remember?"

"Yeah," Zoe said slowly, staring at the picture. "Now I do."

Outside, the tree rustled in the wind. Jubilee watched it carefully. *There!* For a moment, he saw a shimmering; a change in the light.

"Where are you going?" Belinda asked him, as he stood up.

"Is there a bathroom here?"

"Sure," she said, waving to a side door. "It's wheelchair friendly."

He hesitated, watching Belinda's charcoal-smudged, bandaged hand moving quickly on the paper. An creature with sharp teeth and bent spine was slowly emerging. "That's good," he said abruptly.

She frowned at it. "I'm not sure ..."

Jubilee went into the small bathroom, then remembering that they might not see him exiting, popped his head out the door. "If this door opens and there's no-one there," he said, "don't panic."

They stared at him.

"Okay, so now I've told you," he said, and felt stupid.

✵ 23 ✵

JUBILEE OVERHEARS A
CONVERSATION

IT WAS a good thing he'd warned them, because as it was, Chrissie jumped as the bathroom door opened.

"It's okay," he said. "It's me."

"Jubilee?" Zoe asked, reaching toward him. "Is that you?"

He took her hand. Her fingers were warm and he squeezed them gently. "It's okay. I'm here."

"I can't see you. Why can't I see you?"

"It's a new tech," he said, hoping the normality of her voice would soothe them. "Camo, it's called. C-A-M-O. Helps to hide the wearer."

"It works," Belinda said dryly.

Chrissie took a deep breath. Her face was pale. "For a moment, I thought you were a ghost."

"Nope. Only me," he said, and she half-smiled, her eyes tracking to his voice. But there was no recognition in them, none at all, and that, he thought, was the strangest thing.

He glanced at the tree. And there, settled into the branches, just as it had been before, was the thing. The creature. He could see it clearly now: long claws, sharp teeth, and golden, glowing eyes. Was it an alien? Jubilee caught himself on a half-laugh. Aliens were only in the movies.

He crept closer to the window, but the thing didn't move. Like the girls, there was no recognition in its eyes; it didn't seem to see him. He huffed out, thinking hard.

"What is it?" Zoe asked.

"It's still there," he said tightly. "In the tree. Doesn't seem to see me, though, but I can see it clearly now. Must be something to do with the Camo." But he had no idea what.

The creature was watching the girls intently, like a cat watches a mouse.

"I can't see anything," said Chrissie, staring at the tree. "Are you sure?"

"It's hidden," he said. "Okay. I'm going outside now. You girls, stay here. Pretend everything's normal, you understand?"

"You think it can understand us?" Belinda asked.

"I don't know," he said. "But just in case."

He glanced at the motionless creature again. Belinda's sketch was surprisingly accurate.

"Where are you going?" Belinda asked.

"Getting my rifle," he said grimly. "I don't trust that thing. You saw what it did to that bird – I'd be a darn sight more comfortable with a weapon."

The girls glanced at each other.

"Okay," said Belinda, after a long pause. "But when you get back, you'd better speak into the intercom. Or we won't know it's you. Hell, this is bizarre. Where are you, anyway?"

"I'm here, behind you."

"Freaky," she said, and swung about to face his voice. "You be careful out there, you hear?"

"I'll try," he said and pushed the button for the elevator.

"The door will lock behind you," said Belinda.

He opened the door slowly, hoping the creature wouldn't

notice the movement. But it wasn't looking at him. From what he could see, through the shadowy bulk of the pine, its attention was directed back at the studio windows, and the three girls inside. He moved slowly, silently, into the welcome shade of the trees. The creature above him hadn't moved, so it still didn't seem to be aware of him. Strange, how it was so much easier to see it now. What was this Camo, that it could make the hidden visible?

He crouched down, pressed invisible fingers into the soil. Its rich, piney scent was familiar, and he inhaled it with relief. Taking a deep breath, he looked about, and realized how much the world had changed. A gray mist covered everything, seeping through the ground, hiding the tops of the trees. Small sounds: the rustle of the leaves, birdsong, traffic noises were all muffled. Above, trees stretched skeletal fingers, and the light was dim. Yet the creature in the treetops glowed, bright as a beacon. It sat motionless on the branch, a claw-tipped hand resting lightly against the trunk of the tree.

If he narrowed his eyes, he could just make out the garage and the studio windows, but now they looked strangely wavering, insubstantial in this land of gray. It was like being under water. What had Whittaker said, about the trial of the tech? The platoon that disappeared? Jubilee took a deep breath – the thought of disappearing forever into this alien landscape made him feel ill.

The trees whispered faintly, as though exchanging comments. In early trials, the platoon had reported strange sights and sounds. *Stop it! Get a grip, man!* A weapon. That's what he needed. Yes, he'd be better with a rifle in his hands.

Moving through the Camo-world (as he began to call it) was surprisingly easy. Man-made barriers, like walls, were insubstantial as smoke, so he could walk right through them. Trees, though, were not, and must be detoured around. It seemed, mostly, that artificial objects grew less substantial in this gray, dream-like landscape, but living things remained. Trees, therefore, could be climbed, but walls could be walked through. He walked right through the swimming pool as though it didn't exist; his feet didn't even get wet. Finally, he reached the hedge that bordered the driveway, where he stopped. *What the–!*

Crouched beside the hedge, half-hidden by fog-like foliage, was another of those creatures. Like the one outside Belinda's studio, it had clawed hands and feet. It was motionless. If it hadn't blinked he might have thought it was a statue. It made no sign that it was even aware of Jubilee's presence, so he crept towards it, keeping the hedge between them. Seen up close, it looked like a gargoyle.

Just then, the door of the house opened, and Val, carrying a pair of scissors, walked down the steps. The creature's nostrils flared as its eyes tracked the woman. Jubilee tensed.

A shout from the doorway. "Val!"

Riccardo stood there with one hand in a pocket and his belly out-thrust. He wore Bermuda shorts and a Hawaiian shirt. The colors were probably garish, but here, seen in the Camo-world, they were monochrome.

"Where's the new girl?" Riccardo called.

Val turned back to him. "You mean Zoe?"

"Zoe, yeah. Where is she?"

"Isn't she in her room?"

"Her room? Okay, I'll look." He turned to the door, then paused. "Where's her room?"

"Next to Chrissie's."

"And that's – where?"

Val pointed to the northeast wing of the house. "Third door along."

Riccardo left, and Val went to the garden bed in front of the house. Slowly, she selected flowers, snipping their stems and neatly arranging them into a bunch in her hand.

"VAL!" Riccardo shouted loudly, reappearing.

"Mr King?"

"Perhaps she's in the bathroom. Did you ask Chrissie?"

"Chrissie's not there, either."

"She can't have gone far. I'll come and look."

Riccardo's phone rang, and he stood outside, talking loudly as Val returned to the house. "Yeah, what? No. I can't. Tell him I don't care what they're paying. I just can't. Yeah, no. I'm real busy right now." He stopped, nodded, and said, "Tell you what. Give me a call in, say ... oh, three months. I should have time then. Okay? Okay, right. Yeah, good talking to you too." He put the phone back in his pocket, turned to go.

Just then the golden creature stirred, straightened from its crouch, and leaped over the hedge.

"Ricky," it called. "Oh, Ricky!" Its voice sounded like the wind in dry grass; like the hiss of a snake.

Jubilee froze, squatted into the shadows, and hoped the Camotech worked.

Riccardo turned slowly, one hand on the door. Obviously he could hear the creature, but judging by his wide-eyed stare, he couldn't see it. "Who's there? Where are you?"

"I'm here," called the creature, licking its lips with a disconcertingly pointed tongue. "Oh Ricky, I'm just here." It bounded up the steps, stopped at the top, its face directly in front of Riccardo's. "Can you see me now?"

Riccardo jumped back. "What the hell!"

"Don't be frightened, Ricky," said the creature. "I'm only a messenger."

Riccardo patted his forehead with a handkerchief. "Hell, you nearly gave me a heart attack! Okay, what's your message?"

Evidently Riccardo was familiar with this thing, whatever it was.

"Evan, my master, sent me."

"All right. Yeah. What does Evan want?"

"You have a debt that's not yet paid, Riccardo King."

"Tell Evan, that's not my fault. I didn't even know about the girl. He shouldn't blame me."

"Evan does not care about things like blame, and fault. He only cares about the favor. He did a favor for you, Riccardo King, and not a small one. And so now you owe him. Evan says: he will collect on the debt."

"Yeah, yeah," Riccardo grumbled. "It's not a big deal. I'll sort it out, you know."

"Evan says: you will do nothing. He is already sorting it out."

"What? What does he mean?"

"The girls have already visited him."

"They what! No way! That wasn't part of the bargain."

"The bargain has changed, Riccardo King. You changed it."

"Now, listen. I didn't even know about the girl. Her crazy mother never told me about her. It's not my fault."

"Fault is irrelevant. Evan is concerned with what is, and what is not."

"Look, okay. I tell you what. In three months, you can have her. How about that, okay?"

The creature shook its head. "Oh no, Riccardo King. That is not how it works."

"How it works?" Riccardo panted. "I'll tell you how it works." Without warning he swung a punch. But the creature ducked easily, and pushed him backward with a clawed hand.

"You choose violence?" it purred, voice silky-smooth, holding him down without any visible effort. "Is this your choice, Riccardo King?"

Riccardo swallowed, his eyes darting to and fro, as though looking for escape. He held up two hands, palms up. "No, hey. No. I was just – surprised. Yeah. You surprised me. Please."

The creature removed his hand, and let him stand. Riccardo

smoothed his hair. He looked ridiculous in his monochrome, poorly fitting shorts.

"Very well. You have three months. No longer. And in that time, Evan will decide."

"Decide what?"

"Which of your daughters he will take."

"Can't he just keep Alice?"

The creature shrugged. "Alice grows troublesome. Perhaps another daughter will be better suited to his needs."

Jubilee wished, right there, that he could pull a gun and shoot both Riccardo and his messenger. Just then, he heard a shout. Down the driveway ran Juan. He seemed to be carrying a metal rod.

"Demon!" he shouted in Spanish. "In the name of the Lord, begone!"

"You need to do something about that one, Riccardo," the creature growled.

Juan panted up to the steps and threw the rod at the animal. With a snarl, the creature bounded up, landing on the roof, where it squatted, glowering and looking more like a gargoyle than ever.

Juan picked up the rod and brandished it at the creature, which hissed angrily.

"Fool! Don't think that little bit of iron will stop us for long."

It scrambled over the roof, up to the ridgeline, dropped down the other side, and disappeared.

Val came out the door. "Are you okay? I thought I heard ..." She stopped, stared at Riccardo. "What happened?"

"Hola, Miss," called Juan, from the base of the steps. He was still clutching the rod like a baseball bat.

"Oh, hello Juan." Val said, and turned to Riccardo. "I can't find her."

"What? Who?" Riccardo asked.

"Chrissie. And Zoe. Both of them are gone."

"And the other one? Belinda?"

"She's gone too."

"Oh, she'll be back," Riccardo said. "Unfortunately. You coming, Juan?"

"*Si.*"

Juan followed him into the house and the door closed. Jubilee went up the steps and picked up the bar, lying forgotten beside the door. It was a common enough reinforcing rod, made of heavy, slightly rusted steel. He bent to pick it up. It was heavy, its rough surface slightly rusted. Jubilee smiled; now he had a weapon, one these creatures feared. Less noisy than a rifle, and easier to carry. With a loping gait, he ran back to Belinda's studio.

24

CHRISSIE DRAWS A DRESS

CHRISSIE HELD up a stick of charcoal. "Okay if I use this?"

"Sure," Belinda said.

"What are you drawing?" asked Zoe, after a while.

Chrissie wrinkled her nose, held the paper up so Zoe could see it, and said apologetically, "It's not very good."

It was the style of drawing a designer might do; the subject was a woman in a dress, but the focus of the image was the clothing, not the person.

"That's the dress I wore," Chrissie said.

"It was green," Zoe said slowly.

"And you," Belinda turned her chair to face Zoe, "wore red."

Zoe nodded. "I thought it was a dream. Until I woke up." She winced at the memory. "And felt my feet."

Belinda smiled briefly. "The first time I've been pleased I couldn't walk." She held up her hands. "The skin's tougher."

"You wore gloves," said Chrissie, charcoal flying in black streaks across the page, "and lace."

Belinda nodded slowly. "That's right."

"What happened to your dress?" Zoe asked. "Mine was on my floor when I woke up. Val had a fit."

"Val?" Belinda said. "What did she want?"

Zoe shrugged. "Something about Riccardo wanting to see me. But then, well the doctor came."

"We didn't want to talk to Riccardo," Chrissie said, still drawing, "so after the doctor we escaped. This is yours," Chrissie added, passing the sketch to Zoe. "I think. Is this right?"

Zoe nodded. "Looks good."

Chrissie considered the drawing. "It's a real classic design," she said admiringly. "It suited you."

"Thanks."

"I wonder what the fabric was. You've still got it, you said?"

Zoe nodded, then swallowed hard. She remembered something.

"Zoe?" said Belinda. "What's bothering you?"

Zoe hesitated, then said: "About last night ..."

Chrissie put down the charcoal. "What?"

"I asked Evan what our dresses were made of. And he said ..." She stopped. No, it was just stupid, wasn't it?

But if last night hadn't been a dream, then what had Evan's reply meant? Belinda and Chrissie were staring at her, their faces puzzled.

Zoe sighed. "He said my dress was made of dewdrops and vampire blood."

Belinda raised an eyebrow. "Now, that's exotic."

"Want to know what he said about yours?"

"I guess."

"The lace was of spiders' silk, and the fabric from beetle skin."

"What about mine?" Chrissie asked.

"Leaves," Zoe said slowly, remembering Evan's soft voice, whispering: *Leaves and limes and blossom fine.* She shivered.

Belinda was laughing.

"What's so funny?" Zoe said.

"Nothing, just. Beetle skin. Ridiculous! Beetles don't even have a skin. They have that kind of hard stuff. What's it called? Chitin? Yeah. Chitin. So: no skin."

"So, what do you think it was made of then?"

Belinda shrugged. "I don't know. It was comfortable, it fitted, it looked good. I'm not the designer." She glanced at Chrissie. "What do you think? Polyester? Silk, cotton? Lycra, maybe. How do I know?"

Chrissie rolled her eyes. "Lycra!"

"Zoe, you recall anything else?" said Belinda.

Zoe closed her eyes, thinking. "There was music," she said, slowly. "Chrissie sang something."

Chrissie looked horrified. "I did *what*?"

"You don't remember?" Zoe asked.

"Hell, no!"

"I remember meeting Evan in the clearing," said Belinda. "And next thing I'm waking up in bed with this weird, creepy-as dress on my floor. And my hands," she held them up, "are like this. Without the bandages, of course."

"Me too," said Chrissie. "Except it was my feet."

"You remembered the dresses," Zoe pointed out.

Chrissie nodded slowly. "But it wasn't a conscious memory, you know? Only once I held the charcoal. It was like drawing something I'd seen in a dream. Yeah, exactly like that."

"It was like that for me, too," said Belinda. She held up the picture of Evan. "Except all I remember is him." She stopped, turned. "What is that noise?"

❧ 25 ❧

JUBILEE FIGHTS A MONSTER

STILL CARRYING THE STEEL BAR, Jubilee ran toward the studio. He didn't want to think about what he'd overheard; no space to process it right now. But soon, he knew he'd have to work through it, and try to understand what the hell was going on.

Running through the Camo-world was different to moving through the real. His feet were invisible, so he had to focus intently on the sense of the earth under his feet and the noises about him, just to keep his balance. The weight of the steel bar didn't help. He wondered what he'd look like to someone nearby; would they see a steel reinforcing rod bobbing through mid-air? He stifled a crazy laugh.

He stopped, panting beside the studio. All around, the gray Camo-world wavered, but there, above, the golden creature sat motionless on the branch, still intent on the studio window. Jubilee squinted at it, trying to judge distances through the eerie fog. It would be about ten feet up, he reckoned, so how to draw it down to him? Perhaps he should have gone for his rifle. Even a knife would help.

Just then, the creature lifted its head, as though smelling the air. It glanced about uneasily. The steel, he thought, it smells the steel. Which didn't make sense, but hey.

He crouched beside a bush and experimentally waved the bar in the air.

"Here boy," he whispered, "nice devil."

Stupid, crazy even. Yet the creature shifted restlessly on its perch. Slowly, he crept closer, until he was just below the tree. Up in the tree, the creature hissed.

"Come on down," Jubilee whispered. "Come to papa."

The thing was glancing left and right, as though seeking a quick exit. Jubilee grasped the rod like a club.

"I can smell you, human," whispered the creature. "I know you're there."

Seemed pointless then, to stay hidden.

"So come on down," called Jubilee, tightening his grip.

The thing grinned, displaying sharp teeth, and peered down from its perch. "Where are you, man-thing? You delicious little creature. Come closer, and I will eat your brains, pop out your eyes. Come nearer, oh yes, come to me."

It sniffed, moving restlessly. Jubilee felt grateful for the nebulous protection of the Camo. Should he climb the tree? But there were no easy footholds, and anyway, up in the branches he'd be at the mercy of the creature. So he said nothing, just waited.

Jubilee waved the rod experimentally. The animal tensed, one clawed hand gripping the bark. He knocked the steel against the trunk; the creature flinched. Again, harder. Like a woodsman, attacking a tree. Again, and again, and again. Beneath the blows, the pine tree shuddered, and fine fragments of bark scattered.

"Come down," Jubilee called recklessly. "Come down! I will fight you!"

Again, he smashed the bar against the tree trunk. Crazy really, he'd never be able to knock down a tree with a reinforcing rod.

"You fool!" the animal jeered. "I will return with my brothers, and we will feast on man-flesh."

"Empty threats," Jubilee scoffed. "Why don't you come down, now, and fight me? Since you're so brave?"

The creature hissed again. Jubilee thumped the tree in reply. Quite suddenly the creature bounded down the trunk, running down it like a squirrel. Jubilee was almost too slow, for the thing moved as fast as a cat, gripping on with hands and feet, until its face with those pointed teeth was poised directly above him.

But again, it couldn't see him, it could only make out the steel, and it didn't want to be near that, did it? He swung the metal bar at the creature. It ducked, and spat and hissed. Crouched on the ground, almost as though it was uncertain.

Now! He swung the steel bar hard, like it was a club, like it was the butt of a rifle. Muscle memory took over, and he was back in the Congo, on a jungle track, with a jammed rifle. The enemy were coming; he had no time. Ricochets of whining bullets; his partner screamed and fell. Behind him, leaves scattered, as from the underbrush a rebel, all sweat and rolling eyes, was on him.

Shouting, Jubilee raised the metal rod, just as he'd done with his rifle butt, and smashed it down, hard, trying for the enemy's skull.

Spinning faster than the Congolese, the animal darted back. Its eyes were surprised, and suddenly fearful. Jubilee stepped closer; *quick, quick,* and thud! The rod connected, hard, and the thing screamed, so loud his ears rang.

Jubilee swung again, into the thing's head, and again, into its side. The animal screamed once more, then crumpled, still. He poked it with the bar. Was it faking? Gradually, he grew aware of the smell: smoke, like something cooking. Roasting meat. Poked the creature again with the rod, and where the tip of the rod made contact, smoke rose up. He touched it again and it writhed, groaning.

Again, he touched it, and it curled into a fetal position. Jubilee paused – what should he do with this thing that was neither human nor animal? But as he hesitated, smoke burst in a cloud from the creature's body, and it screamed in a high voice, full of agony. He waved the rod to break up the smoke.

The screaming grew louder, a dreadful wail, and the thing gripped his ankle with desperate claws. "Help! Please!"

He kicked it away. "Get off!"

The creature's eyes rolled back into its head; its golden skin cracked into fine black lines; it gasped once, then burst into flame.

Wide-eyed, Jubilee backed away, clutching tight to the steel bar. Had he done *that*?

The agonized screaming went on and on, until finally, mercifully, it fell silent. And there, where once something had lain, was a blackened, burned piece of ground. The bark of the pine tree was rimmed with black soot. Of the creature, nothing remained but a pile of ash.

He looked down at the reinforcing steel in his hand with respect. "Damn," he whispered. "Holy shit."

"Jubilee?" It was Zoe, her head and shoulders out the window.

"It's okay," he called, then realized she couldn't see him. "I'm all right."

She sagged in relief. "That awful noise – what was it?" She wrinkled her nose. "And what *is* that smell?"

"I'll explain later," he said, feeling suddenly exhausted with the backwash of adrenaline. His hands were shaking. "Please, open the door."

"It's like something burning," she said, and pulled her head in. She added something he couldn't catch, then reappeared. "What's happened to the – whatever it was. The thing in the tree. Is it still there?"

"It's gone," he said, staggering tiredly to the door. The latch clicked and he fell inside. Closing the door behind him, he pulled the hood off, and blinked in relief as the world returned to normal.

Standing at the glass door, still half inside the Camo-world, all he could see was a blackened area of forest. All traces of the brief conflict had disappeared. The creature was evidently invisible in death, just as it had been in life.

Later, he escorted the girls back to the house.

"Are you sure you're okay?" Zoe whispered to him, as slowly they crossed the wide lawn to the back door. "That noise we heard? What was it?"

He wasn't sure what to tell her. What would she know of war, of the feeling of beating a living creature to death? Jubilee shook his head. Words were too hard.

She took his hand, squeezed it gently. "Well, I'm glad you're okay."

He smiled, grateful for her presence. Then glanced about, for who knew what might be watching. He'd declared himself an enemy, and the creature, whatever it had been, was certainly not alone.

The rear door to the house swung open. "There you are," said Val, in relief. "I was about to send out a search party."

That evening, he lay in bed unable to sleep. Every time he closed his eyes, flaming demons rushed at him, claws outstretched. Sighing, he struggled from the obscenely high thread-count sheets. He'd make himself a sandwich.

The phone rang just as he was spreading jelly on white bread. He was reverting to childhood.

"What the hell you been up to?" Whittaker said angrily.

"Good to hear from you, too."

"King's threatening to sue."

"Let him," said Jubilee shortly. "Found out something real interesting about him today."

There was a pause, then Whittaker, probably alerted by

Jubilee's voice, asked, "Hey, you okay, man?"

Jubilee stared out the windows at the distant lights of LA, so frigging normal. He felt like laughing at the thought of explaining the events of the day to Whittaker.

"That platoon," he asked instead. "What happened to them?"

"Platoon? What you talking about?"

"Camo," he said. "They disappeared?"

A pause. "You tried it out, then."

He nodded. "Yeah. I did."

"I warned you not to."

"Yeah. So. The platoon. What happened?"

"They disappeared," said Whittaker. "All of them."

"How many soldiers?"

"Four," he said. "Five, maybe. I think."

"Small platoon, then."

"Experimental tech," said Whittaker, like that was an explanation. "You sure you okay? You sound funny."

He pushed a white curtain aside, stared out at the shapes of the trees, blowing in the wind. "I'm fine, I guess. So, no-one found anything? Like, remains or something?"

"Much as I heard," said Whittaker, "no-one found anything. The tech worked then?"

Jubilee took a deep breath. "Yes. Oh, yeah."

"Holy shit, man." Whittaker stopped for a moment. "What you gonna do, then?"

"You know," said Jubilee, suddenly realizing this was true, "I have no frigging idea." He took a bite of his sandwich. The familiar flavor of peanut butter and jelly filled his mouth, and for a moment he was only six years old, back in Mom's kitchen and safe. He sank onto a white leather sofa with a feeling of relief.

"Whittaker, something's wrong," he said.

"Meaning?"

"I ..." He shook his head, took another bite. "Hard to explain."

How could he tell Whittaker about the golden monsters that surrounded the house; the girls that disappeared, returning with bleeding feet; or the baby that had never returned at all. No, Whittaker would say he'd gone mad. Worse still, he'd pull him off this gig. Then Jubilee would never find out what was happening here.

There was something going on, that was certain. And worse still, seemed he'd been put here for a reason: the old women, the strange appearance of Camo tech; all pointed to destiny at work. He nearly choked on his sandwich at the thought.

Whittaker was talking again. "King, he's going on that you abducted his daughters."

"What! You're joking?"

Whittaker laughed. "He says you took all of them. I said he should be impressed at your stamina." A pause. "Care to tell me what really happened?"

"It's ..." Jubilee groped for the word, "complicated."

"You're okay, though?"

"I'm fine. All good." He swallowed the last of the sandwich. "Hey, wait," he said, struck by a sudden thought. "The platoon. That disappeared. What weapons did they carry?"

"Not sure," Whittaker said. "You want me to ask around?"

"Yeah, please."

A pause. "You think you need weapons? Anything in particular?"

"Perhaps."

"Okay. I'll check it out, get back to you."

The phone clicked as Whittaker hung up. Jubilee sat a moment, thinking and listening to the silence, and nearly jumped out of his skin at the knock on the door. Getting to his feet, he retrieved the steel rod, holding it loosely in his left hand as he opened the door. On the step stood Juan, holding a wrinkled sheet of paper.

When he saw Jubilee, he tugged off his hat. "Senor. I saw light on. Sorry, is late."

"That's okay." Jubilee opened the door wide and set the steel down. "You want to come in?"

Juan shook his head, and passed him the paper. "I find it, Senor."

"What's this?" asked Jubilee, unfolding the sheet, smoothing it flat. "A map?"

"*Si*. You ask for a plan, Senor. I find for you."

Jubilee had forgotten his earlier conversation. Amazing, the effect of an action-packed day.

"This is a plan of this property?"

Juan nodded, traced a rough line with his finger. "Is wall, Senor. See, follow hill down to river."

"There's a river?"

"*Si*, in the valley."

"Sure you don't want to come in?"

"No, Senor. I ... very busy now, Senor."

"Sure, gardening. Right."

"Here is wall," said Juan, tracing the outline with a grimy fingertip. "To river."

Seemed like much of the property was half-hidden from the house; below the house lay acres of valley, all encircled by the wall.

"This part, he is wild," said Juan, pointing to the area below the terrace. "No garden here." Jubilee could see a network of tracks crossing the sloping wilderness and converging on a large clearing.

"This property – it's huge!" Jubilee said.

How much would this place be worth? More than he, or all his soldier-buddies together might make in a lifetime. Hundred million, he thought. At least.

Juan nodded eagerly. "*Si*. Twenty-five acres."

Jubilee whistled, then pointed to the open clearing where the tracks converged. "What's here?"

"That place? Nothing – just a tree fall over," said Juan, his tone dismissive.

Jubilee picked up the paper. "Can I take this?"

Juan nodded.

"Just a moment," called Jubilee, as Juan turned to leave. He picked up the metal bar that he'd set beside the doorframe. "Can I keep this too?"

Juan hesitated, and on his face Jubilee saw wary comprehension. Then the man lowered his eyes. "Senor. Be careful."

"Sure," said Jubilee, and closed the door.

Next morning, Jubilee struggled back into Camo. Seemed safer to explore the property that way. Taking the closest track, he headed down the hill, carrying the steel rod, just in case.

At first, walking on a slope was hard; difficult to place an invisible foot without stumbling. But eventually, he learned to trust his body, and then he could move faster. He felt like a ghost, drifting through a dream-like landscape.

To his relief, he saw no more strange creatures. What were those things? It was as though everything he'd ever known had been shaken and turned on this head. That there were creatures who could walk and talk like men while being patently not human felt deeply, profoundly shocking. He had entered a reality for which he had no words. So Jubilee walked numbly, setting one foot in front of the other, and found relief in the familiarity of movement.

Then the track entered a clearing, and the weary numbness shattered. He stood, mouth agape, staring. Where before everything had been gray and silent, this space in front of him was full of color and noise. Everywhere he looked was brightness and gold; the very air seemed to shimmer.

"Hello," said a soft voice.

Jubilee stepped into the clearing slowly. He had to shade his eyes, the light was so bright. At first he could only make out a silhouette of a torso and head, but slowly the brightness dimmed and the figure solidified into the shape of a young woman, seated on a tree trunk in the center of the clearing.

She smiled and beckoned him forward. "Come," she said. "Don't be afraid."

Her voice was gentle, almost melodic. Obediently, he stepped forward, into the bright, color-filled clearing. The dream-like feeling of unreality increased as he stood, so filled with awe that he forgot to be afraid.

She was very young, perhaps in her teens, with brown skin and brown eyes. When she glanced his way, warmth touched him gently. If he could, he would have fallen at her feet and worshipped her, but when he went to move she held up one slim hand, and he stopped, unable to move.

"I won't hurt you," she said, gently

He nodded, for he felt she spoke truth. Or at least, the truth as she understood it, for something told him that she might indeed hurt him, and badly, too.

A butterfly landed on her knee, and sat there quietly, wings opening and shutting like a beating heart. She extended her index finger, and the butterfly climbed on board. She passed it toward him, but he could only stare.

"What's the matter? Haven't you ever seen a butterfly before?"

"Of course I have," said Jubilee. "But not one as large as that."

She lifted up her hand, and the butterfly opened its wings in benediction. "He is very rare," she acknowledged. "But rare things are beautiful, are they not?"

The dream sense returned, stronger than ever. "Things that are common can be beautiful, too."

She laughed. "Oh, we have a philosopher."

"Who are you?" he asked. "What do you want?"

The butterfly shook itself free of her hand, and flew up into the sky.

"I bring you a message," she said, and crossed the clearing toward him. Placed a palm flat on his chest. Through the tough Camo-skin he could feel it burning. "The message is this: Riccardo King is not your concern. And neither are his daughters."

"Riccardo King is my employer."

She shrugged. "Nevertheless." She hesitated. "For your own good, soldier, do not disregard this warning. You may not get another."

He covered her hand with his own. "Who are you?"

She smiled a little sadly. "A lost soul," she whispered. "Just a lost soul."

Abruptly, she vanished. In front of him was an empty clearing, gray and cold. Putting his hand to his cheek, he realized with some surprise that it was wet with tears.

26

JUBILEE EATS A HIPSTER
HAMBURGER

WHITTAKER CALLED HIM LATER. "You were asking about the platoon?"

"You got something?"

Whittaker cleared his throat. "Not on the phone. Gotta meet. You remember the burger place round from the Lilac Tree? Jimmy's?"

"I think, yeah."

"Eight o'clock," said Whittaker, and put down the phone.

Jimmy's Burgers!

The neon sign flashed through the LA dark. Beside the door of the restaurant sat an old woman. Eyes downcast, palms cupped. In front of her, a chipped bowl and a crudely lettered cardboard sign: *Homeless. Please Help!* It was the exclamation mark that got Jubilee; seemed an unrealistic expression of optimism. So he dropped a folded bill into the bowl.

"Thank you, dearie," said the woman, in a cracked voice, and grinned up at him.

It was the Latino woman, one of the three who'd given him the Camo.

Jubilee started. "You!"

"What did I say? You have a kind heart," she said in a satisfied tone, and retrieved the money from the bowl.

"Hey," said Whittaker from behind, and clapped him on the shoulder. "You're on time! Impressive."

"This your friend, dearie?" asked the beggar-woman.

Whittaker stopped, surprised, then half-smiled at the old lady. "That's right, Ma'am. Been friends a mighty long time."

She nodded seriously. "Very good. This one, he need a friend." She pointed a gnarled finger at Jubilee. "Tell me soldier, you try our gift?"

Ignoring Whittaker's puzzled face, Jubilee nodded slowly. "I did."

"You like where it took you?"

He shook his head. "No, Ma'am. I did not."

She nodded. "*Bueno*. No mortal should."

"What's she talking about?" Whittaker asked, over Jubilee's shoulder.

The old woman grabbed Jubilee's hand. Her grip was surprisingly strong. "You meet *him* yet?"

Whittaker's face was frozen with astonishment. Jubilee could almost read his thoughts; this stranger, this beggar, how dare she?

"You mean Riccardo?" Jubilee spoke quickly, before Whittaker could react. "Yeah, I've met him."

She shook her head. "No. No. Evan."

The name was familiar. Something the girls had said ... But he shook his head.

"You will," she said, and released his hand. "I give you another gift, soldier. You must seek the gardener."

The gardener? Juan? Jubilee frowned, thinking this through. Why Juan? "He had reinforcing steel." Which had proved effective against the creature.

"Iron," she said, nodding. "*Si*. They hate the iron. The gardener knows. Ask him."

"What's she talking about?" said Whittaker, irritably.

"Nothing. Thanks," Jubilee said.

"You're welcome," she said in a sing-song voice, and held up the bowl to Whittaker. Rattled it invitingly.

"All right," snapped Whittaker, and took a bill from his wallet.

She smiled guilelessly. "Thank you, good Sir. Blessings be upon your house. May you and your wife be united in peace." She winked at Jubilee.

Thunderstruck, Whittaker stared down at her. "You!" He lunged for the money.

Too slow; too late. One minute she was there: the next – gone. The cardboard sign with its optimistic exclamation mark blew away in the wind.

"What!? Where did she go?" Whittaker said, staring about as though he might spot her among the crowds. Jubilee grabbed his sleeve.

"Leave it," he said. "Come on. Are we going to eat or not?"

Whittaker subsided, muttering.

As Jubilee opened the door to the burger joint, he heard the old woman whisper from the empty air. "Be very careful, soldier. Evan, he has great power. You must take care."

Jimmy's Burgers was packed with hipsters sporting expensively maintained beards, and Jubilee felt immediately out of place.

"What was that about?" Whittaker asked as they queued at the wooden counter to place their order.

"Long story," Jubilee said.

"What'll it be, gents?" asked the girl at the till.

"Two burgers and fries," said Whittaker. "And a beer. You want a beer?"

Jubilee shook his head. "Coke, thanks."

They settled into their table, sipped their drinks.

Whittaker wiped froth from his upper lip. "That woman? What was with her?"

"How would I know? She's crazy."

"Here you go," sang the server, depositing their orders in front of them.

Whittaker glared at him suspiciously, and squirted ketchup on his fries.

"So," Jubilee asked. "What did you find out?"

Whittaker was still frowning, but at the question his face cleared. "That platoon," he said in a low voice. "You asked about weapons." He glanced over his shoulder, and said in a low voice, "for the first tests, they carried standard issue: M4, Sigs."

Jubilee frowned. "Really? Why?" Ordinance would have to be carried on the outside of the suit, making any weapons immediately visible.

"Yeah, pointless," agreed Whittaker. "But you know the army." He bit widely into his burger. "This is good!" Licked his fingers, and in a muffled voice added: "Anyway, after the first trial, they dropped the standard issue armaments."

"So what did they carry instead?"

Whittaker dabbed at his lips with a paper towel. "Yeah, so this is where it gets weird. My contact says, metal. They were big on knives."

"Commando knives? Wouldn't they still be carried on the outside of the suit?"

"Smaller. They had hinge-knives, like switchblades, carried in wrist or ankle holsters. The smaller ones fitted into pockets."

Jubilee nodded slowly. "Okay. Makes sense."

"One of the guys was into MMA; insisted on carrying a katana in a back sheath, and nunchakus. Like something from a frigging comic strip." Whittaker shook his head, then added, "Guess the powers that be decided that since the soldiers were the ones putting their lives on the line, they could make the call on weapons."

"Nunchaku? As in the movies?"

Jubilee couldn't believe it. Relying on two sticks between a chain? Whatever those soldiers had seen, it must have made them desperate.

"Crazy, right?" Whittaker said, finishing his burger. "Hey, you're not eating."

"In a minute," said Jubilee. "You said – their weapons were metal. Any kind of metal? Like, did that matter?"

Whittaker's brow cleared. "Yeah, that's right. Steel, iron. Something like that."

"No carbon fiber?"

"Ha! No. They wanted weight, I guess."

Jubilee nodded, and started on his fries. They were crisp and salty, just the way he liked them.

"That old lady," Whittaker said, glancing over at his shoulder at the door. "What she said–"

"She's just some crazy. Forget it."

"Just, Teena and me, we're still trying for a reconciliation."

"Hey, that's great."

"Yeah." Whittaker finished his beer, held up the bottle. "You want?"

Jubilee shook his head. "No, thanks."

When Whittaker stood up, Jubilee grabbed his wrist. "You want to get back with Teena?" He took the bottle from his friend's hand, tapped it on the table, and glanced at Whittaker significantly. "You have to slow down."

Whittaker glared down at him angrily, and Jubilee tensed. But the moment passed as his friend sighed, then sat heavily.

"You okay?"

Whittaker had his head in his hands. "Yeah, I guess." His voice was muffled.

"You want some Coke?"

Whittaker sighed, took a sip and made a face. "Too sweet." He glanced at Jubilee, then glanced away.

"When are you catching up?" Jubilee asked.

"Huh?"

"With Teena?"

The troubled look on Whittaker's face disappeared, and he smiled. "Tomorrow. We're going away for the weekend."

"Dirty weekend!"

"Too damn right," Whittaker said, then added, "thanks."

"No problem, man."

Jubilee ate his burger. It was cold.

"Riccardo King," said Whittaker, after a moment.

"What about him?"

Whittaker made a face. "He's shady. There are rumors."

"Rumors of ..."

He shook his head. "I'm looking into it. Just, watch your back."

In three months you can have her. Jubilee shivered. Whatever King was up to, Whittaker was right. The guy was shady.

"You okay?" Whittaker asked.

"Fine," Jubilee said, wiping his fingers.

Whittaker considered him, then grinned. "Oh, and I got something for you."

Without warning, he reached into a pocket and plonked a switchblade on the table.

"Shit, man!" Jubilee said, and grabbed at it before a hipster could spot it and scream.

"Try it, go on."

Jubilee hesitated. With a mental shrug, he depressed the catch. Click! Out swung the blade, shiny-bright and deadly sharp. "Nice," he said, turning it, feeling the balance.

"Sweet weapon," agreed Whittaker.

"Is this for Teena? Like a peace offering?"

"Ha! No way. Ain't going to give that woman anything sharp. It's for you."

"Me? Well, thanks, I guess." Jubilee picked it up, The weight was nice, and yeah, it would be great for Camo, looked like it might just fit in the thigh pocket.

"Thing is, this ain't from me." Whittaker rubbed an eyebrow. "My buddy slipped it to me. That platoon that disappeared? This was left in their weapons locker."

"Shit, man!" Stealing from the army was a big, big No. It was always the guys in the front line who got caught short. Fatally.

"Hey. I get it." Whittaker held up his hands in agreement. "Normally, I'd never. Just, he – well, he wanted you to have it. My contact. Thing is, his girlfriend was in that platoon that went missing. If you could find out what happened to Myla, I know he'd sure appreciate it. That's her name. Myla Franks."

Jubilee hesitated, then pushed it into his back pocket. "I'll think about it."

"Be careful, man," said Whittaker.

"Sure," Jubilee got up. "You can finish my fries."

"Thanks, but no thanks," said Whittaker, eyeing the cooling pile with distaste.

"You want her back?" said Jubilee firmly. "Then lay off the beer." He hesitated. "I don't like this."

"It's not from Supplies," Whittaker said quickly. "It's special stock. No-one else would want it."

"It's not that."

"Then what is it?"

"It's the obligation," said Jubilee, and left the restaurant.

"Hey," Whittaker called, as he pushed open the door, "I'll be in touch."

"Sure."

Beside the door, a figure wrapped in grimy blankets lay on flattened cardboard. It stirred as he passed and a filthy face peered up at him. With relief, Jubilee saw this was no-one he knew. No-one at all.

Waving for a taxi, he felt a mad fury. It wasn't the gift of the knife that made him angry, no, nor the removal of the weapon from the army supplies. It was that with the gift, Whittaker had placed him under an obligation to a nameless supply officer. Now, like it or not, Jubilee felt honor-bound to return to the gray Camo-world.

27

IS THIS WHAT IT'S LIKE, HAVING SISTERS?

EARLY EVENING and the three of them had gathered in the family room at the front of the house. Behind the glinting turquoise of the pool lay the city of LA, half-hidden by the haze. The sky was turning pink, and in the distance the street lights were coming on. Kind of cool to watch the city becoming outlined in light.

Chrissie and Zoe were reclining on opposite corners of an enormous couch. Chrissie thumbed lazily through a fashion magazine as Belinda sketched. Her pencil, skimming across the paper, made a soft scraping sound.

Zoe's feet throbbed relentlessly. Today had been so bizarre. Belinda had been so sure there was something in that tree – but Chrissie couldn't see it, and neither could Zoe. She frowned. Jubilee had seen something. And there had been that awful smell.

Well, at least she'd run into that kind soldier again. One positive to come from this bizarre day. And he was even nicer than she'd remembered. How strange to think that he was her bodyguard. Weirder still, that she even needed a bodyguard. She shook her head at the unexpectedness of it. Jubilee had gone into the city to meet a friend. He'd said she would be safe if she stayed indoors, and she'd said she wasn't going outside; she wasn't going anywhere until her feet stopped hurting.

The door opened and Riccardo came in. Chrissie stiffened and Belinda closed her sketch pad.

From his frown, Riccardo was obviously annoyed. "Why did you disappear like that? I thought the doctor made it clear – no walking until your feet healed."

Belinda pointed at her wheelchair. "You talking to me?"

"Don't be stupid," he snapped. "I meant *them*." He indicated Chrissie and Zoe.

Chrissie didn't lift her eyes from her magazine. "We were okay."

"We didn't go far," Zoe added.

He rounded on her. "And I thought *you* had more sense."

She shuffled guiltily. "I'm sorry."

Belinda swung her chair about, and scowled at her. Belinda, Zoe realized, probably never apologized.

Riccardo sighed. "Well, never mind. At least there's no lasting damage." Reaching over, he yanked Chrissie's magazine from her hands.

"Hey!" she said.

"So what happened last night? Where did you go?" He held up the magazine. "No, don't tell me. Let me guess. You have no idea."

"Actually," said Belinda, "that's precisely true."

He rolled his eyes. "Sure. So, now I know why you were so keen to get together this morning: you were hatching a crazy-ass story. What do you mean, you don't remember?"

Belinda wheeled over to the window. "It's the truth. We don't remember."

"And what about that useless piece of shit of a bodyguard?" Riccardo grumbled. "My daughters disappear and where is he? Asleep, that's where he was." He grunted then, walked over to the marble fire mantel, and stood, moodily surveying the gold-painted pine cones placed on the artificial coals. "And now he's disappeared."

"He's gone to meet a friend," said Zoe.

She felt protective of Jubilee. Back in the bus depot, there had been something empty about his eyes; like he'd lost part of himself. Men like to be up and doing, Mom had said, ain't good for them to have nothing to do. A job, Zoe thought, might help fill up that emptiness. Besides, she owed him.

Riccardo's face softened. "I forgot what a big change you've had this last week, Zoe. I guess it is all strange: me, your sisters, this house."

Chrissie picked up her magazine, thumbed through the pages. "Sure. I bet it's real strange."

"What does that mean?" Riccardo asked.

She shrugged. "Nothing."

"Anyway, since you're supposed to be resting," Riccardo said to Zoe, "let's make use of this time. Been wanting to record you ever since that damn competition. Now's our chance." He rubbed his hands together. "You said you've got some of Charley's songs?"

Zoe nodded. "Some. But–"

"Great. I'll check my files too." He left the room abruptly, calling for Val.

"Do you think," Belinda said slowly, "he seemed *relieved* when I said we couldn't remember?"

"He didn't press the point," Chrissie said.

They sat in silence. Chrissie turned the pages of her magazine. Seemed like all that closeness in the studio, the sisterly chats of yesterday, had disappeared in the face of this moody silence. Swish, swish, went the pages. What had Chrissie said earlier? *He never pays attention to us.* But that was hardly Zoe's fault. If this is what it's like to have sisters, Zoe thought, I can live without them.

Zoe set her feet on the floor. Bit her lip at the pain. I've waited all my life for this chance, she thought, and I'm not going to let some sulky girl get in my way.

Taking a deep breath, she stood up. After a brief moment the pain settled enough to let her move. And if she kept her feet rolled out, so she was walking on their outer edges, it wasn't so bad.

"Where are you going?" Belinda asked.

"Where's Riccardo's studio?"

The sisters exchanged a glance, then: "That way," said Belinda, pointing to the door.

"First left," Chrissie said.

"You sure you're all right?" Belinda asked.

Zoe shrugged. "Hopefully." She wished Jubilee was here. She could do with a friend in this place. Someone she wasn't related to.

When she reached the door to Riccardo's office, she heard voices. Zoe hesitated. Should she knock?

"I don't know what to do," said Riccardo. "Tell me what to do."

"You make bargain," a man replied, "but words are tricky. *They* tricky."

It was the little gardener, Juan, with the soft Hispanic accent. *You're welcome, Senora.* What was he doing in there?

Riccardo sighed. "All right, all right. You make your point. But you heard what that thing said. We've got to do something."

"You try get out of a bargain with *them*? Is very dangerous. They watch you, they know if you cheat."

"They do?" Riccardo sounded worried. "Are they watching us now?"

"I wear iron," said Juan, as though this was an answer.

"Iron," said Riccardo thoughtfully. "Juan, buddy, you think that might help?"

"I don't know. Maybe."

"If it works, I'll owe you."

"No!" The gardener's voice was harsh. "You owe me nothing. *Nada.* No more debts."

"Okay, okay. Sheesh, it was just a figure of speech."

"Words important," Juan said. "Have power." There was the sound of a door opening. "I think about it, yes? But no promises."

"I appreciate it. Thank you."

The door closed, and the room went silent.

In the hallway, Zoe hesitated. Through the door she heard the soft tap-tapping of a keyboard.

Come on, girl! Squaring her shoulders, she took a deep breath and knocked.

"Come in," Riccardo said. As she opened the door, he raised his eyebrows. "Hey, Zoe. Are you sure you should be up?"

"My feet are feeling better," Zoe lied. "And I thought, since you were talking about recording, I'd come have a look – if that's okay."

Riccardo gestured to a chair. "Sure, it's fine. Please. Sit down." He considered her for a moment, then said, "Do you have your singing voice on?"

"Now?" She tried to keep the excitement from her voice. Taking a deep breath, she aimed for studied nonchalance. "Yeah. Sure."

"Excellent." Glancing at his watch, he got to his feet. "I can spare an hour. Once I've seen what you can do, I'll book the session guys."

Zoe stared at him in excitement. She'd never been able to afford real-live musicians before – she'd always had to make do with software.

He seemed amused by her reaction. "It *is* music, sweetheart."

"I thought you'd just ... I don't know. Run a loop or something."

"Better with the real thing, don't you think?"

"Oh yes." She nodded fervently. "Definitely. Absolutely."

Holy cow! Real musicians! In a real, honest-to-god recording studio!

"Through here," he said, opening a door and snapping on lights.

A mixing desk, bright under spotlights, stretched away like the console of a 747. Half-hidden in the darkness stood shadowy microphones and music stands. The room smelt of stale smoke, and with its flat echoes, it felt peculiarly empty. In front of them was a wide window. Riccardo's reflection drifted, ghost-like, across its dark glass.

"Sound booth," he said, pointing at the window. "I got an overdub room too. If I need more, I hire a suite."

When Riccardo snapped on more lights, reality struck: here she stood, in a recording studio! Zoe smiled. Pausing in the doorway, she wished Charley could see her.

Riccardo, Charley had said, *he likes being generous. You treat him right and there ain't nothing he won't do for you. Smile, be nice. Not too difficult, is it? Ah, but keeping it up: that's the hard part. That's the part I could never manage.*

28

RECORDING TIME

RICCARDO SETTLED himself at the mixing desk. "Okay. So, I'm thinking simple, but effective. Old school, kind of Nina Simone meets Carole King." He glanced at Zoe. "You know Charley's early songs? You sang them with your Mom, huh? You ever take the melody?"

"Sometimes. Sometimes the harmony. Whatever we felt like, really." Her eyes stung, but she wasn't going to cry, not in front of him.

Once, when Zoe was about seven, Charley had leased a convertible because: *Baby girl, I know we ain't got the money, but – hell. Everyone should ride with the wind in their hair once in their life.* They had driven all the way from Nebraska to the coast, riding the freeways with the top down. Wind combed their hair as they'd sang their hearts out. Zoe remembered it so clearly: the sun on the sea, and the smell of the brine. And Charley's voice, high and clear, like a lark.

"It's okay that you miss her. Charley had a beautiful voice." Riccardo's voice was low, persuasive. "You have it too. The way you sing, your range, the clarity of your tone. One of my biggest regrets is that I never made an album with her. Wish I had." He clapped her on the shoulder. "Your voice is a gift. Believe me. We'll make something that would have made make your mother proud. All right. Let's make a start, shall we?"

He opened the door to the sound booth, snapped on more light and tugged over a high stool. "Here. Better for your feet."

Awkwardly, Zoe perched upright, tried not to fall off.

"Okay?"

She nodded. "I think so."

"Great. So, your job," he said, handing her a set of headphones, "is to wear these, sing like an angel, and do whatever the hell I tell you to do."

Zoe swallowed, put the headphones about her neck. Riccardo adjusted the microphone so the round pop filter sat in front of her like a target. She tugged the headphones on and the world grew instantly silent.

Riccardo gave her a thumbs-up, stepped into the mixing room and made a face at her through the glass.

At first Zoe felt like a fish in a tank because of the high window that looked directly into the mixing room. All she could see was Riccardo at the desk, his big hands moving quickly across the dials, head nodding in time with the beat. Behind him, LEDs flickered.

He issued soft commands that rang in her headphones, so it was like he was standing right behind her. At first this was disconcerting, and she had to stop herself from turning her head.

Again from the top; hold the A; more emphasis on the second syllable, okay?

She'd do whatever it was he'd asked, and he'd either nod, or frown, and ask her to repeat. Sometimes he'd sing the melody into her ears: "Like this, yes?" and when she did it right he'd smile in approval.

Time and again his phone rang, and he'd break off what he

was doing to take a call. Once, Val had put her head around the door, but he waved her away. The studio had no external windows so the process seemed to exist outside of time; there was only the two of them, just her and Riccardo, locked in this creative space. It was exhausting; it was exhilarating. She wanted it to last forever. But eventually, her throat and belly began to ache from sustaining the pitch and her feet were one long continuous throb.

"You look pale," said Riccardo. "Go get something to eat. We'll do this again next week."

"Next *week*! But I thought …"

He shook his head as his phone rang again. He glanced at the number. "I'm booked for the next few days." Said into the handset: "King here."

Zoe thought of the killer-silence of her sisters. "What am I going to do? For a whole week?"

"Hang on a minute." He covered the phone, waved a hand toward her, like it wasn't his concern if she had nothing to do. "Rest. Swim. Relax, sunbathe, whatever. Recharge your batteries. Have a holiday."

She made a face. She couldn't swim, not with her feet bandaged.

"You could do some practice," he offered. "There's a piano in the music room."

"You have a music room?" she said, then bit her lip. *Obviously* he had a music room.

"Actually, yeah," he said. "That's a good idea. I won't be able to get the session guys for at least three weeks, so you may as well get some practice in."

Reluctantly, Zoe nodded. She could do that, she could practice. "Okay."

"But first, you gotta get some rest, all right?"

She nodded.

"Good girl." He returned to the phone. "Yeah, sorry. Fire away.

No, no, that's um ..." he pinched the top of his nose, as though thinking, "... Zoe. Yeah, my oldest kid. Yeah, that's the one." He added to Zoe, "Hey, do me a favor? Find Val for me, will you?"

Was it Zoe's imagination, or had he just forgotten her name? "Yeah, sure," she said, getting up off her stool. Hell, but her feet hurt.

Slowly, she hobbled back to her room. The doors to Chrissie's and Belinda's rooms were closed. Reaching her room, she flopped onto her bed with relief.

"Mew," said Helen, jumping up beside her.

"Hey girl," said Zoe, running a hand across the cat's smooth gray fur. "Where you been? You settling in okay?"

As though in answer, the animal curled up beside her. Lying beside the purring cat, Zoe stared up at the white, white ceiling. She felt she might fall up into it, float away, weightless. It had been hard, trying to reproduce Mom's voice, but somehow she'd succeeded. Listening to today's playbacks had almost been spooky, because her voice had resembled Charley's so closely.

Zoe wished she'd had a chance to sing her own songs. She didn't want to be an echo of her mother. Perhaps, if they had time, and Riccardo was willing, she might be able to do that. Perhaps.

She tugged her duffel out from under her bed and felt in its side pocket. There, half-hidden, was the USB that held her songs, recorded on her mixer in her bedroom. Such a tiny thing to hold such magic! She lay back on the bed, USB clutched in her left fist.

Next morning, Zoe's feet had improved, so she decided to try a gentle walk to the gate, check out the street, perhaps. But the gate turned out to be locked, needing a keypad code to open it. A code she didn't have. Which meant that if she exited the property, she wouldn't be able to open the gate again. Although she wouldn't make it far – the way her feet felt, likely she'd end up slumped on a sidewalk, waiting for Val to pick her up in her shiny white car.

To either side of the metal gate stretched the white wall,

topped with broken glass. It seemed to go on forever, down into the valley. Looking at the gate, so shiny and high, she wasn't sure who the wall protected: was it the people on the outside, or those within? I guess it's whoever has the key, she thought.

Through the palms, she saw a small white building. Was it a gatehouse? Like, for a chauffeur or something? But Riccardo didn't have a chauffeur. Or did he? She hesitated, wondered if she could ask whoever lived in it for help.

On cue, Jubilee stuck his head from a window. "Hey! You okay?"

Feeling like a fool she replied: "Um, not really."

"You know what it's like to practice something, day after day, month after month, until it becomes second nature?" Jubilee asked. Glancing at Zoe's feet, he added: "Are you sure you shouldn't be resting?"

"I've had more than enough rest, thank you," she said.

They were sitting on a terrace outside his miniature house, drinking sodas and enjoying the sunlight. He couldn't have a beer, he said, because he was working, but he dragged out two recliners and raised a sun umbrella, so it felt like being on holiday. Zoe felt guilty that she wasn't practicing, but whatever. Hadn't Riccardo told her to take a break?

Jubilee sat on the edge of his recliner, soda in hand, chatting to her. He was bare-chested, which was a mite distracting, because he was *built*. Clearly, he worked out.

Shading her eyes with her hand, she squinted at him. "You were asking about practice. Are you talking martial arts? Or any skill?"

"Any skill."

"Well then, sure, I know what it's like."

"How so?"

"Music. Hours and hours of practice," she said, and took a long, cool sip.

"Playing what?"

"Piano. Sax. Flute. Violin."

He raised his eyebrows. "Any instrument you *can't* play?"

She laughed. "Oboe. Trumpet."

"What about that, I don't know, that kind of guitar. Like with all the strings. The Beatles used it."

"The sitar? No, not that, either. I really am useless. You play anything?"

He shook his head.

"So, what do you know about practice, then?" She poked him with a bandaged foot.

"Nothing," he said, resting back on an elbow, and watching her from half-lidded eyes. "I'm too lazy."

She snorted. "So, what's a lazy-ass guy like you doing here, then?"

"Security detail," he said, finishing his soda. "You want another?"

"I'm good, thanks." She glanced at the house behind him, and the soda in his hand. "Security work seems pretty sweet, these days."

He half-smiled. "Seriously," he said, "you shouldn't be walking about here, not by yourself."

"Why not?" She stretched out on the recliner, and aware of his attention, spread her arms wide.

"You forgotten that thing – in the tree?"

"I never saw it."

"Well, I did," he said, and something about his tone made her sit upright. "And I tell you, it wasn't friendly." He held out his hand. "If you've finished your drink, I'll take you back to the house."

"You think it's that dangerous? I mean, there's a locked gate and everything."

He paused. "I don't know. And that's enough to get me worried."

As they walked back to the house, Zoe leaned on his arm. She went extra slowly, because she was enjoying the play of his muscles beneath her hand. A butterfly bobbed past, blue wings shimmering in the sunlight.

"You want to go out," he said, "you let me know, okay?"

"Why? You want to come with me?" She was flirting, and she didn't care.

Jubilee glanced down at her and she saw, deep in his eyes, that he knew what she was doing, and appreciated it. But his tone was serious. "I'm employed to keep you safe."

"You think I'm in danger?" She meant it to be funny, but now the words were out there, and she couldn't pull them back.

"I hope not." He put out a finger for the butterfly, but it kept flying.

"Where are you from?" she asked. "LA?"

He smiled, shook his head. "South Side. Chicago. Where were you raised?"

"Cheyenne County, Nebraska." She laughed suddenly. "I was the only black girl at my school. Only black girl in the district."

"You get picked on?"

"A bit," she said quietly, remembering. She'd tried to flatten her hair, brushing it for hours and hours, so hard that her scalp ached. And the kids at school, asking if her skin was dirty. She took a deep breath. "Yeah. Some. What about you?"

He shrugged. "Chicago gets a bad press, but South Side ain't so bad. Folk look out for each other, you know?"

"Your people still live there?"

As they reached the house the butterfly disappeared into the shrubbery.

He shook his head. "Dad got cancer. I was in the Congo when he died."

"I'm sorry to hear that," Zoe said, recognizing the pain in his eyes. "Your mom?"

He shook his head. "Dementia. She's in a home. I visit, but she don't know me."

"Oh man. That's tough."

"Yeah, well." He paused, gave her a shy smile. "I don't talk about my family much."

Zoe nodded. Talking about home and family allowed people to make judgments about you. Safer to keep your background hidden.

"Listen. From now on, if you want to go out, let me know. I'll come with you. Don't go walking." He squeezed her shoulder gently. "I'm serious. This place," he glanced behind him, at the hills, "there's something weird here."

"What do you mean?"

He said nothing for a moment, then: "Where do you think you went? That night."

She shook her head. "I don't know."

"That's what worries me," he said quietly. "That you don't know. Better be safe. Besides," he added, "you got a real nice car. So if you want to go out, I'm happy to drive you."

"Okay, so you don't care about me. You just want my car."

He shrugged, mock-serious. "Well, I guess."

"Thanks," she said, laughing.

"Hey, don't get me wrong. You're great-looking and everything, but hey, that Mercedes!"

She punched him on the arm as they reached the house. Jubilee helped her up the steps, and they stopped at the door.

"Thank you," she said awkwardly. "For the soda and everything."

"No problem." He paused. "I mean it. If you need a break from luxury, you let me know."

Rising early next morning, Jubilee stepped out onto the terrace to watch the sunrise. Best time of the day, before the air got too hot, when things still smelt fresh and clean.

Behind him, someone spoke. "Soldier. You be careful."

He turned quickly. It was Juan, his face half-hidden by an ancient straw hat. He wore a pair of battered coveralls and carried a pair of clippers. A grimy red bandana was knotted about his neck. He pulled out a fistful of worn house nails. "For you." He pressed them into Jubilee's palm. "You help Miss Zoe yesterday." He tapped Jubilee on the chest. "You good man."

"Um, thank you," he said, weighing the nails. "What are these for?"

"Is iron." The gardener glanced about warily, and half-whispered, "*They* not like iron."

"You know who *they* are?"

Juan shook his head. "Senor, best to be quiet." He gestured to the grubby roof nails. "Tell no-one I give you."

"Okay," Jubilee murmured, and added, because the man seemed to expect it, "Thank you."

"*De nada.* Wear next to skin." Juan pointed to his sock, as worn and tattered as the rest of him. "Me, I wear here."

Jubilee blinked. "You want me to put nails in my *sock*?"

Juan put a finger to his lips. "Remember. They not like. You go anywhere," he pointed at Jubilee, "you wear iron. Okay?"

Jubilee was reminded of a briefing in his first year, when he was still doing Basic. The instructor had been a grizzled sergeant, a half-PTSD half-psycho with one hell of a service record. "Pay attention, men. What I'm about to tell you will save your life."

They had expected a deep secret or a special ninja trick.

"Get to know the locals," said the psycho. "They know the conditions better than you – hell, they *live* in them. If a local ever offers you advice, then you better damn well listen."

"Okay." Jubilee rolled down his sock, inserted the nail, then rolled the sock back up. The metal pressed against his skin, but luckily, the point was dull. "Iron, is it?" he said, bending over. "What about steel?"

But when he straightened up, the gardener had disappeared. Jubilee sighed, put the rest of the nails in his breast pocket and went inside to grab breakfast.

Over the next week, as her feet slowly healed, Zoe kept out of Jubilee's way. Get too close to someone, that's when you get hurt.

"Meow," said Helen, winding about her legs.

Zoe tugged the comb through her hair. She wanted to braid it into cornrows. She liked that look and the clicking as she shook her head.

"Mew!" said Helen, commanding attention.

Zoe picked her up. "Girl, but you're heavy."

Helen struggled free. "Meh," she said, reprovingly.

She trotted to the door and stared at it until Zoe opened it for her. "You got me trained," she said, as Helen squeezed out through the narrow gap. "You coming to my practice today?"

The cat hesitated as though considering the offer, but her answering meow was non-committal. Zoe sighed. Great. Another day alone with Riccardo's piano. She made a face. She was over that piano.

Val was in the kitchen, spooning granola into a bowl. "Hi," she said, as Zoe came in.

"You been for a run?" Zoe asked.

This morning Val's hair was loose, her face flushed. She wore jogging pants and a crop top. Her abs were rock hard.

Val shook her head. "Pilates."

"There's a reformer here?"

"In the pool house," said Val. She lowered her voice, moved closer to Zoe, which felt kind of creepy. Zoe tried not to back away. "*He* was there."

"He?"

"You know," said Val, and when Zoe stared blankly at her, she added in a whisper: "the bodyguard." She fanned her face. "Watching him work out made my heart beat twice as fast."

Zoe stared. What was Val thinking? She was way too old for Jubilee. "Where's Chrissie?" she asked. "I've hardly seen her this week."

Val took skim milk from the fridge. "'Designing,'" she said, making air quotes with her fingers. Glancing over her shoulder, she whispered, "Personally, I doubt there's any actual design work happening."

"So what do you think she's doing?"

"Absolutely no idea. I don't see her wearing anything new afterward, though." She took a mouthful of granola.

"And Belinda?" Zoe asked "What's she up to?"

"Who knows? That girl's a law unto herself. She's probably out in her studio. Where are you going?"

"Piano," said Zoe, stacking her dishes into the dishwasher. "I have to practice."

"Good luck," said Val, raising her cereal bowl in salute.

The piano, a white concert grand, was set on a dais in the music room. Red velvet curtains, tied back with gold braid, moved slightly in the hum from the air-conditioner. The room was icy-cold. Zoe liked it this way, because it kept her awake.

As she'd done for the past few days, she began with scales. Charley, who'd taught piano, had made Zoe learn scales and arpeggios as a kid, on and on, so boring. Finally, Zoe had flat-out refused to sit at the stool, unless Mom promised to teach her actual music.

"You think this ain't music?" Charley said, and raised an eyebrow. "Baby, scales are the basis of music."

Zoe was sulky. "I don't care. They're boring."

Charley had sighed. "All right. I teach you a song, then you do your scales. Okay? Deal?"

Zoe, five years old, considered the offer carefully. Finally, she nodded. "Okay. But they've gotta be a *proper* song."

"Baby, I'll teach you Bach."

"Who's he?"

"Only the greatest composer that ever lived," said Charley.

"It's a proper song?"

"Definitely."

So at five Zoe began her musical education with *The Well-Tempered Clavier*, by J.S. Bach. Which had still felt a good deal like scales, but Charley insisted otherwise.

Scales over, Zoe sat back. She wanted to work on her own pieces first. She'd been thinking over Jubilee's question: *You get picked on?*

After that, seemed the lyrics just built themselves.

Casual Cruelty

> *The casual cruelty,*
> *Of a girl at school,*
> *Ain't no one as cruel,*
> *As those girls at school.*
>
> *Everywhere I go I feel eyes on my back,*
> *Eyes on my back,*
> *Eyes on my back.*
> *Everywhere I go,*
> *There's eyes at my back,*
> *But I walk tall anyway.*
>
> *My teacher, rich and white,*
> *Calls me 'cool';*
> *Like I'm a freak*
> *To the girls in school*

Everywhere I go I feel eyes on my back,
Eyes on my back,
Eyes on my back.
Everywhere I go,
There's eyes at my back,
But I walk tall anyway.

They talk about my hair,
My skin, my house,
But the girls at school,
Can kiss my ass.

I will not fear; will not fear.
And I walk tall anyway.

Yeah, everywhere I go I feel eyes on my back,
Eyes on my back,
Eyes on my back.
Everywhere I go,
There's eyes at my back,
But I walk tall anyway.

Loving the tension between the sadness of the verse and the anger of the chorus, Zoe left the piano and picked up her guitar. Verse with a four-chord progression, I-V-vi-IV. Not sure about the chorus.

She searched the room for blank score sheets, opening and closing closets until finally she found them heaped messily inside the piano stool. She sat on the floor, guitar on her lap and back against the sofa, and hummed the melody through. Then the piano, where she played the song phrase by phrase, and wrote it down on the score. Lots and lots of erasing and scratching out, until the melody was there.

Returned to her guitar. Tried different strum patterns, unsure. Might sound better with more beat? Sang the melody again, louder this time. Anger caught and held and she stood up, slung the strap about her shoulders and sang LOUDLY. Now it was a protest march, with the muted strum acting as percussion. And all of a sudden, there was her song, brand new in the world. Perfect and shining sweet.

Glancing out the window, Zoe realized half the day had slid by in the creation of her three-minute musical masterpiece. She was supposed to be working on Charley's songs, not her own.

Reluctantly, she returned to the piano, just in time to see the handle on the door turn slowly. She hoped it wasn't Riccardo. Should she be apologetic, or defiant? Didn't she have a right to play what she wanted? An excuse was building on her lips as the door swung open – to reveal an empty corridor, and improbably, a floating steel bar.

She stared at it, unable to think; unable even to move. *What the hell?*

Jerkily, the bar moved forward into the room. She swallowed back deep, almost irrational fear. Could the house be haunted? The bar stopped, just in front of the French doors, and a man's voice uttered a soft curse. She recognized the voice.

"Ju-Jubilee?" She licked dry lips, tried again. "Is that you?"

The steel bar was floating diagonally upright, about six feet up off the floor. When she spoke it twitched, and seemed to spin slightly. It looked kind of like a baseball club, clutched ready for a pitcher's swing. Hands shaking, she reached out to touch it and hit something.

"Careful," said a voice.

Not something. Someone.

The metal bar moved, and above the roaring in her ears, Jubilee's voice asked, "Zoe? Are you okay?"

She nodded weakly. Refused to look up at that floating piece of metal.

The hand on her shoulder felt normal, and she focused her mind on that. "Are you really here?"

She felt him squat in front of her, except she couldn't see anything, only empty air. But she was sure, when she closed her eyes, there was someone there: she could feel his presence. Zoe reached out with two hands, connected with a head, and hit ...

"Ow," Jubilee said. "You got me in the eye."

❦ 29 ❦

JUBILEE IS STARTLED BY THE
SUDDEN APPEARANCE OF A CAT

JUBILEE HAD BEEN WALKING the grounds every day for the past week or so. The estate was huge, and much of it was difficult to access, almost wilderness, so he took his time. Finally, he figured he could find his way pretty well, even the dark.

He wanted to explore unseen, so he wore Camo. Just as he'd thought, the switchblade fitted neatly into his pocket without affecting the invisibility. He still missed his rifle. Something about holding it in his hands felt calming. Eventually, he went back to the steel bar. After all, it was narrow enough that it could be hidden behind things, and besides – and this was a significant advantage – it actually seemed to work against those damn creatures. Except, he hadn't quite factored in the effect it might have on others.

He'd heard Zoe singing, and had followed the music inside. Stupid. He should have said something first, not freaked her out like this. For a moment, he thought she might faint. "Zoe? Hey, Zoe! It's only me."

A silver-gray cat crept around the door. "Meow."

"What the hell?" Jubilee asked. "Who are you?"

Zoe laughed shakily. "That's Helen. Helen, come here."

But the animal wasn't looking at her. Standing at the French doors, it stared out at the garden, before scratching on the glass. "Meow!" it said, imperatively.

Jubilee pushed the French door open and in one bound, the cat was through, making for the bushes. And then he saw it, the thing that had drawn the cat's attention. Half-hidden beneath green leaves, a monster crouched. It had red eyes and clawed hands that looked capable of tearing a cat in half.

The cat, Helen, crouched a few feet from the creature. Her fur was erect and her ears were flat on her skull. The monster hissed, stamping angrily, but the cat wasn't deterred. She hissed back, then opening her mouth, *yowled*. It sounded like a baby crying, or a declaration of war.

Jubilee, with an increasing sense of unreality, stifled a laugh. You had to admire the animal's nerve. He gripped the metal bar tight, just as the cat yowled again and leaped for the monster. They both fell into the bushes and for a confused moment, all he could see was branches moving about. Above their rustling murmur he heard the howls of an angry cat, and more hissing. The branches swayed again, hard, and there – no, surely he was imagining it.

Jubilee ran forward, squinting into the melee. "What the–"

For a moment he thought he'd seen a tall woman in a silver dress in the clearing beyond the shrubs, and the monster, all teeth and claws, cowering at her feet. Then the woman stamped her foot and the monster turned and ran. Jubilee stood, amazed. Then suddenly his vision was impeded by falling leaves. No, not leaves – hundreds of butterflies.

"How gorgeous!" Zoe said from behind him, and held out her hands to the small creatures.

"Meow," said a small voice, and astonishingly, there was the cat.

"Is she yours?" he asked, then remembered he was still invisible, so he tugged back the mask, rolled it down to his neck.

Zoe stepped back, clearly startled at seeing his face appear in midair.

"It's all right. It's only me."

"Christ!" she said, still holding the cat tight. "What is this?"

"New tech. Remember?" He took her right hand in his, and squeezed it gently. "See? I'm here. It's okay."

Taking a deep breath, Zoe returned the pressure of his fingers. "The invisibility suit, right?"

"Right," he said, smiling.

"I'm sorry for getting freaked before. Seeing stuff floating in mid-air – I thought the place was haunted."

"Meow," said the cat. It jumped from her arms and darted into the undergrowth. They heard a hissing yowl.

"Shit!" Jubilee said. He retrieved his hand, pulled the glove back over his fingers and rolled the mask back into place. "I gotta go."

Seizing the metal bar, he followed the cat into the undergrowth. The creature was perched in a low tree, one scaly arm locked about the trunk. It paid no attention to him; its gaze was focused on the cat crouched at the tree's base. But when Jubilee flung the bar at it, it shrieked and grabbed at the trunk. With a howl it tumbled from its perch. It leaped up, quick as lightning and hissed.

Jubilee swiped at it, but the thing ducked, whip-quick. He feinted; another swipe. It crouched, as though about to pounce. As he thrust forward like a swordsman it scrambled backward, eyes fixed on the bar, alight with sudden fear. Gripping the solid metal rod tight, Jubilee swung it like a baseball player. With a dull thump, the bar connected with the creature's head. Silently, it fell to the ground.

He poked the steel rod into the creature's body. A tendril of smoke snaked upward; he stabbed again, harder. The creature writhed, and screamed, and burst into flame. He stepped backward and stood panting.

From inside the house came a piercing scream. *Zoe!* Jubilee hurdled the still-burning monster, and burst through the open doors into the music room. Another of those devil-creatures held Zoe. Teeth poised above her neck, its eyes glared mockingly at him. Jubilee heard himself shouting. No time to think, no time at all; the creature was bending its head. Its teeth grazed her neck.

In a blur of silver-gray, the cat raced past him. Zoe, clearly terrified, was struggling; writhing and pushing. She couldn't see the thing, but still she fought against whatever it was that held her imprisoned. A cloud of butterflies surrounded him, small wings brushing in dry rasps. Jubilee tried to swipe them aside, but their bright wings seemed to flow; it was like trying to stop the ocean.

"No!" he screamed.

As he reached the threshold, the butterfly cloud lifted, spinning out the door. He ran forward.

"Zoe! Zoe!"

She lay semi-conscious on the floor with the cat, Helen, beside her. Above them both stood another girl. Her dark hair crackled with energy; her brown eyes were bright. A butterfly with iridescent blue wings perched on her finger.

"Zoe!" he knelt beside her, felt her cheek. It was ice cold.

"She'll be all right," said the stranger. A flick of her hand and the butterfly flew up, into the high shadowed ceiling. "She's had a fright, that's all."

Jubilee frowned; something about the girl felt familiar. She was looking at the cat, so he had the strangest feeling the girl was addressing the animal, not him.

"It's the music that draws them," she told the cat. "The creation of music. It's like a magnet. And here, the barrier between the seen and the unseen is fragile. You must guard her closely."

"I'm sorry," he said. "I didn't think."

She raised her eyebrows. "What? I'm not talking to you."

"Meow," interrupted the cat.

"I *can't* be nearby all the time," said the butterfly girl. "This is your problem."

"Meow."

"Yes," she agreed. "That's a good idea." She surveyed Jubilee. "You could use him."

"Use me? How?"

The cat glanced up at Jubilee. Perhaps it was his imagination, but somehow he felt the animal had considered him, then discounted his aid.

"You do?" She considered him carefully. "No, I think he has potential."

Jubilee felt himself flushing. "Well, thank you very much."

She half-smiled. "They want her. Zoe. You must stop them."

"*They*? Who are they?"

She nodded at the cat. "She knows. Ask her."

A cat? She wants me to talk to a frigging cat?

"Jubilee?" murmured Zoe. She turned closed eyes toward him. "Is that you?"

"How are you feeling?"

He slid an arm beneath her shoulders, lifting her head and shoulders from the floor.

"Remember," the strange girl said seriously. "Keep her safe."

And from nowhere came butterflies, pouring into the room like a cloud of fluttering, trembling jewels. They swept up and around, wings brushing faintly against him. Jubilee bent protectively over Zoe, and she smiled up at him, as though she could see him. Her face was worryingly pale, and her eyes were still closed.

"Are they – butterflies?" she whispered, as the creatures passed above and around her.

He nodded, then remembered she couldn't see him. "Yes."

"Meow," said the cat, and Zoe sighed and sat up.

"I think," she said carefully, "you should keep talking. Just so I know what you are."

"What do you want me to talk about?"

"Tell me about your suit. What's it called again?"

He helped her to her feet. "It's called Camo."

"As in camouflage?" She smiled. "It's pretty good."

Take care of her, the girl had said. Jubilee closed the French doors and locked them.

"It's new tech," he said.

"Can you take it off? So I can see you?"

"I could. But that might be embarrassing."

"Embarrassing? How?"

"I've nothing on underneath," he said.

"So?" she asked, and laughed.

❦ 30 ❦

RICCARDO AND THE MOON

RICCARDO IS UNEASY. Time is passing. Soon, it might be too late for the music. If Zoe is taken ... No. He can't think that; mustn't think that. He needs her. Or rather, he needs her voice.

But the musicians aren't ready. Heard from them yesterday, very apologetic. They were running late, had another recording gig.

"Sorry man. You know how it is."

He wanted to scream. *Don't you understand? This is important.*

But Riccardo has gained wisdom over the years. Better to swallow the anger. He must have these particular musicians; they are the only ones with the power, the energy, to make what he wants.

Funny, of all the women in his life, the only one he misses is the one who left him. Charley. He shouldn't have let her go. He sighs. No point in crying over past sorrows. Aunt Carlotta used to say that. At the time he'd thought she was just a crazy old woman, but perhaps the old woman was right. Regrets ain't good for nobody.

He looks up at the moon, sailing arrogantly above the hills, tingeing the clouds with silver. One, two days until it's full, perhaps.

Zoe's ready; he's heard her practicing. She knows the songs, understands their timing. So. He could lay voice tracks down early. Just in case. *Then, after the full moon, we'll see.*

Anyway, who knew? Evan might take Belinda.

I should be so lucky, thinks Riccardo. Flicking the stub of the cigar into the bushes, he steps inside the house and pulls the curtains against the moon.

31

JUBILEE HEARS RUMORS
ABOUT KING

A WEEK LATER, Whittaker called. "Told you I was checking on King? Got something you need to know."

"Like what?"

Whittaker hesitated. "I'm sending you a link to an app. Put it on your phone, go outside the property. Then call me back."

What the hell? Jubilee thought, as a link appeared on his phone screen: *Cone of Silence: Secure Calls.* Jubilee shook his head at Whittaker and his paranoia. Still, he did as instructed and drove to a nearby park. Sitting at a picnic bench in the sun he installed the app.

Whittaker picked it up at the first ring. "Johnson? That you?"

"Course it's me. Why the secrecy?"

"I owe you an apology. I do security, not investigations. Still, I should have asked around."

"Whittaker. What you talking about?"

"King, man. You told me to dig around, find out about him. I found something."

"Hey, this is Beverly Hills," Jubilee said, waving a hand at the mansions behind the park. "Everyone got secrets here."

"Not like this," said Whittaker. "No, not like this."

Jubilee sat up. "Okay, tell me. These rumors. What are they about?"

"His kid? The one who disappeared?" Whittaker lowered his voice, "Rumors are, it wasn't the wife. It was King. And," he added, "they say he works with someone big."

"Big? What does that mean?"

"I think, drugs. You know what King does to folks that cross him?"

"What?"

"Poison."

Jubilee stared at the phone.

"King don't like you, he gives you this special drink that takes you on a one-way trip to heaven. He calls it some sort of sports drink, like a smoothie or something." Whittaker snorted. "Crazy!"

"This is a joke, right?"

"Could be. I don't rightly know." Whittaker hesitated, then added, "You want to leave, I understand."

For a moment Jubilee was tempted to walk away. He'd spent near on ten years in trouble spots; surely that was enough for one lifetime? But Zoe might need him.

Jubilee shook his head. "No. No, I can't. Don't forget, you signed a contract."

"True." A sigh. "Okay. Now listen. Only thing King cares about are his daughters. So you better be careful around them. Respectful, you understand, but keep your distance."

Helen, Zoe's cat, pranced from a patch of weeds. Seeing Jubilee, she rubbed her head against him. Absently, he bent and tickled her chin.

"Johnson? You there?"

He straightened. "I hear you."

A red butterfly floated past, and Helen leaped for it. Too slow. She missed, and the thing floated free.

"And don't go drinking nothing King gives you, you understand?"

"I understand. Don't worry, I'll be fine. Hey, how did the date go? How's Teena?"

"She's great. It went real well, man. Real well," said Whittaker. There was a smile in his voice.

"Congratulations in order?"

"I wouldn't go that far. Things definitely looking up, though."

"That's good, man. I'm happy for you."

"Thanks. I'll call you later, okay. You keep alert, soldier."

"Will do. And don't worry, I'll call if I need you."

❧ 32 ❧

BELINDA'S CAR IS AN ALFA ROMEO

ZOE WANTED to try out her new car. On opening the hanger-like door, she felt a sick excitement at all the shiny, expensive metal. As well as Zoe's Mercedes, the garage contained: Val's white BMW, a yellow Porsche, a Mini Cooper and a couple of cars she couldn't see clearly. In the nearest corner of the garage, Belinda was stuffing a bulky gym bag into the trunk of a red Alfa Romeo coupe.

"You want a hand?" Zoe asked.

"Thanks," said Belinda, and passed her the rattling, over-full case.

"Nice car."

Belinda shrugged noncommittally. "It's okay." She eyed Zoe for a moment, and added, "You free at the moment?"

Zoe nodded. "I was going to go for a drive."

"By yourself? Tell you what, why don't you come with me?"

"Where you going?"

Belinda grinned wickedly. "Ah, ha. Not telling. It's a mystery."

Zoe hesitated.

"Oh, come on. It'll be fun."

Zoe sighed, then ... what the hell. Might be good to spend some time with her sister. "Okay."

"Great! Get in, get in."

The interior of the car smelt like money and leather. Zoe settled into the seat uneasily. Belinda heaved herself from the wheelchair to the seat, slipped a catch on the wheels, and unlocked them from the frame. She stuffed them and the wheelchair cushion into the rear seat, then turned to Zoe. "You able to hold something for me?"

Zoe nodded.

"Okay. Then take this." She passed Zoe the metal frame.

Zoe turned it about on her lap, trying to figure out the easiest way to hold it without being jabbed by an axle. "It's not that heavy, is it?"

"Carbon fiber," said Belinda, and slammed her door closed. "Ready?"

She didn't wait for Zoe's response but flicked the start switch, and the car roared into life. Belinda gunned the engine, then shot from the garage with a squeal of tires. Juan, clipping an irrigation line onto a faucet, jumped clear just in time.

"Sorry!" Zoe shouted over her shoulder.

Belinda turned on the stereo and heavy bass pulsed. When they reached the gate she glanced in her rear mirror, made a face. "What does he want?"

Jubilee had emerged from the gatehouse. He was yelling something that Zoe couldn't hear over the stereo. But she knew what he'd be saying: she shouldn't be going out without a guard.

"Let's go," she said quickly.

Belinda shot through the opening gate, as Jubilee waved at her to stop.

"He doesn't look happy," Belinda said, with a sidelong glance.

"Just drive," said Zoe.

They raced down the hill, Belinda easily navigating the tight curves of the road. A tan sports car came toward them, traveling fast up the steep slope.

"Holy heck!" Zoe said, turning to watch it pass. "That was a Ferrari!"

Belinda raised an eyebrow. "I take it you're not used to supercars?"

"You kidding? I see these, like, all the time. Matter of fact, my teacher has two."

A sleek sports car, wasp-like yellow and black, pulled out to overtake. Belinda glanced at Zoe. "Shall we permit this?"

"Fine by me," said Zoe nervously.

But Belinda laughed, and with a surge of power, the Alfa Romeo shot forward. Zoe clutched the seat and closed her eyes. For a too-long moment the two cars raced together down the hill, fighting for supremacy. Zoe opened her eyes just as the yellow car made it to safety in front of them. Turning in his seat, the driver flipped them the bird, then sped away.

"Asshole," said Belinda.

"You know him?"

She nodded. "Friend of Riccardo's. Done him some favors."

"Favors? Is he in the music business?"

Belinda laughed dryly. "Favors, as in drugs, booze. Girls. Boys. Whatever. Our father, he's not fussy."

Zoe hoped Belinda was joking. "Gross."

"Hey, this is Hollywood. If you've got money, you can buy anything you want," Belinda said, and pulled to a halt at the lights, turned right, following the signs to the freeway.

"How are you driving this?" Zoe asked, curious.

"See this?" Belinda said, pointing to a lever on the steering column. "It's a throttle. All the controls are hand operated. Kind of like a racing car."

"Cool," asked Zoe. "Hey, have you always lived here? With Riccardo?"

"Mostly, yeah. I was with Mom when I was tiny. Moved here later, was about, oh, four or five."

"Did your Mom just hand you to Riccardo or something?"

"Yeah. Something like that." Her flat tone gave nothing away.

"You and your mother, you're not close?"

Belinda shook her head. "Nope."

They were driving beside a wide drainage ditch. At its base ran a trickle of blue water that shone bright in the LA sun. "Where are we going?"

Belinda glanced sideways at her, half-smiled. "You'll see."

After half an hour they turned off the freeway and took a couple of turns so quickly that Zoe lost her bearings. They drove past a strip mall with graffiti on walls, men in baggy sweats on street corners, and girls wearing bright headscarves. An old man in a wheelchair watched traffic from beneath the brim of a red fedora. He waved at the car, and Belinda waved back.

"You know him?" Zoe asked.

"Joey Smith. Nice guy."

"You come here a lot?"

"Sure do," Belinda said, and turned right, into a side street. "See that tagging, there?" She pointed at painted blue letters on the blacktop. "*OTC*. Original Town Crip. This is their turf. Joey Smith, he keeps an eye on the cars that come and go. Anyone he doesn't know, he tells the OTC."

Zoe glanced nervously at Belinda. "You're kidding, right? Will he tell them about us?"

"Maybe," said Belinda. Glancing at Zoe's face, she laughed. "Nah, I'm joking. I told you; Joey knows me. Don't worry. I ain't going to get you killed." She drove slowly past a chain-link fence and turned left, into a weed-strewn yard. At the far end was an abandoned building, covered in vines and tagging.

"Here we are." Switching off the engine, she said, "We're early. They'll be along soon."

"The OTC?"

Belinda grinned. "No. My helpers." She opened her door, and asked Zoe to pass her the chair.

Zoe handed the frame across and Belinda set it on the ground. She retrieved the wheels from the rear, snapped them into position and flipped the brake levers on. "Can you grab my bag from the trunk?"

"Yeah, sure."

Getting out, Zoe sniffed the air and smiled at the faint seatang. The gym bag felt surprisingly light as she hefted it onto her shoulder.

"Yo! Girl!" called Belinda. "You coming?"

"What is this place?" Zoe asked, as they neared the building. Plaster peeling from the walls gave the place a mottled, diseased look. Long grass grew in cracks in the concrete and on the roof, a length of guttering clanked mournfully in the wind.

"Used to be a shoe factory. Closed down about twenty, thirty years ago. Couldn't compete against cheap imports. Any other part of the city, it would have been turned into apartments." Belinda took a key from her pocket. "Not here." A low ramp led to a wooden door.

"How long have you been coming here?"

"I guess, about a year."

"Riccardo know?"

Belinda shook her head. "And don't you tell him, okay?"

"Hey," Zoe held up her hands. "It's your business."

"It's way more than that," said Belinda, seriously. "This is an art project. It's *my* art project."

Zoe stared at the battered façade. "You're joking, right?"

"Shouldn't judge by appearances," said Belinda, and wheeling up the ramp, unlocked the door. "Come on." Shoving the door open, she wheeled inside.

"Wow!" said Zoe, staring. They were in a high-ceilinged

entrance chamber. At the sound of her voice, pigeons took flight, wings clattering. Cracks in the floor tiles spouted grass and low bushes, and the place smelt of damp and mold. Once a receptionist might have greeted them here, but now the place was derelict – but the walls! Ah, the walls were amazing.

"You did all this?" she asked Belinda, turning slowly.

Spray art poured across the walls, merging with the cracking plasterwork and rotting wood. On the wall opposite a rat chased a cat through a door, and she followed the image into the next room, where a girl in a red cloak picked up the cat. A soldier, rifle at the ready, paced beside her. Further along the image changed again: now trees, aqua and blue speckled, grew into a dense jungle. Yellow and black birds flew through the branches, and the girl disappeared into the foliage.

"You like it?" asked Belinda, wheeling along behind her.

"It's amazing!"

"It's not all mine. I had help."

"From who?"

"Kids, mostly. The birds are mine." She pointed at a small figure half-hidden in the forest, "and the witch." She considered it critically. "I'm still working on her, though."

Zoe peered closer at the image. She could just make out a skirt, a pointed hat.

"We lock the doors to keep it secret. But once we've finished we'll open it to everyone. Would make a great rave location, don't you think?"

Taking a deep belly breath, Zoe sang a clear A. The echoes were clear and high, like a cathedral. She sang a scale: *doh, ray, mi, fah.* Stopped, smiling at the sound. All that concrete made for great echoes.

"Oh yeah," she said. "It's cool."

"This is the main area. But there's more. I'll show you."

Although the art was amazing, the whole place gave Zoe the

creeps, so as they moved down a long corridor, she followed close to her sister. Half-rotten wooden doors opened at intervals, and at the end a broken window let in dusty light.

"Do you ever get people in here?" she asked.

"People come here, obviously," said Belinda, indicating the walls. They were painted with a thick green vine, its thick trunk looking vaguely snake-like. Below the vine, butterflies, half-hidden in the shadows, floated.

"I mean, homeless people?"

"I've never seen anyone, no."

Piles of rubbish along the walls meant the hallway was narrow, so Belinda went in front. "Anyway, don't worry. Most of the home-less guys are harmless."

"*Most*. Thanks."

Belinda grinned over her shoulder. "Scared?"

"Yep."

"That's part of the fun. In here," and she pushed her way into a stairwell. Newspapers and pizza boxes lay forgotten behind the staircase.

"And rats," Zoe asked nervously. "Are there rats?"

"Probably. I can't go up the stairs, obviously. The kids do this part."

Here the walls were covered in a different style of spray art: butterflies with human heads, blue hearts, black diamonds. Above them, on the landing, a tiger in a pink baseball hat roared a silent warning.

"You want to take a look? Go on, check it out."

Zoe hesitated. "You know, I think I'll pass."

"Coward! It leads up to the roof. Great view, they say. I'll wait here."

Reluctantly, Zoe climbed the stairs. Past the tiger, and a soldier in a black gas mask. Her footsteps echoed.

"I go outside here? Through the fire escape?" she called.

"Yeah." Belinda's voice floated upward.

Zoe pushed down the bar on the fire escape and shoved against it until it opened. She emerged onto a flat roof, and braced the door open with a brick.

"What do you think?" Belinda hollered.

From here Zoe could see across the freeway to the ocean. The sun was warm and smelt of traffic and sea spray.

"It's amazing!" she yelled.

A concrete ledge formed a low wall in front of her. She climbed onto the narrow ledge to see further. Above, the sky seemed to go on forever, blue blending into space. She wished she had wings. Opening her arms, she closed her eyes and felt the brush of the wind on her face. How easy it would be, she thought, to let go? She wondered if she would spiral down like a seed.

When a hand grasped her ankle she flinched.

"Careful, *querida*," said a gruff voice. "It is a nasty fall."

From a pile of old rags a face emerged; an old woman with a weather-beaten brown face and missing front teeth. Her fingers, clenched about Zoe's ankle, were tipped with long, yellow nails that stabbed into her skin like tiny knives.

"Hey!" said Zoe. "Let go."

"Please, *querida*. Come down."

When the woman released her ankle, Zoe stepped down from the ledge. "Who ...?"

The woman emerged from the rags like a phoenix. "Me? I am Carlotta." Her Hispanic accent was strong, and her voice was husky, like someone who'd spent a lifetime smoking. "And you are Zoe."

The woman was familiar. How?

"It does not matter how I know your name," said Carlotta impatiently. "I am here to help you. And you are, I have to say this, very silly."

"Excuse me?"

"You have a very nice man to watch over you, yes? A guard?"

"You mean Jubilee?"

That gap-toothed smile – yes, this woman was definitely familiar. Zoe frowned, trying to remember where she'd seen her.

"*Si*. Jubilee. Him. You have run away from him. That is silly."

"I haven't run."

"No, but you have. Me, I know this." She wagged a finger at Zoe. "Tsk, tsk, you are foolish child. You have silly phone on you, yes? Young people, you always have these tiny phones."

Zoe blinked at her. "You mean, my cell phone?"

"*Si, si*. You ring him. Tell him where you are. He worry about you." When Zoe hesitated, Carlotta tapped a foot angrily. "What you wait for? Go on! Call!"

"Oh, okay." She fumbled her phone from her pocket – it was on silent. Instantly, ten missed calls came up. All from Jubilee. "Shit!"

Carlotta peered over her shoulder. "I think he not pleased with you. You call him, yes?"

"Okay, yeah." Zoe tapped reply, then held her phone up, like a student showing homework to her teacher. "See?"

The phone rang. "Jubilee." Just his name.

"Um, hello. Hi. Were you trying to reach me?"

"Zoe? Where are you? Are you all right?"

"I'm fine. It's okay." She glanced over at the old woman, who was sitting on the edge, inspecting her hideous nails. "I, um, sorry I left you behind."

"Silly girl. Tell him where you are," hissed Carlotta.

"Where are you?" Jubilee asked.

"Belinda says it's an old shoe factory."

"Where?"

"Um, I don't know exactly. Somewhere near the sea."

"Zoe?" Belinda hollered from the stairwell. "Who are you talking to?"

"Just a minute," she said to Jubilee. Covering the receiver with her hand, Zoe shouted down through the open door, "It's Jubilee."

"What does he want?"

"He wonders where we are."

A pause, then, "Did you call him?"

The old woman shrugged at her.

"Um, yeah."

"Jesus!" Belinda said. "Why did you do that? Shit, shit shit! Hang up. Hang up."

Carlotta stood up, and with surprising strength, dragged the phone from Zoe. "Soldier," she said, "you mus' come soon."

Zoe could hear him asking: "Who the hell is this?"

"Language," said Carlotta reprovingly, and tossed the phone off the roof.

"Hey!" Zoe lunged for it, but the phone was already gone, smashed into the concrete of the parking lot.

"ZOE!" shouted Belinda. "What are you doing?"

Carlotta put her finger to her lips. "Do not tell her about me. She not need to know, not yet."

"Hurry up!" And now, Belinda sounded seriously angry.

In the distance, Zoe thought she could hear car engines revving and heavy bass thumping. Perhaps Joey Smith had called the OTC.

"I have to go," she said. Who *was* this old woman? Why were her dark eyes familiar? Zoe hesitated, remembering: the waves breaking, and the sunlit shore. "The apartment in Venice," she said slowly. "That was you, wasn't it? Who are you?"

Carlotta grinned at her, and the smell of exhaust and the noise of bass and engines grew louder as she unwound herself from her many shawls. Then, with an agility unexpected for her age, the old woman leaped onto the concrete roof that rimmed the edge.

"No!" gasped Zoe, suddenly realizing how it must have looked when she had stood there.

But Carlotta only smiled. "Be brave, *querida*." She closed her eyes, then flung herself out into space, jumping into the blue.

Zoe screamed.

"Zoe!" Belinda called. "What's happening?"

Hands to her mouth, Zoe went to the ledge, stared down at the pavement below. There was no sign of the old woman: no body lay broken. A pigeon flew past her, toward the sunlight.

"Zoe!"

"I'm coming," said Zoe, and leaving the roof, she closed the door behind her.

With a sense of unreality she went down the stairs. One foot after another; all the way down. It had been the same woman, she was sure of it. *Take the key*, she'd said. *I hope you don't mind cats.*

What had just happened? Perhaps it had all been her imagination. She glanced down at her arms: red half-moon crescents marked where the old woman's nails had gripped her.

"Finally!" Belinda said, as she reached the bottom. Her eyes narrowed. "What happened? Are you okay?"

The old woman, falling, arms outspread ... Zoe felt suddenly dizzy; thought she might be sick. She closed her eyes. "I–"

"You look pale. Sit down. Here, on this step. Don't worry, it's not too dirty. Come on. Sit."

Slowly, eyes still closed, Zoe sat. Outside, car engines roared and horns sounded.

Under her breath, Belinda swore. "I have to go," she said. "Will you be okay?"

Zoe nodded heavily. She still felt sick. But outside in the parking lot she heard the sound of heavy feet. "I'm fine. Really. Belinda, when you go outside, tell me if you see anything strange."

Belinda stared. "Strange, as in?"

"I don't know. Just, weird." Like a dead old woman. But what if she wasn't dead? What if she was just badly injured? "There might be someone there."

"Yeah, I can hear them."

"No, I mean, like a person who's fallen."

"Fallen? What do you mean, Zoe? Fallen from where?"

"The roof. Look, I think I saw something. Just, can you look, okay?"

"All right," said Belinda slowly, then wheeled away. She stopped, glanced over her shoulder at Zoe. "Hey, don't go wandering about. Some parts of the building aren't safe."

Zoe nodded weakly. She really didn't feel like exploring. "Okay."

Belinda's wheels moved steadily through the building, and from outside came the thudding bass of the car stereos. Gradually, Zoe's nausea eased. This building: the smells, the echoes, the dusty light – all felt unreal. Perhaps her encounter with that woman had been a dream; perhaps she'd just imagined it. Zoe rubbed the nail marks on her arms. They too were fading.

There was a rustle in the corner. Her breath caught. *Oh my God! Rats!* She sat bolt upright, stock still. The noise stopped.

Then it returned, strongly. It was definitely coming from the corner, below the stairs. There was a figure on the wall there, a painting of a man with golden eyes. From the corner came a sudden pattering, like the passage of many small feet.

Zoe jumped up. *I'm not staying here, not with rats.*

A voice spoke, out of the darkness. Little more than a whisper, but still she heard it clearly. "Tonight, my dear."

Outside, the stereos cut off, and the silence seemed louder. Under the stairwell was nothing, only shadowy darkness. "Soon, you will be mine."

"Who's there?" She hated the quivering fear in her voice.

"You know. Me." On the wall, the figure moved. The golden eyes blinked.

No! It's not possible! She stared into the shadows. Her heart raced as in front of her the painting on the wall detached itself from the plaster, and stepped toward her.

"Hello child," he said, and stroked her cheek. "Zoe, isn't it?"

Zoe ducked back from the chill, white palm. Outside, someone laughed, and the stereo began again: thud, thud, thud. A noise of reality. Her head cleared and Zoe remembered.

"Evan," she whispered.

He examined the paintings on the wall. "What a *fabulous* place. So atmospheric, don't you think? Who did it, do you know?"

"Why do you care?" Zoe asked.

He knelt to examine the butterflies. "Now, these are intriguing." He touched a blue wing gently with his finger; it came loose in his hand. He stood up slowly.

"How did you ..."

He waved his hand; the butterfly lifted into the air and flew toward the window at the end of the long, dark passageway. Some seemed to free themselves easily from the paint; for others it was harder, and they struggled for a time before coming loose.

Evan seemed as amazed as Zoe. Staring wide-eyed at the creatures he asked: "Did you do this?"

"Not her. This is my doing." A woman spoke from the gloom.

Evan tugged at his collar. "You! What are you doing?"

"Listening. Apparently, you consider *her* –" she pointed at Zoe, "interesting."

Evan stepped back as, trailing shadows, the woman advanced toward him.

"Now, now," he said, "you know I didn't mean it."

"Well, we shall find out, won't we?" She took his left hand in hers and lifted her arm high. The knuckles on her hand turned white as she squeezed Evan's fingers.

"Stop it!" he cried. "Stop!"

"You will leave her alone – you'll leave all of them alone."

"I have a right," he cried, panting. "I have a right."

"Only until the contest is decided. Yes?"

He nodded. "All right. Yes."

Slowly, she released him.

He wiped his forehead. "You drive a hard bargain."

"I had a good teacher," she said.

The woman approached Zoe, her skirt dragging through the detritus on the floor. "You must take care."

"I've already said I'll leave her alone," Evan said sulkily.

"Not you. Girl, beware of King. If he gives you something to drink – don't."

Zoe remembered Charley's warning: *You cannot trust him.*

"I'll be careful," she said seriously.

"Good." She turned to Evan and offered him her arm. "Well? What are you waiting for? Come along."

Evan sighed, put his hand on her elbow and the couple stepped forward into the wall. Zoe stared at the plaster in disbelief. There stood two figures, silhouettes of a king and queen. She rubbed the paint with her fingers. They wore crowns and cloaks and – she peered closer – were those blue-gray paint specks *butterflies*? She retrieved a fragment from the floor. It looked like a dead leaf.

"I told you not to go exploring," said Belinda.

Zoe glanced up quickly. "Did you paint these?"

Belinda wheeled over to her, inspected the grimy wall. "Hmm. I don't think so." She peered closer. "Strange. You'd think I'd remember. Hey, how are you feeling now?"

"Better, I think."

"Good. Come on, I want you to meet someone."

"Is it okay out there?"

"It's fine."

"You didn't see–?"

Belinda shook her head. "All normal."

Zoe sighed in relief. So the old woman had been all her imagination. "What about the noise – is that, like, gangs?"

Belinda laughed. "Gangs? You thought those were *gangs* outside?"

"I guess I wondered, yeah."

"Girl," said Belinda, wheeling down the corridor, "if there were gangs out there, there'd be all sorts of crazy shit going down by now. Nah, those are just my friends. Come on. I've told them you're here."

"Oh. Okay."

Still holding the butterfly, Zoe followed Belinda. Was she hallucinating? Was she going insane? Things like people stepping out of paintings, old women disappearing in midair – such things could not be, not in the real world.

"They don't like surprises here," said Belinda, over her shoulder. "But now they know about you, they're cool."

On her palm lay a dead butterfly, wings folded. It felt thick and rubbery, like dried paint. They entered the reception room, where shafts of warm sunlight fell in bright patches on the broken tiles. When she looked at her palm again the painted butterfly had disappeared, but her palm was streaked with gray powder.

"Zoe?" Belinda stopped. "What is it?"

"Nothing," she said, brushing her hands together to shake off the residue. "Nothing at all."

Outside the front door stood a small group. Most were Black or Latino, all about her own age. Belinda pushed her chair gracefully down the ramp, did a sideways slide at the bottom, and waved her hand with a flourish to Zoe.

"And here she is! My one and only step-sister." Made a face. "Okay, maybe one of my two step-sisters. Anyway," hands in the air, "ladies and gentlemen, boys and girls: Zoe Banks!"

The crowd burst into cheering applause.

"Oh man!" Zoe groaned. She'd forgotten what this felt like.

"You rock, girl!"

"Hey, Zoe!"

"Zoe, over here!"

"Go on, meet your fans." Belinda grinned.

"You! You set me up."

Belinda shrugged. "People like you; they appreciate your art. Ain't nothing to be ashamed of. Why don't you go say hi?"

"I'll get you for this," Zoe said.

"Sure, sure," Belinda said. "But later, okay?"

Zoe went down the ramp into the smiling group of strangers. Hands shook her own, faces smiled.

"Hey, I'm a huge fan!"

"Go girl!"

"Love your music."

"Thank you," she said, blinking back tears. "Thank you so much."

A red Mercedes pulled into the lot. She blinked at it – that car sure looked familiar. At the wheel sat Jubilee.

"Uh oh," said Belinda, waving at him. "Someone sure looks annoyed."

"That's *my car*," said Zoe. "He's driving my car!"

Jubilee came over to her, pressing through the crowd. "You okay?"

"Sure," she said.

"When you called me, and then we got cut off–"

"Dude," said Belinda, "she's fine. Don't get so worked up."

Jubilee put a hand on Zoe's shoulder. "What are you doing?"

"Just meeting my fans," said Zoe. It felt weird: she had *fans*! People liked her music!

"Oooh, she's got a maaan," someone called.

"Hey, big boy. Why don't you give her a kiss?"

"Go on, go on! Kiss, kiss, kiss."

Jubilee grinned at the crowd, as Zoe, embarrassed, hid her face in his chest.

"Listen to them," said a gravelly voice. "Do as you're told, *querida*."

Zoe glanced up, staring. It was the old woman with the gap-toothed grin.

"You!?"

"Girl, you hear them? So, what you waiting for?" Carlotta said. "Better you kiss him."

Jubilee winked at her. "I'm game if you are."

She laughed, so he bent his head and kissed her. His lips were warm and gentle and, as the crowd shouted approval, Zoe kissed him back.

❦ 33 ❦

ZOE IN AN ARGUMENT

ZOE STOOD AT THE POOLSIDE, staring out at the view. Seen from here, the lights of LA sparkled like fairyland. Had she imagined the old woman, the paintings that came to life? But Jubilee – ah, he was not imaginary. She touched her lips and smiled. In the blue-green glow of the pool lights she could make out Chrissie's figure, walking toward the house where Belinda sat alone in the family room, watching TV. Chrissie seemed to be carrying something in her cupped hands.

Zoe didn't feel like talking, and moved back into the shadows. Jubilee had insisted on driving her back to the house, and then Riccardo had seen them arrive, so they'd had no space to just talk; to figure out what had happened between them. Riccardo had grabbed her, and she'd spent the next few hours in the sound booth, laying down vocal tracks until her throat was raw.

Worst thing was, none of the songs were what she wanted to sing. They had been Charley's songs. But after today, everything had changed. There were people who liked Zoe Banks, who wanted to hear her music. Zoe had half-suggested this to Riccardo, but he'd shaken his head so angrily that she'd backed off.

Chrissie knocked on the French door, and Belinda wheeled over to open it. "Where have you been?"

Zoe moved closer. She was too tired to start a conversation, but it was nice to hear voices, to know there were people nearby. It felt normal; safe. After today, she could do with a bit of normality.

"Where have you been?" Belinda asked.

"Working," Chrissie said. "Where's Zoe?"

"With Riccardo. They're recording."

"Now? This late?"

"It's only nine." Belinda said.

"He never normally works in the evening, though."

"He's in a hurry. He's working to a deadline."

"We all are," said Chrissie.

"Yeah, that's how it feels, isn't it?" Belinda wheeled over to the terrace windows, stared out at the night, like she was looking for something. Zoe stepped backward, into the dark.

"Full moon tonight," Chrissie said softly.

Belinda nodded.

"Are you scared?"

Belinda shrugged. "I guess."

Chrissie let out her breath. "Yeah, me too."

"I just wish it was over."

"What about Zoe? How's she taking it?"

"I don't know. Something weird about that girl. Today, I took her to my project."

"You took her *there*? What! Are you nuts?"

"You sound like the bodyguard. Jubilee," said Belinda . "I thought it would be good to get away, you know. This place, it's so *intense*."

Chrissie shook something from her cupped palms and set it on the sofa, just behind the curtain. Voice slightly muffled, she asked. "What did she think of it?"

Zoe crept closer to the window. If they were talking about her, she definitely wanted to hear.

"She liked it, I guess. Just, something weird happened. She was up on the roof; I was down below, right? I really wish there was an elevator, so annoying. Anyway, I hear voices. When I ask her, she says she's talking to Jubilee. But that's not what it sounded like to me."

"How did it sound?"

"Like there was someone up there with her. But there's no-one up there, ever. Then she comes down, all white and shaken and says there might be a body down in the lot."

"A *what*?"

"She thought someone jumped off the roof."

"And was there? A body, I mean?"

"Of course there wasn't," said Belinda.

"You think she imagined it?"

"I don't know, that's the thing," said Belinda. "Something else weird too – I could swear the paintings had changed. You know the ones in the hallway? The forest and the butterflies?"

"They give me the creeps."

"You're a coward. They're *friendly* butterflies. Anyway, when I went back, some of them had disappeared."

"Probably you miscounted."

"Of course I didn't," said Belinda sharply. "I know every inch of that goddam wall."

There was a pause, then Chrissie said, "Juan says that Zoe's like Alice."

"Like Alice? What does that mean?"

Chrissie shrugged. "I don't know."

"Another thing," Belinda said. "You know about Jubilee?"

"The hot bodyguard? What about him?"

Belinda glanced sidelong at her sister. "He likes her."

"So? I like her. Zoe's nice."

In the darkness, Zoe smiled.

"I mean, he *likes* her."

Chrissie's eyes widened. "As in, like like?"

Belinda nodded. "As in. They kissed."

Chrissie laughed.

"It's not funny." Belinda glanced behind her, at the empty room, and added, so quietly that Zoe could barely hear: "What if Riccardo finds out?"

Chrissie's smiled faded. "Someone needs to warn her."

When Zoe tugged the door open, the two girls jumped.

"There you are," said Chrissie. "Want to see what I've been working on?"

"What do I need to be warned about?" Zoe asked. "I heard you talking."

The two girls exchanged a glance, then: "Hon, look. I made you this," Chrissie said, and handed her a long string.

"What is it? Belinda asked, wheeling over. "Hmm. A necklace." She inspected the black pointed pendant. "I like it."

"You do?" asked Chrissie, sounding pleased.

Zoe refused to be diverted. "Is Jubilee in danger?"

"When did you make this?" Belinda asked, picking up the fine leather of the necklace, so the pointed pendant dangled, pointing like a dagger toward the floor.

"Careful! It's sharp," Chrissie said.

"You're changing the subject," Zoe said.

Belinda held the pendant close to her face and squinted at it. "Hey, it's a nail! You put a nail on a chain."

Chrissie nodded. "It's the old kind, made of solid iron. There's one for each of us. Juan says, wear them tonight."

"Juan?" Zoe asked, annoyed. "What does he have to do with this?"

"You've changed things," Belinda said. "Shook things up. We were fine before you came. We knew what to do, how to stay safe."

"Stay safe?" Zoe asked. "How do you mean, *safe*?"

"It's not her fault," said Chrissie.

"I think it is," Belinda replied. "All the weirdness began after she arrived."

"Who are you calling weird?" Zoe said, angrily.

"It's you, just being here. That's the problem."

"*I'm* a problem!" Zoe snorted. "What about you?"

"What about us?" Belinda asked.

"Oh," Zoe said sarcastically. "Nothing. Only that you have this life of totally *ridiculous* privilege. Your cars, this house – just look at it! You're so used to it you don't even see it. You dabble in art and design and you call it work! And now you're complaining, because I'm here and I'm doing something with my time. And because I'm working with Riccardo, you're jealous. Because I'm working with him, and he's never asked you to do it. That's it, isn't it?"

She stood, panting. Chrissie's face was pale, and Belinda looked frankly furious.

Oh shit, Zoe thought, and swallowed. *What have I done?*

"You think we're lazy?" Belinda said slowly.

She shook her head. "I'm sorry."

"You know nothing!" Belinda said, and wheeled about.

"I said I was sorry."

"You patronizing bitch!"

"I–"

"*You* try life in a chair," said Belinda. "See how you like it. Before you come in all judgmental." Her eyes sparked with anger. "You think you're so wonderful, just because you're poor and we're not?" She snorted. "And that bodyguard? Don't get too fond of him. Because one day, he'll be gone. And you won't even see it coming." She threw the door open and was gone. There was silence in the room.

"Chrissie? I'm sorry."

In a low intense voice, Chrissie said: "You should be more careful."

"Chrissie, I–"

Chrissie shook her head. "Don't. Just don't." She left the room too, leaving Zoe standing beside an open door, a black pendant in one hand.

"There you are," said Val briskly, coming into the room. She was carrying a metal water bottle. "I was looking for you."

"I'm going to bed."

"This early?" She looked searchingly at Zoe's face. "You do look tired. Riccardo said he'd been working you hard." She held out the water bottle. "Here."

"What is it?" said Zoe, taking the container. The metal was cold to the touch.

"It's from Riccardo."

"For me?" Zoe went to unscrew the top.

Val put out a hand. Her fingernails were painted with silver glitter. "No, not for you. It's for the bodyguard."

"Jubilee? Why?"

Val pouted. "Riccardo says he might need it. Riccardo's into nutrition, you know."

Zoe shook her head. "I didn't know."

"Yes, well. Apparently, it's full of amazing seeds and stuff. And he wants you to take it to the bodyguard. Make sure the fellow drinks it."

Inside the bottle, the liquid sloshed gently.

"Riccardo's very insistent," said Val. "So I think you should take it *right now*."

There was something weird about Val tonight; her eyes were glassy and her speech was slurred. Had the woman been drinking? "Val? You sure you're okay?"

"I'm fine," said Val, smiling fixedly. "Off you go. Remember – make sure the bodyguard drinks it."

"Um, okay," said Zoe. The flask burned, cold in her hand.

Val stood in front of the French doors, silhouetted by the pool lights. "One thing, dear?" Her voice was calm, emotionless. "Riccardo's always watching." She giggled, high-pitched and awkward. "In case you're tempted to disobey him."

"Right, okay," Zoe said. This was getting more and more surreal. "No disobeying him. I understand."

Val nodded.

Zoe walked along the edge of the driveway, keeping to the grass so her footsteps made no sound until she reached the irrigation line, so carefully placed by Juan that morning. She stopped. Looked about. Satisfied no-one was following, she turned on the faucet and sluiced out the contents of the flask. She washed away the remains and sluiced out the flask again. Once she was certain it was clean, she refilled it with water.

"This is for me?" Jubilee said, sniffing the contents of the flask. He wrinkled his nose.

"It's from Riccardo," said Zoe.

"Hey," he said softly, putting an arm about her shoulder. "Are you okay?"

"The girls, my sisters. I said," she shook her head. "Shit, what did I say?" She put her head against his and whispered, "Val says *he's* watching." Quickly, almost desperately, she reached up, kissed him. "I have to get back."

"I guess it is a little late." He put the flask in the fridge. "Tell Riccardo, thanks."

"I think you're supposed to drink it now."

"Okay." He drank it down slowly, and handed the flask back to her. "Here you go. Satisfied?"

She nodded, eyes large in her face. "Thank you."

He hesitated, then lifted her hand, pressed her knuckles to his lips. "Shall I walk you back to the house?"

"No, no. I'll be fine." She squeezed his hand, and whispered: "At midnight, come find me."

She took the flask back to the house, put it on the kitchen bench.

Val looked up, yawning. "Okay?"

"Fine. He drank it. Just as you asked."

"Good, good." Val rubbed her eyes. "Sorry, I'm just so tired."

"Go to bed then."

"But it's still early."

"If you're tired, though?"

"True," Val said, her voice slurring. "I've been working so hard. That's what it is, work."

"Sleep well," said Zoe, and watched her go. Helen stalked into the kitchen, and Zoe addressed the cat. "Okay, so it worked. Now what?"

The cat rubbed against her legs, purring.

"Yeah, I know," said Zoe. "Now we wait."

❧ 34 ❧

MIDNIGHT AND MOONLIGHT

HELEN BATTED at Zoe's hand with a barely sheathed claw. *Wake up!*

"Ouch!" Zoe said, tugging her hand away.

The clock by her bedside said eleven-thirty. Silver moonlight shone through a gap in the curtains and fell on the lace dress that lay across foot of the bed. Zoe shivered – it had definitely not been there earlier. She sat up, rubbing her arms and feeling powerless. She didn't want to put the thing on: didn't want to disappear into the night. Yet already she could feel the garment calling to her.

Helen woke with a yawn. The cat took one look at the garment and stalked across the bedsheets toward it.

"Hey," said Zoe, picking her up. "It's only a dress. It's not going to hurt you."

"Meow," complained Helen. She slid from Zoe's arms and landed gracefully on the floor.

Zoe had to admit the dress was attractive, if you liked that sort of thing. It was a classic style, almost like a ballet costume, with a full, faintly glimmering skirt, tight-fitting bodice and cap sleeves. And of course, when she tried it on, it fitted perfectly.

The black pendant, laid out on her bedside table, caught her eye. Who would have ever thought Chrissie might make something so edgy? Zoe clasped the chain about her neck and settled it under her bodice, where it nestled in the secret place between her breasts, cold against her bare skin. She was ready.

Taking a deep breath, Zoe opened her door and nearly screamed when a dark shape moved in the hallway. It was Belinda, half hidden in the dark.

"Good. There you are," Belinda said.

Embarrassed, Zoe said nothing. What should she say? Should she apologize, or proceed as though nothing had happened?

"Time to go, girls," said Chrissie, closing her door.

Chrissie wore a sheath dress of black satin. A fur stole encased her shoulders; her lips were deep red. She sashayed down the corridor in spiky stilettos like it was a catwalk.

"I like your outfit," said Belinda.

Chrissie smiled, and turned slowly. "Thank you." She peered into the shadows, where Belinda sat, half-hidden. "What are you wearing?"

Belinda sighed heavily, and wheeled into the moonlight. Zoe bit her lip and tried not to smile.

"It's awfully ... pink," said Chrissie, after a long pause.

"I was going to say, sparkly," said Zoe.

"Pink *and* sparkly," Chrissie said.

Belinda made a face.

"It suits you," said Chrissie quickly.

"Yeah," Zoe agreed. "You should definitely wear pink sparkles more."

Belinda scowled. "Right then, are we going?"

Zoe pressed the pendant into her skin; the sharp end pierced her flesh and cleared her mind. Almost abruptly she saw herself standing between her sisters in a lace ballgown.

"I'm going to wear shoes," she announced, and darted back into her room. Thrust her feet into Converse.

"That's an interesting look," said Chrissie.

"I don't care," said Zoe, tying the laces. "I'd rather be comfortable."

"Wait for me," said Belinda quickly, and turned her chair.

"Where are you going?" called Chrissie.

Belinda paused, one hand on the doorknob of her bedroom. "You guys changed your outfits. I don't see why I shouldn't."

"Oh, but you look so sweet," Chrissie said.

Belinda stuck out her tongue.

"Thank you," said Zoe to Chrissie, as they waited.

"What for?"

"The necklace. It's really cool."

"You like it?"

"Like it? I love it!" Was she being too enthusiastic? She patted her chest. "I'm wearing it now."

"Good," said Chrissie. "Juan said, keep it against your skin."

"What I said earlier," Zoe said, in a rush. "I shouldn't have. I'm real sorry."

Chrissie considered her for a moment, then nodded. "That's okay. Anyway, we should have told you."

"Told me? About what?"

"What do you think?" Belinda asked. She'd knotted a black gypsy shawl about her waist, obscuring the pink netting.

"Interesting," said Chrissie, and raised her eyebrows at Zoe.

Zoe shook her head. "I preferred the pink sparkles."

Belinda made a face at them.

"The weirdest thing," she added, as she propelled herself along the corridor, "earlier, this shawl wasn't there. But when I went into my room just now it was on my bed. As though I was supposed to put it on."

In silence, they went outside and walked toward the gap in the hedge. Zoe shivered. She didn't want to do this. Yet her feet kept walking, one step after another. She saw movement out of the corner of her eye; it was Helen, half-hidden behind a flowerbed, pacing beside them. The cat glanced at Zoe and lowered one eye, as though winking.

Chrissie stopped, glanced behind her. Traffic hummed in the distance, and far away a clock began to strike.

"What is it?" Belinda whispered.

"I thought I heard ..." Chrissie shook her head. "Never mind."

The air smelt of creosote and pine. Zoe stopped; faint, over the traffic rumble, she was sure she could hear music. Violins and oboes, dancing a jig.

"You okay?" Chrissie asked.

Zoe pressed the pendant and once more, the sharp iron tip pressed into her skin. She nodded. "Yeah."

The compulsion to step through the gap was strong; involuntarily, she moved forward.

The music grew louder.

Chrissie took her hand. "It's okay. You got this."

Zoe shook her head. "I don't know ..."

"Come," said Chrissie, and taking a deep breath, stepped through the hedge.

Almost blindly, Zoe followed. Passing into the narrow gap, she wondered where Jubilee was and how he was faring. Hoped he'd be able to follow.

At least this time she was wearing shoes. Sneakers may not be elegant, but hell, they sure were practical.

❧ 35 ❧

IN CAMO, JUBILEE FOLLOWS

AT A QUARTER BEFORE MIDNIGHT, Jubilee, in full Camo, waited outside the house. He carried the length of reinforcing iron, the folded knife and, for luck, the roof nails, taped just above his ankles. Strangest weapons he'd ever carried.

He squatted in the shadows. Waiting was something he was good at, so he didn't mind the silence, or the Camo-gray. She would be coming; she'd said so.

Finally, the door eased open. In the moonlight, he could see the girls plainly. They were dressed like they were going to a party. He followed them quietly along the driveway, keeping always to the grass verge, so his footfalls would be muffled. Down in the valley a clock began to strike. He counted the notes slowly: *one, two, three.* He stopped. Was that music? *Nine, ten, eleven.* In a sudden flare of light, Zoe disappeared through the gap in the hedge. Jubilee stood in the dark, waiting. Finally, he gave up waiting for her to return, and followed.

On the far side of the hedge, mist drifted from the trees, blurring with the Camo-gray. He couldn't see the girls anywhere.

Jubilee ran down the path. In the dark, the trees resembled

monsters, and small patterings in the undergrowth made him flinch. Clouds raced across the sky; the silver moonlight came and went. Moving with invisible feet at this speed was hard, and several times he stumbled. Once, he fell, and lay breathless. Slowly, he picked himself up, no damage done, and set off. Finally, the path widened and entered a clearing. Jubilee slowed, chest heaving.

The girls stood at the far side of the clearing. Mist, rising from the damp grass, floated like a soft blanket. Faintly, he heard music. Without a backward glance Zoe walked into the thick forest; Chrissie and Belinda followed. Jubilee went too, all of them moving downhill through the trees toward the drumming, thrumming noise. About their feet, mist swirled. Jubilee watched it dully, all his attention focused on moving in time with the beat, until his foot rolled slightly on the rough grass and the nail jabbed his skin and his head cleared.

What am I doing here?

The chill mist, waist high, swirled. It might outline his shape, so he stopped, waiting for it to dissipate as ahead the girls disappeared into the dark. Jubilee stood, watching the empty night.

Gradually, as the drums throbbed and the guitars wailed, the fog dissipated. He crept onwards, seeking the source of the music. Quite suddenly, the melody fell silent and Jubilee heard the rapid wash of water. He smiled, for now he knew where he was. Just below lay the stream and its cave that marked the boundary of Riccardo's land.

Jubilee trod cautiously, his movements fluid, almost dancing. Now he didn't disturb the mist; he flowed with it. He crept around tree roots, bent below gnarled branches until finally, he reached the water. In the muddy bank lay two tire marks. Belinda's wheelchair.

Mist rose from the river, filtering the moonlight and turning the night to silver fire as he traced the tracks into the narrow cave opening. It was hung with long stalactites that looked alarmingly like teeth.

The current increased as the river arrowed into the cave, and drums echoed, drawing him onward. He tried to resist, but it was like pulling against gravity and his feet moved him on until finally, he stood in the ice-cold water of the cave's mouth.

Jubilee shook his head. *What the hell is happening?*

The music swirled with the fog, growing louder, more insistent. Fists clenched, he tried to fight it. But as the beat of the drum merged with the beat of his heart, he knew he had no choice: he had to follow.

With a sigh, Jubilee stepped forward, into the dark.

🎇 36 🎇

JUBILEE TRAVELS INTO
THE DARK

THE STONES WERE SLIPPERY, and the knee-deep water felt bitterly cold so now and again he lost his footing in the dark. But fortunately, the steel bar made a useful staff, so Jubilee prodded his way slowly through the tunnel, the gray of the Camo shifting with the fog. The music had gone, vanished as soon as he walked into the cave. There was more light in here than he'd expected; or perhaps his eyes were adjusting.

Gradually, Jubilee became aware of a rushing, gurgling sound. The current increased and he felt a sudden panic; he didn't want to get caught in the dark. What if there was a flood? He might be stuck here; he might even drown!

Get a grip, man!

He stopped. Counted slowly to ten. In the distance ... was that a light? He walked forward, slowly, slowly. *Don't look at it directly; gotta keep the night vision.*

Gradually the light grew brighter. Now the water was up to his thighs. He stopped, took a deep breath. At least no-one was shooting at him. Yet. A splash of water brushed cold fingers against his face.

Now the current was so strong he could barely stand. Keeping his eyes shaded, he peered ahead; faintly he could make out a white spume of spray where the river formed rapids. He squinted. It seemed to be tumbling over a rock barrier, before falling into ... he blinked. Was that wide, calm surface a *lake*? He could just make out a stretch of silver sand. Using the metal staff for balance, Jubilee waded against the current, and stepped onto the beach with relief.

Clambering onto a low rock, he stared out at the lake. On its far side stood a castle with high, pointed turrets and lamplit windows. Where the hell had the river taken him? One thing for sure, he was definitely no longer inside a cave. Above the rush of water, Jubilee heard laughter and music and there, just below his vantage point lay a low pier, pointing into the lake.

Jubilee jumped from the rock with a smile. A jetty meant a boat, and a boat meant escape.

He crept silently toward the pier, rounded a rock, then stopped. At the base of the long low pier clustered the three sisters. Jubilee sagged in relief: they were safe! Although they seemed to be arguing.

"Be careful! Your wheels," snapped Zoe. "They keep tangling in my dress."

"It's not my fault," said Belinda. "You shouldn't walk so close."

"It's so bizarre," said Chrissie. "I mean, the place feels familiar ..."

"Like a dream," agreed Zoe.

"We've been here before," said Belinda.

"Look!" Chrissie pointed out at the lake. "A boat!"

Jubilee carefully set the metal bar down on the ground, hiding it in the shadows, and tiptoed quietly forward. The girls stared out at the darkly gleaming lake as the vessel grew closer. Finally the boat touched the jetty, the captain threw a rope around a bollard, and knotted it tight.

"Come on," called Belinda, wheeling forward.

Jubilee crept behind Zoe, so close he could nearly touch her. As he passed the boatman the man lifted his head, and sniffed. Jubilee froze, as the boatman set out a ramp for Belinda and bowed her aboard. She wheeled onto the boat, stately as a princess. Jubilee crowded into the stern beside Zoe, careful not to touch her. None of the sisters seemed to notice he was there as the captain withdrew the ramp and cast off.

There was no engine, no sail, yet the vessel moved smoothly out onto the lake. It skimmed lightly across the surface, reflections fracturing in the rippling arrow of its wake.

At the front of the house was another pier, and here the boat moored again. The captain set out the ramp, and Belinda wheeled out onto the quay. The boat swayed in the movement, and Jubilee stumbled.

"Careful!" said Zoe to Chrissie. "You stood on my dress. Be careful."

"For goodness' sake," said Belinda. "No-one hurt your dress, Zoe. At least, not on purpose."

"She's so clumsy," Zoe wailed, and stormed down the ramp. The black-eyed captain paused, then bent to untie the mooring ropes.

"Jubilee?" Belinda whispered.

He said nothing.

"It's okay," she added. "We can't see you. But we know you're there."

"How?" he murmured.

"You made the boat low in the water. And you tore Zoe's dress," Chrissie muttered, as the boat sped away into the darkness.

"Just, be careful," Zoe said. "Please?"

"I'll try," he muttered.

"Okay, girls," called Belinda. "Are we ready?"

The three girls glanced up at the great house. At its lamplit windows silhouettes moved darkly. The moon sailed free of the clouds.

Taking a deep breath, Zoe straightened her shoulders, and linked her arm with Chrissie's. "Right! Let's get this show on the road."

Belinda spun her chair about. In the dim light, Jubilee could just make out the fierceness of her expression. "Soldier, you must find your own way in, you hear?"

"I hear," he whispered, low.

"What if he gets hurt – how will we find him?" Zoe whispered.

What had Whittaker said, earlier? *You get injured, you're on your own.*

"You can't," Jubilee breathed. "I'll find you."

❧ 37 ❧

JUBILEE OBSERVES THE DANCE

JUBILEE CREPT along the low grass of the lake's edge. The moon gave enough light for him to find the narrow path that led to a weather-beaten door set deep in the walls of the great house. Amazingly, when he turned the handle, it opened and Jubilee found himself in a kitchen, a chaotic space of scents and steam.

He ducked from the room before the steam might reveal him, narrowly avoiding a plate-carrying server, and dodged into a wall alcove. He stood for a moment, just watching. This place was like nothing he'd ever seen: a wide corridor paneled with polished wood and flickering lamps that cast moving shadows on a vaulted ceiling. Dimly lit oil paintings hung on the wall, and thick carpet muffled the sound.

But it was the people, rushing about like rats in a maze, who really grabbed his attention. Some were short, compressed with humped chests and protruding chins. Others, tall and thin, seemed almost stretched. A few were beautiful as the stars while some were nightmarishly ugly: scarred or covered in warts. But whatever their appearance, their gold eyes were all the same: split with cat-like vertical pupils. Just like the monster at Riccardo's.

Whatever these creatures were, Jubilee was certain they weren't human. After watching for a time, he left the alcove and tiptoed carefully along the edge of the hallway, trying to keeping out of the way. No-one seemed to notice him; the Camo tech seemed to be holding. He passed openings to other corridors, merging or splitting randomly, and now and again a closed door. He wanted to turn the handle and see what was inside this strange place, but didn't; a door opening by itself might draw unwelcome attention.

Finally, he crossed an empty side passage that seemed to twist strangely. It was lit with smoking candles set in tarnished silver wall sconces, and he followed it cautiously, because the passage was thick with smoke. Jubilee took care not to move too quickly and set it swirling. By now he was alone.

He heard a sound: someone was coughing. He spun about, but the corridor was still empty. The churning smoke formed strange patterns. Faintly, he heard whispering, like someone trying to attract his attention.

"Who's there?" he called, then stopped. Didn't want to give himself away.

Around him, the whispers grew louder. Jubilee shivered. *This place, it's haunted!*

Heedless of anyone who might be coming toward him, he sprinted down the dark hall. Passing a door, he tried the handle, but it was locked. Something brushed against his leg, but when he glanced back, the hall was empty. Fumbled at another door; again, it was locked.

"Hey!" a voice called. "Wait!"

Pulse racing, Jubilee ran on, following the curving line of the corridor. Finally, feeling dizzy, he paused. About him, smoke eddied, forming a shape in the air: a man, with his arm outstretched.

Horrified, Jubilee stumbled and nearly fell. His hand hit something cold: a glass door, half-hidden by smoke. Through the glass, he could see dim figures moving. Desperately, he scrabbled at the handle; to his relief the door opened and he stepped into a room full of dazzling light. As he closed it behind him, an orchestra began playing.

Jubilee found himself at the rear of an enormous ballroom; a vast chamber, crowded with couples and hot as a furnace. Six silver-glass chandeliers, ablaze with candles, filled the room with light. One wall was sheathed in mirrors; along the opposite side were tall windows. During the day he imagined there might be a grand view from them, but now, it being dark, the windows acted as mirrors. So he stood in a churning, ever-shifting midst of dancers. Reflected into infinity they formed a vast, glittering throng.

As the mob parted slightly, Jubilee he sighed with relief – there were the girls, and they were all safe. Well, perhaps not exactly safe, but they seemed okay; they were dancing with the others. At the far end of the room, the glass door opened again and he tensed, watching. But the doorway remained empty. Perhaps there had been a draft.

Navigating around the dancers, Jubilee crept past a marble statue, then settled behind a curtain to watch the crowd. From here, he could see Zoe's exhausted face and patches of dark sweat across her back.

Zoe glanced in his direction and her eyes widened. Following her gaze, a dancer in a blue dress turned quickly. Another did the same, and then another. On the stage, a musician dropped an instrument. The throng of dancers turned toward him, and their eyes – *their eyes!* In the thousand-upon-thousand reflections, their eyes gleamed red.

He stood still as one of the marble statues. His pulse was racing; he slid his hand over his wrist, as though he could muffle the noise. The air seemed hot and stifling. For a moment he felt as though he was back in battle, where the scent of blood lay thick.

When the voice whispered, he was so keyed he nearly screamed.

"You fool! The curtains," it snapped. "They're draping over you. *They* can see your shape."

"Who – who's there?"

"Never mind that now. Quick – there's a statue to your left. Wait beside it; I'll find you. On my mark – Go!"

The window shattered behind him. A gust of wind fanned the curtains wide as Jubilee raced for the statue. Never had he moved so fast. The crowd of dancers, hands outstretched, rushed the curtain just as he reached the marble figure of a naked man with a wreath about his head. Crouching at its stone feet, he tried to calm his breathing, while nearby the dancers ripped the curtains to shreds.

Chrissie shoved Belinda's wheelchair to the far side of the room, away from the frenzy at the windows. The girls huddled together, shielding their heads with their hands. He could see the panic in their faces.

A voice rang out: "That's enough!"

On the stage stood a tall silver-haired woman. Hands on hips, she surveyed the crowd. "What are you doing? Return to your positions!"

The dancers glanced at one another, then apparently chastened, returned to the dance floor.

"Sir," called the woman to the conductor. "If you please?" Her blue-gray dress glittered with crystals and pearls and her mask, made of thin black wire, was severely plain.

The music and the dancing resumed. But the uniformity of their steps had changed: now and again, a partner stumbled, or took a little too long to turn, or moved his head too slowly. Eyes narrowed, the woman watched intently, until, apparently satisfied, she nodded and walked down the steps.

The woman crossed the floor to the sisters. Above the music and the soft tread of feet Jubilee couldn't hear what she was saying, but Zoe's shoulders relaxed, Belinda smiled, and Chrissie nodded. Then the woman took Chrissie's hand and, leading her into the dance, presented her to a man in an elaborate coat of peacock feathers. As the two twirled about the floor, the man's coat flared into lustrous blue-green light.

Zoe shook her head. Clearly, she didn't want to return to the dance. Jubilee's heart ached, and he wanted to help her. But he didn't dare move again, and as he hesitated the woman seized her hand and tugged her out onto the floor, presenting her to a fat man in white velvet.

The woman in the gray dress danced with Belinda, who turned her chair in neat circles as her partner trod a slow, stately measure. Of the three sisters, only Belinda seemed to be enjoying herself, smiling as she spun her chair.

"Where are the others?"

The angry whisper made him jump.

"What others?"

"You know what I said, soldier. Stop dicking around."

This voice was no ghost; this was a soldier! Who had, most likely, been declared missing.

"Are you from the platoon?" Jubilee whispered, and wished he'd thought to find out their number from Whittaker.

"Where you think I'm from? Mars?" the voice snapped. It paused, then added, "You – who are you? Thought you were Chavez. You're not. What's your name?"

"Johnson. Jubilee Johnson."

"Soldier," whispered the voice, "who the hell are you?"

Around and around went the dancers. The musicians sawed at their instruments, never stopping, never slowing. No-one entered the room, no-one left, yet somehow the dance floor grew ever more packed. Belinda and her partner were the only ones with space about them now; he could barely see Chrissie and Zoe.

In whispered tones, Jubilee explained why he was here. Felt kind of stupid, whispering to the air. There was silence, and for a moment he worried that the person, whoever he was, had disappeared.

"Sounds ridiculous," the man snapped.

"Well, all due respect, Sir, but you're MIA."

"MIA? What the hell you mean?"

"You're six months late for your rendezvous."

"Six months! You're shitting me."

"No, Sir."

There was a rustle, like someone sliding down the wall, and now the voice came from the floor. "Six months! You sure?"

Jubilee sat beside him. "What's your name, Sir?"

"Devon Richards," said the voice. "Captain." A hand came from nowhere, poked Jubilee in the ribs. "Sorry," Richards muttered. "Trying to shake your hand. This being invisible, not what they said it was going to be."

Jubilee nodded ruefully. "Ain't that the truth."

There was a pause, and finally Richards said: "Six months. Six months?"

"I'm sorry."

"Not your fault." Richards took a deep breath. "So, that's why you're here – you're looking for us?"

"Um, yeah. I guess. In a way."

"What's your rank, soldier? Your platoon?"

"I was staff sergeant, Sir."

"Was?"

"Not in service any more. Sold out."

"Sold out?" Richards said incredulously. "How you come by the tech, then?"

"I was given it, Sir."

A pause. "By whom?"

Jubilee paused – no way could he explain this. "Sir? All your platoon here?"

"Most are, yes."

"Some?"

The man's voice was somber. "We took casualties."

"Sorry to hear that. How many of you …"

"Five of us left. We lost Jamieson." Richard's voice trailed off. "Geez, six months."

Now and again a clock chimed, marking the hours. As the night wore on, the music raced faster and faster, like water heading downhill. Chrissie danced barefoot, and her feet left red patches on the floor. The spinning of the dancers made Jubilee feel dizzy. He didn't know how much longer he could stay here: he needed to pee; he needed water. He had a headache. Richards said nothing. Perhaps he'd left. As the swaying melody wore on, Jubilee felt caught in a dream. Once or twice his head lolled.

Abruptly, the music ended. Jubilee yawned, rubbed his eyes. A girl carrying a violin appeared on stage. She wore a green hijab fastened with a bronze brooch, but unlike the dancers, no mask.

"Richards? You there? Something's happening."

The girl scanned the crowd and then paused, a look of surprised recognition on her face. Through the crowd, Jubilee saw Zoe's surprised glance; clearly, they knew each other. But the girl said nothing, just tucked the instrument beneath her chin and began to play. And the music, oh it caught Jubilee's heart, made him want to move, to dance and to sing. Getting to his feet, he took one step, another, until Richards's finger clamped about his wrist and held him tight.

"Stay still, soldier."

Finally, the violinist drew the final chords from the instrument. The dancing stopped, and just as the last echoes faded, the clock chimed. Richards counted: one, two, three ... "Twelve o'clock," he said. "Midnight."

"But – it can't be." It had been near to midnight when Jubilee had met the girls.

"Ssh!"

Jubilee stood still, wondering how long he'd been here in this house. *When I get out of here, how much time will have passed?*

The violinist curtseyed, left the stage. A drum beat loudly and on stage a slim girl appeared out of thin air. She wore a golden mask and carried a harp, also gold.

Richards swore.

"Who's she?" Jubilee whispered.

"Don't know," said Richards tensely. "But last time I saw her, *he* arrived."

"He?"

"The boss. Kind of like a king. Name of Evan. He killed Jamieson."

"I'm sorry."

"Ssh. She's going to sing."

Holding her harp, the girl stood at the stage's edge, smiling as the crowd applauded, shouting: "Sing! Sing! Sing!"

When she began playing, Jubilee paused, caught in the melody. The song reminded him strangely of sunlight and smoke and the soft scent of flowers, and for a moment Jubilee forgot where he was; there was only the music. He thought he heard someone calling his name, but when he turned there was nothing, only a marble statue and the reflection of an endless crowd.

As the song's melody faded, Zoe approached the stage. "You call that music?" She laughed. "That's not music."

"Oh, hark at the brave one. She's challenging you, my dove." Through the crowd came a man dressed all in yellow-gold.

"That's him," said Richards. "That's the bastard. Evan."

A blood-red mask hung from Evan's finger and his eyes gleamed with mischief. The crowd moved aside to let him to pass.

"Ssh!" said Jubilee.

Richards subsided, grumbling.

"It's easy to look good when there's an audience in your favor," said Zoe. "When you're in a place you know. You want a *proper* competition? Then let me sing."

Evan jumped neatly onto the stage, and settled on its edge. Swinging his legs, he glanced up at the harpist. "Hmm. Alice? What say you?"

Alice, thought Jubilee. Wasn't that the name of the baby who disappeared?

The harpist smiled briefly. "If she's as good as she says she is – I want to hear her."

"Very well. Girl, name your conditions. What do you want for your prize? Consider carefully."

"If I win, you let my sisters and me go. Let us live normal lives."

"You wish to be *normal*? My dear, why?" Evan asked. "And if you lose?"

"I won't."

"Confidence! I like it," he said. The smile faded. "Ah, but there must be a penalty. Otherwise, it is not a competition. So what will you forfeit, if you lose?"

Zoe said nothing.

His eyes gleamed. "Very well. Your life is forfeit."

Chrissie flung herself at the stage. "No!"

Hands caught her, dragged her back as the woman in the gray dress put a hand on Belinda's shoulder and pressed it gently.

Evan glared. "You wish to say something?" The menace was clear.

Belinda swallowed. "My lord. This is your house."

"Exactly," Evan said. "And I have the right to do as I will in it."

He hesitated, then nodded curtly. "Very well. Make your preparations."

"Your platoon," whispered Jubilee. "Where are they? How fast can they get here?"

"What are you thinking of?"

"I think I can get you out of here. If she wins."

"And if she doesn't?"

"Then we'll need them even more."

Richards paused. "I ain't about to get more men killed for no reason. Who is she?"

"She's ... well, it's complicated. Look. You do nothing," said Jubilee softly, knowing this was true, "you'll be dead, or good as. You help me – then you got a chance."

Richards sighed. "I'll see if I can find them."

The air behind Jubilee felt abruptly empty. At the far end of the room, the door opened and closed. Jubilee settled back to wait, and watch.

"Meoow," said a small voice at Jubilee's ankles.

What the hell? It was Helen, Zoe's cat. He reached down, automatically, and patted her.

"What are you doing here?" he whispered.

Her right eye closed at him, almost like a wink.

❧ 38 ❧

SISTERS TOGETHER, SINGING

ZOE, standing beside the stage, felt curiously remote, like she'd been caught in a most peculiar dream. Then she saw Helen, weaving restlessly around Chrissie's legs, and smiled. How had the cat gotten here? Had she followed them? Seeing the cat definitely made her feel calmer.

"Just so you know," said Belinda to Evan, "we stick together. We're all going onto the stage."

"The deal is that Zoe sings."

"We know," said Chrissie, fluttering her eyelashes, "We just want to keep her company."

Evan nodded. "Very well."

The crowd murmured and shuffled closer. Zoe smiled; she knew that sound. Anticipation.

"Wait!" a voice called from the wings, and onto the stage came Fatima, carrying her violin.

"What are you doing?" Evan said.

"Providing an accompaniment," Fatima said. "You would like an accompaniment, wouldn't you? Alice had a harp, after all. It's only fair."

"Thank you," said Zoe, and as she climbed the stairs, thought: *Alice*. She turned and faced the audience, which from here seemed to extend forever. It's only reflections, she thought to herself. They're not real.

Chrissie was dragging Belinda in her wheelchair, up onto the stage. She grinned over her shoulder at Zoe.

"You'll be fine," she said.

"Can't be as bad as singing for Riccardo," Belinda added.

Zoe smiled at that, because it was true. Then she took a deep breath, a singer's breath, deep into her belly to sustain the note, and the song began:

> *"Remember girls, when we were young*
> *Before we knew the battleground*
> *Before we knew the bad*
> *That was to come*
> *Now stay with me my sisters*
> *As we sing this song*
> *And let us all remember*
> *The past, and all its wrongs."*

Chrissie stepped forward and faced the audience.

> *"If you sell your soul to the devil*
> *Be careful not to tell*
> *For the devil, he won't never*
> *Sell you back your soul*
> *No you gotta live your tiny life,*
> *Gotta live like you don't care*
> *Never caring whom you hurt*
> *Nor listening to your fears."*

Zoe took the melody, as Chrissie's delicate, thready voice

picked up the harmony:

> *"Sing with me, oh my sisters*
> *Together sing this song*
> *As together, we remember*
> *And together we grow strong."*

Belinda wheeled forward to the edge of the stage. Her voice was dark and dangerous and gritty as sand:

> *"But those fears will catch you one day*
> *In the middle of the night:*
> *When you've had too much to drink*
> *Or when you've had a fright*
> *I was just a little girl*
> *When ma, she said to me*
> *Child, careful what you wish for*
> *For wishes can come true."*

The three girls moved together, swaying to the rhythm like a church choir:

> *"Sing with me, my sisters*
> *At the closing of the day*
> *Sing with me my sisters*
> *And together we will pray*
> *Together we will pray."*

Alice stepped from the wings, and joined them. Her clear, pure voice gave Zoe goosebumps; it was like listening to an angel sing. She reached out her arms, smiling, and there stood four sisters, finally together.

"I was just a babe
When I reached this land
I had no choice
I had no heart
I did not understand
Everything was taken
Everything was lost
But there's no loss without a gain
But was it worth the cost?"

The four sisters sang in unison as behind them, in the shadows, a woman with a violin played as though her heart was breaking.

"Oh sing with me my sisters
And join me at my side
For together we grow powerful
Together we will ride
Four of us against the world
We stand together, strong
Sing with me, oh my sisters
Together sing this song
As together, we remember
And together we grow strong."

39

JUBILEE THROUGH A MIRRORGLASS

"Hello?" murmured a voice at Jubilee's shoulder. "Soldier? You there?" It was Richards.

"Sure. I'm here."

"Found them just where I'd left them, who'd have thought it?" he said, as at the far end of the room, Zoe began singing.

"Come on," said Jubilee.

"Hang on a mo. Don't want to lose them again. Yo, Chavez? You there?"

"Here, Sir," a voice whispered.

"Stephen?"

"Sir."

"Franks?"

A woman said softly, "Sir."

Down the line, voices replied, five in all. Four men, one woman.

"Okay, Johnson. Go," said Richards.

They kept to the side of the room, clear of the crowd. Now and again Jubilee caught a red-eyed glare, as though the creatures sensed their presence, but he kept moving until they reached the front of the room where above them, on stage, the girls stood in a circle, their arms about each other's shoulders.

But Evan's face was flushed with anger. He leaped onto the stage, shouting: "Do we allow mortals to dictate to us? Do we?"

The audience roared.

"Quick!" said Jubilee. "Up onto the stage."

"What? Why?" Richards asked.

"Them," he said. "The girls. We have to protect them."

Evan called to the crowd. "We are the masters! They do what *we* tell them!" His eyes blazed. "I made a bargain, and I will not be foresworn. You hear me? I will not be foresworn."

Don't let the tech fail me, Jubilee thought, and crept up the stairs to Zoe. There were tears on her cheeks. Gently he touched her shoulder and she flinched. On the crowded dance floor below, the audience jeered and shouted.

"Hey, it's me," he said gently. "Jubilee."

She exhaled with relief. "Hey. Are you okay?"

The roars of the crowd grew louder.

"I'm fine," he said. "But we gotta get you out of here."

"Come on," he said. "Quickly." He grabbed her hand, pulled her toward the shadows.

"What's going on?" Belinda asked.

"Jubilee," she said. "He's here."

"Hey there," Belinda said. "Wherever you are."

Wheeling about, she followed Zoe. The other girls went too, scurrying into the darkness at the rear of the stage. Below, the crowd howled angrily. A door opened and Fatima peered out. "Here! Quickly!"

Helen zipped between Jubilee's legs and darted through the door, into a dimly lit room. The girls followed the cat; Jubilee followed them while at the rear came the platoon. The room was empty save for a tall mirror in a gilt frame. The cat meowed, and across the mirror glass her reflection moved, silver gray. Fatima closed the door, and locked it.

"Helen!" said Zoe. "What are you doing here?"

"Meow!" said the cat, as though that was a stupid question. Turning, she leaped through the mirror. The mirror glass rippled, and parted like water. The cat vanished. Chrissie screamed.

"Holy shit!" Richards muttered.

"Quick!" Fatima said. "Before they find us."

"What do we do?" Zoe asked.

Fatima gestured to the mirror. "Just walk through it."

"It's a *mirror*," said Chrissie. "You can't walk through a mirror."

Fatima sighed impatiently. "And have you ever tried?"

"Of course not. It's ridiculous!"

"But if you've never tried it, how would you know?"

"I'll try," said Zoe, and put a hand on the glass.

"Do it like you mean it," said Fatima.

Zoe took a deep breath, closed her eyes, lifted up her foot as though to step over the frame, and ... the mirrorglass rippled and let her through.

"Hell!" said Richards.

Outside on the stage, there came a shouting howl, and a scrabbling at the door. The handle turned, and caught.

"Come on!" said Fatima. "Now!"

Chrissie cleared her throat, stepped up to the mirror. Hesitantly, she pushed a foot into the glass. It moved sluggishly, so she disappeared slowly, almost an inch at a time.

Her face, half in, half out of the glass was anguished. "Help! I'm stuck!" The words were muffled.

Belinda tried to grab her, pull her free. The door behind them rattled as fists hammered on it, but Chrissie was stuck fast.

"Help her!" Belinda said.

Fatima touched Chrissie's hair gently; the trapped girl's eyes followed her desperately. "It is okay. You have this," said Fatima.

"Remember: this is only an entry. Think of it as a curtain, if you prefer."

Chrissie's eyes widened, her lips moved. The mirror-silver shimmered again, and she disappeared.

"What happened?" Belinda asked.

"She didn't believe," said Fatima.

"I believe," said Belinda. "I definitely believe. Help me through."

"I'll do it," said Jubilee, and lifted Belinda, still in her chair into the air. With a grunt, he pushed it through the frame.

Fatima's eyes widened, and she stared about the storeroom. "What was that?"

"Tell you later," said Belinda, as she and her chair disappeared.

"Alice," Fatima asked. "Are you coming?"

The final sister, the butterfly girl, shook her head. "Later."

Her soft voice was clear as sunlight and springtime, and for a moment the dusty storeroom appeared full of light. Fatima nodded tightly and stepped up to the mirror.

"Hang on!" said Jubilee quickly. "We need to get through, too."

Fatima stopped. "Who? What are you?"

Behind them, the door shook in its frame, and there was a loud rhythmic thudding.

"No time, no time," said Richards quickly. "Come on, men. You got this?"

"Yes, Sir," said Stephen from behind.

Jubilee felt a rush of air, and was abruptly shoved sideways as the platoon stormed the mirror. The silver shimmered and, for a split second, five figures were clearly outlined by glass.

He took a deep breath. Could he do this? He felt a hand touch his, glanced back.

Alice smiled at him. "Thank you," she whispered.

"You can see me?"

"Of course. Thank you. For taking care of them."

The door cracked. Clawed hands pushed their way through, grabbed for the handle.

"Hurry!" Fatima said.

"Go," said Alice, and pushed him into the mirror. The silver glass parted, ice cold and burning, and then he was gone, tumbling head-first into – somewhere else.

Panting and dizzy, Jubilee lay on the wooden floor of a cramped storeroom. Behind him, Fatima stepped from the gilt-framed mirror, and trod on his foot.

❧ 40 ❧

ANOTHER FORM OF HELEN

Zoe opened her eyes. She was lying on a battered leather sofa in the middle of a book-lined room. A young man, carrying a cup of tea, was watching her intently. As her eyes opened, he smiled. "Hey there. How you going?"

He seemed familiar, so Zoe smiled wanly. "I'm not sure. Where am I?"

"*Scheherazade Dreaming*. The store. You remember it?"

"Oh," she said, and sat up. "You're–"

"Hassan. Fatima's husband." He handed her the cup and saucer. "This is for you."

"Thank you," she said. The steam from the teacup rose in a white spiral to the roof. The delicate porcelain clattered softly; after a moment she realized this was her hand, shaking.

"Not everyone finds the mirror-door easy," he said. "Don't worry. The chill will pass. Drink your tea. And look, it's a lovely day."

He opened the stained-glass front door, revealing a view of – Zoe blinked. This was definitely not the courtyard she remembered. Outside, a blue-green lake shimmered in the sunlight. A gull darted past, screaming, and at the lakefront, children squabbled over stones. Rounded hills reached toward a clear blue sky, and at the far end of the lake lay snow-topped mountains.

"I remember the store, yes," she said going over to the door. "But not this view. Is this – am I in a dream?"

"Who knows? Sometimes it's hard to be sure."

Still holding her tea, Zoe stepped from the store, keeping one hand on the doorframe, just in case the world moved again. *Scheherazade Dreaming* in gold letters above the door front – but how?

"Hey, Zoe," Belinda called, waving from the sidewalk. "You want an ice cream? Chrissie's getting me one. Amazing flavors – they even have licorice, can you believe it?"

Zoe blinked, then shook her head. "Um, no. Thanks." Turned to Hassan. "Where are we?"

"Don't you like it?" asked Fatima, emerging from a door at the rear. "Me, this is one of my favorite stops."

"Stops? What, are we on a bus or something?"

"We move around a bit, yes."

"Sheez!" The lack of sleep, the general weirdness of what had once been a perfectly sane world made Zoe feel dizzy.

"Actually, an ice cream's a good idea. Protein and sugar. Help with the shock," said Hassan.

"I don't want an ice cream, thank you," said Zoe.

"What flavor?" asked Fatima.

"I don't–"

"Vanilla," said Hassan. "That's your favorite, Zoe. Right?"

Zoe nodded. "But–"

"Vanilla," Fatima nodded. "Okey-dokey." She danced down the step and disappeared down the street.

"Don't worry, it's real good," said Hassan. "They make it fresh."

Jubilee, looking amazingly chirpy, trotted along the sidewalk toward them. "Can she get me one, too? Zoe!" He opened his arms, and she fell into them. "How are you going?" he murmured to her hair.

She was too busy hyperventilating to reply.

"I'll ask," said Hassan, setting off after Fatima. "Hey, take care of Zoe, will you? I think she's ..."

What he thought disappeared into slow, revolving spirals. The bright sunlit lake seemed to darken; the world shrunk as Zoe toppled slowly to the ground. Fortunately, Jubilee caught her in time, but the teacup fell from her hand and fractured into thin shards.

Zoe focused on his eyes, so close to hers. "Are you? Is that really you?"

"It's me," he said, smiling. "Who else were you expecting?"

She shook her head, closed her eyes.

"Hey, you're all right," he said, helping her down the steps to a low wooden bench. He settled her in the sunlight. "I know, it's a shock. Took us all a while to adjust."

"Where are we?"

"New Zealand. Or so they say."

"New Zealand!" She bit her lip. "What are you ..." She blinked at him. "Jubilee? *What* are you wearing?" It looked like a bathrobe of yellow silk. When he turned she saw red dragons embroidered across the back and blue flowers along the sleeves.

He flushed. "Um, yeah. Hassan – that's his name, right? He offered to lend me his clothes, but we're hardly the same size. And it was either this, or something even weirder. You wouldn't believe the clothes they have in there. Zoe? You feeling better now?"

She nodded slowly. "I guess."

He put an arm about her shoulders and pulled her toward him. She rested her head on his shoulder. Where ever she was now, it couldn't be that bad, not with Jubilee here.

"I think I'm dreaming," she said.

He smiled down at her. "Good dream?"

"It is now," she said smiling, and he kissed her slowly, his lips soft and warm, and so wonderfully normal and delicious that she closed her eyes and gave herself to the moment. After all, this was a dream. You can do anything you want, in a dream.

"Uh-hmm," Fatima said. She was standing in front of them, holding two dripping cones. "Vanilla." She handed the white one to Zoe. "And licorice." This was dark purple, and went to Jubilee.

Zoe laughed. "Licorice?"

"What's so funny?" said Jubilee, and took a bite.

Methodically, Zoe licked the melting ice cream from the edge of the cone. If this was a dream, she was going to go with it. "I'm sorry about your teacup," she said.

"Don't worry," Fatima said, gathering up the porcelain fragments. "I can make them into something new."

"Like what?"

"Mosaics," she said. Carrying the broken china in her cupped hands, Fatima disappeared into the store.

Across the road, Zoe saw Belinda, Chrissie and Hassan sitting at the edge of the lake. Chrissie laughed, smiling in the sunshine, and Belinda, finishing her ice cream, tossed the paper napkin into a trash can. A tall woman with silver-blue hair and heavy black sunglasses came up to them, and they welcomed her as though they knew her. Zoe stared – something about the woman's stance seemed familiar.

Fatima settled on the bench beside them. "It's nice for Hassan to have company. I think he gets a bit bored with just Helen and me."

"Helen?" Zoe asked, wonderingly. "Is she here?"

"Sure," said Fatima, pointing at the group beside the lake. "Look."

"Where?" Zoe shaded her eyes against the sun. "I can't see a cat."

Fatima laughed. "She's not always a cat. Right now she's

talking to your sister. Chrissie. She's a big fan of her designs, you know."

The silver-haired woman and Chrissie were deep in conversation, Chrissie nodding from time to time.

Zoe choked on her ice cream. "You're telling me, that person over there is sometimes a ...?" She stopped. No. That was just too unlikely.

Sensing Zoe's stare, the woman smiled and waved. As though she knew Zoe already, as though they were old friends. Zoe sighed. The day just kept getting weirder.

Fatima patted Zoe's shoulder. "It's okay. Took me a while to get used to it, too."

Taking a deep breath, Zoe got to her feet. "Right. Well, I'm going to talk to her." She turned to Jubilee. "Are you coming?"

"He can't," said Fatima. "I need him to help get the others sorted."

"The others?"

"Long story," said Jubilee, unfolding himself from the bench. He put an arm about her shoulders, kissed her again. "Don't worry. Go see your sisters. And the cat. Or whatever she is." He pushed the small of her back gently. "Go."

"Helen?" asked Zoe, holding out her hand.

The tall woman shook it. "How are you? Lovely to finally meet you."

She wore sunglasses with heavy black frames, and her silver-gray hair had a hint of blue.

"Were you–" Zoe asked, then stopped. "Are you–"

Helen smiled. "A cat? Occasionally, yes. Do you mind?"

Zoe shook her head numbly. "No, not at all. It's fine. If you need too ..." She swallowed.

"You poor thing," said Helen. Her voice hinted of Ivy League and country clubs and up close, her smoky-blue tunic seemed expensively chic. "You've had a tiring day, haven't you?" She took

Zoe's arm. "Come. Sit down, before you fall down." She nodded to Chrissie. "Thank you, dear. That's very helpful."

Chrissie grinned briefly at Zoe, then darted away toward Belinda and Hassan. The young man was pushing Belinda's chair toward a narrow quay, where boats bobbed in the light waves, and children threw bread into the water.

The breeze coming off the lake was chilly, but the sun-warmed stones of the lakeshore were warm on Zoe's legs. The air smelt of fresh water and snow.

"What's it like, being a cat?" Zoe asked, running her hands through the gravel. It whispered softly. Closing her eyes, she lay back on her elbows. She could sleep here, on this warm bed of stones. And when she woke, everything would be normal, and everything would be okay.

"They're very clean animals, cats. Not at all like dogs. Independent, and good hunters; it's exciting being a cat."

Zoe nodded, accepting this. I might enjoy being a cat, too, she thought. Except for having to lick myself clean. Although, if I was a cat, would I care?

She considered this sleepily, as the waves sucked and sighed along the shoreline.

"Besides, being a cat allows me to keep an eye on Evan. After all, a mother likes to know what her sons are doing. Sometimes, he doesn't even know I'm watching."

Zoe opened her eyes. "Wait – Evan's your *son*?"

Helen nodded.

"And were you a cat when you had him?" Would that make Evan a cat, too?

Helen laughed. "Oh no." When she stretched and yawned, the likeness to the cat seemed strong. "This isn't my true shape either. Although," she frowned, "I do think it is my favorite."

"Oh," said Zoe, numbly.

"It's the hands," Helen said, tipping her palm uppermost. "So very useful."

"What is your true shape then?"

"I barely remember. When we're young, we change shape all the time. Rather as you would change your clothes; all shapes are ours. But as we grow older, generally we settle to one, maybe two forms. Changing shapes is tiring, you see; hard to remember which limbs go where."

Chrissie and Hassan stood on tiptoe at the jetty's edge. They were peering down at the water, fascinated. Belinda laughed at them, took some bread from a tiny girl in pigtails. As she threw the bread into the water, a dark shape rose from the depths. Chrissie shrieked.

"What are you?" Zoe asked suddenly.

"Humans," Helen said. "Always trying to categorize." She sat up, hugged her knees. The wind blew her fine hair about her face, and she looked very ... normal. "You want a name? A label?"

Zoe shrugged. "It might help, yes."

"In ancient times, we walked with you, and you worshipped us, called us gods. We were fascinated by you, your short lives and your endless curiosity. We thought this harmless." She stared out at the lake and the quiet mountains. "But you took fire and flint and made weapons from them. Iron and steel: metal that burned. But your art; your music – that, we love." Helen glanced over her shoulder at Zoe, eyes hidden behind her glasses. "In truth, we are afraid of you."

"I don't understand," Zoe said. What did all of this have to do with Evan? And why was Helen sometimes a cat, and sometimes a person? "I'm sorry. I guess I'm thick. Just, what you're saying makes no sense."

Helen patted her hand. "Believe me when I say – we never meant to cause you harm."

Hassan pushed Belinda along the towpath, shouting loudly.

The wind blew her hair back from her forehead, and she laughed. Chrissie scampered behind them, spinning in wide circles as she ran.

"It's nice to see them happy," said Helen. "My dear, I'm here to right old wrongs. And to beg forgiveness. You see, my son caused you great harm."

"Hassan?"

"Hassan? He wouldn't hurt a fly."

"Evan, then."

She nodded. "Evan."

❧ 41 ❧

JUBILEE LONGS FOR REALITY

JUBILEE WENT INTO THE STORE, past the counter and into the store-room. Save for the large mirror, the room seemed empty, but it *felt* occupied. Crowded, even.

"It's okay," he said loudly to the air. "You're safe now."

There was a rustle, and on the floor a scrap of paper moved. "You sure?" Richards asked.

"Hello. He's right," Fatima said. She was leaning against the door frame behind him. "Here, you are safe."

"Her headscarf," the woman whispered suspiciously. "Sir, she's a Muslim."

"I am no radical," Fatima said indignantly. "I will not hurt you. Why can I not see you?"

"Where are we?" Richards asked.

"New Zealand," Jubilee said.

"Ah, I remember – new tech. I read about it," said Fatima, sounding intrigued. "C-A-M-O? Do I have that right?"

"We just call it Camo," Richards said. "New Zealand? You sure?"

"Scheherazade knows where she is," Fatima said.

"New Zealand? Why the hell New Zealand?"

"I don't know," Jubilee said honestly. "Fatima? Why New Zealand?"

"It's an island," Fatima said, like this was an answer. "Very interesting to see this tech. I thought it was just a story, yet look at you here. Or rather, I cannot look at you! You are totally invisible!"

Richards sighed. "Johnson? What the hell is going on?"

"Um," said Jubilee, rubbing his nose, "We're in the back room of a store."

"A *store*?"

"Yep. Got some weird name."

"*Scheherazade Dreaming*," Fatima murmured. "As in Arabian Nights."

"Like that helps," Richards said wonderingly. "What the hell, a store in New Zealand?" He sighed. "Franks, you'd tell me if I was going insane, wouldn't you?"

"Sir," said the woman, "could be we're all insane. But way I think is: at least no-one's shooting at us."

Fatima straightened. "Can I make you some tea? Something to eat, perhaps?"

"Ma'am," Richards said. "I for one can't wait to get out of this suit. Do you have any spare clothing?"

There was a murmur of agreement from the platoon.

"It's Fatima," she said, and smiled. "Certainly. I will see what I can find."

The air shimmered and slowly, five faces appeared. Weirdest thing he'd ever seen, Jubilee thought: heads, emerging from thin air, as the soldiers slowly peeled back their Camo hoods.

There were four men and one woman. The woman must be Myla Franks, the one Whittaker had mentioned. The men sported thick beards, and Myla had her hair pulled back tightly in a ponytail. Their faces were gaunt and their eyes ... Jubilee looked away.

"You would like a shower?" called Fatima. "There is plenty of hot water."

"I think I've gone to heaven," Myla muttered, before calling, "Yes, please!" Her face floated from the room.

The men peeled their suits away. Their bodies were streaked with dirt and sweat, and they seemed thin as famine victims. One was Latino, one African-American, the others white. They all stank. Putting a hand over his mouth, Jubilee backed from the room.

Fatima appeared behind him. "She is in the shower. Oops," she said, as Richards tugged the suit over his hips. "I will wait outside." She thrust towels into Jubilee's hands. "Here. I have placed some clothes on the counter."

"More bathrobes?" Jubilee asked, gesturing to his own bright costume.

She shook her head. "Not at all."

Seated on folding wooden chairs, Fatima and Jubilee waited outside the store for the platoon to finish showering and changing. Fatima had propped the glass-fronted door open, and now and again the doorbell rang softly in the breeze. Passersby skirted around them, glancing at the store with interest, but no-one ventured inside. The building seemed anchored to the pavement, like it had always been there. Jubilee shook his head. Seemed insane that a store could move, but hey. He'd seen weirder things in the past few weeks.

"This place, what do you sell?" he asked.

"Software. Web design."

"You're kidding!" The building with its tiny glass windows and hand-lettered sign, looked old fashioned. Like something out of Harry Potter; definitely not a place for computers.

"We sell other things too."

"Like what?"

"Old books, curios, antiques." She shrugged. "Magic. Dreams. We sell dreams as well."

He nodded blankly. Dreams. That made more sense. "So, why the moving about?"

"I'm sorry?"

"I mean, the store. You said it moves, right? Why?" How does a store just get up and move? Once upon a time, the world had kind of made sense. Jubilee missed that time.

"Why? I think she just likes to see the world," Fatima said, patting the plastered wall.

The five platoon members crowded through the door, Richards at the front. Richards was shorter than Jubilee had imagined; thin and wiry. The soldiers, hair still damp, wore an odd assortment of clothes: jeans, shorts, cargo pants. Stephen wore a tux.

Myla, in a bright orange tunic, stared out the lake, wide-eyed. "Holy shit. It's real. It's freakin' real."

Richards surveyed the place with interest. "Very nice. New Zealand, you said?"

"I thought it was a dream," Myla said in a wondering tone. "It's like I've been asleep, and just now, I've woken up."

"Sir," said one of the soldiers. "Shouldn't we be trying to get home?"

"Tell them what you told me," said Richards, to Jubilee. "How long we been away for."

Jubilee stood up, uncomfortable at all the hollow eyes focused on him. Wished he could break this more gently. "You been MIA for six months."

A shiver went through the troop.

"You're kidding," said Myla. "Six months? Six freakin' months?"

Jubilee shook his head. "Not kidding, no. Ma'am, I was given something." Taking the knife from the pocket of his gaudy bathrobe, he passed it to her. "This yours?"

"Yeah," Myla said. "Sure, it's mine. Thought I'd lost it." She pressed the catch; sunlight glinted on the blade. "Where you find it?"

"I was given it," Jubilee said. "By a friend who had a contact in a supply depot. From what he was saying, sounds like this contact hoped the knife might find you. I was angry with him for taking it. I think I was wrong." He shrugged. "Anyway, thought you might like to have it back."

Myla's eyes narrowed, then slowly, she began to smile. "Thank you."

"Yeah," said Richards, "Thanks."

The rest of the platoon murmured their agreement.

"So," Richards said, rubbing his palms, "How do we get home?"

Beside the lakefront, Zoe sat up and waved at Jubilee. Helen helped her to her feet, and together they walked toward the store. Even though Zoe must have been tired, she moved as gracefully as a dancer.

"She likes you," Fatima said quietly. "I can tell."

"You'd met before," Jubilee asked, remembering the recognition on Zoe's face. "How? When?"

"I told you," said Fatima. "The store gets around." She glanced at Richards. "Your transport is being organized. But in the meantime, can I get you some food?"

The soldiers grinned. "You freaking kidding?" said Stephen. "Me, I could eat a horse."

Later that day, a battered minivan drew up outside Scheherazade Dreaming. The driver, an old woman with gold hoops in her ears, rested one elbow on her open window.

"*Hola!* You call for taxi?" she called.

"Oh no," said Helen.

"What's wrong?" Richards said. "Thought we were going to the airport."

"Yes, well. Something may have changed with that little plan." Helen went out onto the sidewalk. "What are you doing?"

The taxi driver grinned at her through blackened, broken teeth. "Hark at you, always so fancy. Don't see why you're surprised. Should have known I wanted some of the fun."

"Fun? Is that what you call it?"

"Of course. Is fun."

"You can't take them. You can't even drive."

"Sure I can. How you think I get my taxi license?"

Helen sighed. "All right. Just be careful, okay?"

"I'm always careful, me."

"Mr. Richards," called Helen. "When you're ready."

The platoon assembled on the pavement as the driver watched them with inscrutable eyes.

"Ma'am," said Richards to Helen. "You sure these are okay?" In his left hand he held a US passport.

"*Si*," said the taxi driver. "They fine. Get in."

Richards did so, looking confused and slightly annoyed.

"You take them straight to the airport, you hear?" Helen said.

"*Si*, of course," she said, and waved at Zoe. "Hey girl! You okay?"

"Yes, Ma'am," said Zoe. "I think so."

The old woman glanced quickly at Zoe, then at Jubilee. She winked at him, grinned, then gunned the van. The platoon waved from the windows as the van jerked an erratic path down the street.

"Will they be okay?" Chrissie asked, leaning against the door frame.

"They'll be fine," said Hassan.

"But those passports – where did they come from? And those

air tickets, how do you know they'll be okay? What if they get caught at security?"

"Scheherazade knows what she's doing," said Fatima.

"That woman," Zoe said to Jubilee. "The taxi driver? She helped me get my apartment."

"What apartment?"

"In Venice. I had a cat, too. Helen." She frowned at Helen. "You. In my apartment."

Helen, seated primly on the edge of the sofa, smiled at her.

"I've met her too," said Jubilee.

Chrissie and Belinda were in a side room, busy with something. Now and again Jubilee heard a sudden burst of laughter. Fatima and Hassan were clearing away the remains of the meal, carrying the dirty dishes into the storeroom. What they did with them there, Jubilee had no clue. He sighed, then leaned back on the curiously comfortable sofa. Seemed little point in worrying over dishes. More important things to consider. Like, how were they going to get home?

The bell jangled. When the old taxi driver stuck her head around the door, the dark scent of tobacco wafted into the store.

"You!" said Zoe. "We were just talking about you."

"*Si*, I know. So I came – better you ask me your questions, no?" She stepped into the store.

"The soldiers? They all right?" Jubilee asked.

"But of course." Carlotta tapped the pipe on the counter, then returned it to her mouth and puffed. Blue smoke rose about her head. "You looking good, girl. Got yourself a nice young man, I see." She winked at Jubilee.

"That suit," Jubilee asked. "The Camo. You gave it to me. Where was it from?"

Carlotta shrugged. "Old woman like me find stuff lying about all the time." She turned to Helen. "Is time. Turn the doors."

"Is it safe?" Helen asked.

GHOSTLY MELODIES

Carlotta shrugged. "Safe? Maybe. Perhaps. Who knows? But is time."

"You're coming with us?"

Carlotta, puffing largely, shook her head. "I have a job to do."

"Inge," said Helen. "You know where she is?"

"She try to hide. Ha!"

"Well, don't be long. We don't know what Evan will do next."

"Oh, we do," said Carlotta and turned to leave. As she opened the shop door, the bell jingled merrily.

"There were three of you," said Jubilee.

"Jubilee?" Zoe asked. "What are you talking about?"

"Old women, at Venice Beach. They gave me that – that suit. The Camo."

"The invisibility suit?"

He nodded. "It was her." He gestured at the door. "The one with the pipe. And ..." he turned to Helen, "you. I think." He frowned, remembering. "You looked different, though."

Helen smiled, but said nothing.

"And someone else. She had an accent. Was she German?"

"Austrian," said Helen, and turned her head, calling: "Chrissie, Belinda. I need you seated. Hassan and Fatima, it's time."

Austria was next to Germany, wasn't it? So, close enough. Jubilee frowned, trying to remember the woman's name.

"Inge," said Helen. "Her name is Inge." She took a small red leather volume from a bookshelf and passed it to Hassan. "*Gulliver's Travels*, isn't that right?"

Hassan nodded, taking the book.

"My grandmother's name was Inge," Chrissie said, coming into the room behind Belinda. "She was Austrian. Why?" she said, catching Jubilee's expression. "What is it?"

"I know you have questions," Helen said to Jubilee. "But now is really not the time. I'm sorry. Listen everyone: Evan may feel our return. You must be on your guard."

"That's why we're in New Zealand?" Belinda asked. "Because it's an island? And Evan can't travel over water?"

"Very good," said Helen.

"And because of this lake," said Hassan, nodding at the open door, where the water sparkled blue-gold in the sun. "That hill you can see there? It's actually an island."

"And on that island," said Fatima, "lies another lake."

"Rings of water," Hassan agreed.

Helen nodded. "An added protection."

"Why do we have to go back?" Chrissie asked. "If Evan's looking for us? Shouldn't we just stay here?"

"Water will not keep him away forever," said Helen. "And we must finish this. Evan must be stopped."

"I don't understand," Belinda said.

"Nevertheless," said Helen and handed the book to Hassan. "Best you all take a seat, I think. This may get a little bumpy."

Somehow, they all managed to squeeze onto the sofa, except for Helen, who settled into the leather armchair and Belinda, in her wheelchair beside her. Helen pushed the brakes on and winked at Belinda as Hassan stood by the counter top, the book in his hands.

"You have this, honey?" Fatima asked.

Hassan opened the book. He thumbed through the gold-rimmed pages, faster and faster, until they formed a fan-shaped gold blur above the open covers. His head, his hands, were still; only the thin pages moved.

Zoe sank into her seat. Her legs and her shoulders felt stuck fast, too weighty and cumbersome to move.

The only noise in the room was the shush-shush of the pages flicking. The others sat, still as statues; even the dust motes floated immobile. Then Zoe caught a flicker of movement out of the corner of her eye and with difficulty, turned her head. It was a butterfly, iridescent blue, flying free.

Abruptly, movement and sound returned, and Zoe felt suddenly lighter. She took a deep breath, relieved to feel her body again.

"Honey? Are you okay?" Fatima asked, one hand on Hassan's shoulder.

He was leaning against the countertop, panting heavily. "I'm fine," he said, gulping. "It's hard work, that's all."

"You did well," said Helen. She took the book from his hands, snapped it closed, and returned it to the shelf.

Going to the shop door, she pushed it open. Outside, the daylight had disappeared, along with the lakefront and the cafes and the passersby. In front of them stood the plastered house of Riccardo King, white against the dawn sky.

"We're home," Chrissie said wonderingly.

"You said Inge was your grandmother?" Jubilee asked.

Chrissie nodded. "She died when I was three." She turned to Helen. "Are we really here? At home?"

Dead? Jubilee remembered the three old women, seated on the park bench, talking to him. But the cop couldn't see them, hadn't even noticed them. He shuddered. Inge, Helen – even Carlotta. They were all *freaking ghosts*! He felt sick.

"Meow," said a small voice, and a silver-gray cat darted out the door.

"Helen!" said Zoe, leaping after her

Jubilee stumbled out the open door. The damp grass was cool underfoot and the soft breeze smelt of pine and jasmine. There, in front of him stood the store, looking for all the world like it had always been there, like it had been built in this grassy clearing. Above its door, picked out in gold letters were the words: *Scheherazade Dreaming*. Behind him, the hills loomed, purple against the lightening sky.

"Jubilee," Zoe called, from the edge of the clearing. "Are you okay?"

He swallowed against the rising nausea. "I don't know," he said, voice drifting like the wind.

He had a sudden nostalgic longing for the army, where the world was logical and rational and could be understood.

"I'm sorry," he mumbled. "It's all just too weird." He backed away.

Jubilee turned and ran, away from the creepiness of the store; away from Zoe and her sisters. They called out, but he ignored them. He was running back to reality, because that was what he wanted.

✵ 42 ✵

RICCARDO DRINKS ORANGE JUICE

INSIDE THE HOUSE, Riccardo is seated at the breakfast bar, drinking orange juice and watching the dawn. As Belinda wheels by, he frowns. He'd hoped Evan might have kept her.

I should be so lucky, he thinks sourly, sipping at his sun-bright juice.

"Hi, Daddy," says Chrissie softly.

"Hey, baby," he says, relieved she's okay. "You have a late night last night?"

She sighs. "You could say that."

"I'm going to bed," Belinda announces.

Zoe rushes into the kitchen. "Anyone seen Jubilee?"

And now Riccardo feels a sudden release. Zoe's back, so now he'll be able to finish the recording. Good thing he didn't cancel the session guys.

"Who? Oh, the bodyguard." Another sip of ice-cold juice. It tastes sweet as sin; he licks his lips. "He'll be in his quarters, I imagine. You gave him that drink?"

She's staring at him like she doesn't know what he's talking about; as though she doesn't remember, or like she's never followed his orders and given the over-muscled idiot the drugged drink.

"The flask," he says. "The drink. Remember?"

"Oh. Yeah. Yeah, he got it."

He lays a hand on her shoulder, it feels warm beneath his fingers, and her flawless brown skin is soft, so soft. He rubs it with his thumb. Zoe shivers at his touch, and bites her lips nervously. God, but she's gorgeous. Nearly as nice to look at as Charley. Charley, who'd run away with this child – his daughter – in her belly, and in so doing made him into a liar.

"You sure you gave him the drink?" he asks.

She nods quickly.

"Good girl," he says, and pats her cheek. She looks away. "So, no problem, then. I know where he is."

"Where?"

"In his room. Asleep."

Her eyes sharpen. "Why? Was there something in that drink?"

"Not at all," he says smoothly, draining the last of the orange juice. "Just, he looked tired is all. But don't let's worry about him. What about you? Are you ready?"

"Me? What for?"

"The musicians, of course. The session guys come today."

"Musicians?" she asks, blankly. "Oh hell! The musicians!"

"Don't tell me – you forgot?" He shakes his head, mock-serious. "Yeah, they're here today. Ten."

"Ten!" she glances at the clock on the cooker. "That's only four hours away." She swallows. "I don't know ..."

"What do you mean, you don't know?" he asks, pressing his thumb harder into her shoulder and felt an obscure pleasure as she winces. "Come on! I need you focused."

"She needs to sleep," says Belinda from the kitchen doorway. In the half-light she looks ugly as a toad. "We all do. Let her go."

Riccardo glares. "Go away. This is nothing to do with you."

"It's okay," says Zoe quickly. "Really. Belinda's right, I am tired. It's been ..." She swallows. "It's been a real long night. Tell you what," she adds, smiling brightly, "how about I have a nap? Say, until nine? Then I'll be okay to play, sing, whatever."

Riccardo glances over his shoulder at Belinda, scowling at him from the doorway. Something in her gaze makes him hesitate and he lets his hand fall.

"Sure. Don't want you too tired, after all." He hesitates, wondering if he should add something about putting her to bed, but Belinda wheels her chair forward and nearly hits him with her footplate, so Riccardo has to step back, and the moment's lost.

43

ZOE AND THE MUSICIANS

"THAT CREEP!" Belinda was so indignant she seemed to be steaming. "You see the way he looked at you?" She pushed her chair angrily along the corridor.

Zoe shook her head; she was way too tired to think straight. They passed Chrissie's door, shut tight. That look on Jubilee's face as he'd left. Like it was all too much ...

"Not leaving you alone with him," said Belinda grimly.

Something scratched at the inside of Chrissie's door. A moment later it opened, and the silver-gray cat eased into the corridor.

"Meow," said Helen, rubbing her head against the wheelchair's front castors.

Belinda bent and patted her. "I'm glad you're here," she said. "You know what Riccardo's like, don't you?"

"Meow." Helen trotted along the corridor, scratched on Zoe's door, and gave her a look: *let me in.*

Belinda let out a sigh of relief. "Perfect."

"But I don't want her on my bed," said Zoe.

"Too bad," said Belinda. "She's your guard cat."

When Zoe opened the door, the cat dashed into her room and jumped onto the bed. Zoe eyed her in irritation. "Don't get too used to it," she muttered. "That bed is mine."

"Zoe," Chrissie said sleepily, from her doorway. "What's with Jubilee?"

Zoe sighed. "I don't know." That look on his face, just before he'd turned away. "I should check he's okay."

"Talk later. Sleep first," said Belinda firmly.

"But, did you see his face? He was totally freaking out."

"Meow," said Helen firmly, and pressed her face against Zoe's.

"Go away," said Zoe, pushing the cat.

"He's a big boy, he'll be fine," Belinda said.

"He's got a friend. Whittaker," Zoe mumbled, settling onto the pillows. Gods, but this mattress was comfortable. When Chrissie pulled the blanket up over her shoulders, she gripped her sister's wrist tight. "Can you call him for me? Promise?"

"Sure," said Chrissie. "I'll do that."

"You got the number?"

"I'll find it. Don't worry. Get some sleep."

The alarm pulled Zoe from a confused dream of purring cars and red-eyed monsters. Her eyes flicked open; she couldn't breathe! Panicked, she pushed aside the sheet. There was a thud.

"Meow!" Helen yowled from the floor.

"Serves you right," Zoe said, and killed the alarm.

She felt weirdly disorientated. How long had she slept for? Cracks of daylight shone through the base of the curtains, and the clock on her phone said 9:30. She stretched, yawned. Only a couple of hours, but still, better than nothing.

The door opened, and Val peeped around the edge of the door. "I thought I should check on you. You sleep okay?"

Zoe nodded. "I guess. Yeah."

"You better get up," Val said, coming into the room and

pushing back the curtains. Zoe winced at the sunshine. "Riccardo asked me to be sure you're awake."

"Can I – do I have time for a shower?"

"Don't be long, okay?"

Zoe stood under the hot water, trying to work out what to do first. Call Jubilee, she thought. That was what she would do first. Check he was okay. But when she emerged from the shower, Val was tucking Zoe's cell into a day bag.

She glanced at Zoe curiously. "What time did you get in?"

Zoe toweled her hair hard. "I don't remember."

"Strange thing," said Val, as they walked down the corridor to the kitchen. "Normally I'd be out late too, you know? I mean, what's the sense in going to bed early? But last night," she shook her head. "I was so tired." She sighed, worry lines creasing her perfect forehead. "I don't know, maybe I'm getting old. What do you think?"

Zoe shrugged.

"True," said Val, "I mean, I am only thirty-five." She tugged open the fridge. "Can I get you some granola? Milk?"

"Thanks."

"They're called Altdim," Val said to the fridge.

"Sorry?"

"The session guys. Short for Alternate Dimension. Here you are."

"Thanks," said Zoe, taking the bowl. "Cool name."

"You're welcome," Val said, and smiled. "Coffee?"

"I'm good thanks," said Zoe, mumbling through a mouthful of cereal. "Hey, have you seen Jubilee? You know, the bodyguard?"

Val shook her head. "Not yet. You want me to tell him you're asking for him?"

"Please. Yes. I'd really appreciate that."

Still feeling half-asleep, Zoe plodded through the house, toward the recording studio. Outside, the bright California sun made the pool sparkle and she paused, watching the ripples ebb and flow in the breeze. Outside, Juan pushed his wheelbarrow along the gravel driveway, the gravel tumbling against the tires. The look on Jubilee's face, yesterday. Zoe pulled her cell from her bag, but Riccardo opened the door to the studio just as she was about to dial.

"Ah! There you are! I was just coming to get you," he said. "Well, come in, come in." He glanced at his watch. "They'll be here soon." He opened the door to the mixing room and ushered her in. "Take a moment to warm up, okay? Once they're here, we'll be straight at it. Session guys charge by the hour."

"Like lawyers?"

He grimaced. "Yeah, kind of."

She played a scale, sang it softly, as he went to the door. Hopefully, she could call Jubilee, check he was okay. She went through her vocal routine, waiting for Riccardo to leave.

Through the open door, she saw a matt black van draw up. On its side, in gothic letters was written *AltDim*.

"Here they are," he said, sounding relieved.

"Yo! Ricky, man!" A short fat man stood on the threshold. "You waiting for us?" He wore a black sleeveless vest and black tattoos etched his arms like scrimshaw.

"Perfect timing," Riccardo said, waving him in. "Tom, this is my daughter. Zoe. Zoe, Tom."

"Well, pleased to meet you, I'm sure," said Tom, waddling forward. His accent was thick Irish and his belly protruded forward over black jeans. Quickly, he grabbed her hand, shook it hard. It felt like shaking a slab of meat. "So, what you got for us, Ricky-boy? Shall I get the lads to set up?

"Yeah, in here, in here," said Riccardo, waving him into the room. Suddenly, the mixing studio felt cramped.

Tom ran a professional eye over the desk. "This new?" He inspected it with a professional eye. "Nice, Ricky. Very nice."

"Thanks."

"Tom? What do you play?" Zoe asked.

"Me?" Tom swung around. "Drums, mostly. Bit of electric guitar. Bit of the keyboards. Bit of everything. But mostly, I'm a drummer boy, so I am." He chuckled wetly. "The little drummer boy, so they call me."

"We getting the others in or what?" said Riccardo irritably.

"Hark at him," chuckled Tom comfortably. "Restless as a tick on a dog." Cupping his hands about his mouth, he bellowed. "HOOI! Youse guys a-comin?" Shook his head. "Pack of slarkarses, pardon me French, love."

As if to make up for the rotund Tom, the other musicians were rake-thin, with scrawny arms and pale, pale skin. Evidently, they spent their life indoors. There were five of them, including Tom, but Riccardo either didn't know their names or couldn't be bothered to introduce them, and Zoe didn't like to ask. There was a guitarist, bass guitar, drums, keyboard, and one who seemed to play everything from sax to flute. She sat on a stool in the corner of the mixing room, watching them set up in the recording studio. They moved quickly, unpacking instruments and setting up music stands like they'd done this a thousand times.

"You want me in there?" she asked Riccardo.

He shook his head, settled himself behind his mixer. "Not yet." Into his mike he said, "Okay. Start with the lullaby."

Through the glass, Tom pulled on a pair of white gloves and raised his drumsticks. "Count off. A one, two, three, four."

The way they took the melody and melded it; it felt like magic, just listening. They ran through the first verse a couple of times, Riccardo adjusting the levels, getting the feel of the sound. When they stopped Zoe realized she was smiling.

"Nothing like the real thing, is there?" Riccardo said, addressing her reflection in the window. He made a rotating movement with his hand and abruptly, the musicians fell silent.

"Well?" he said to Zoe, when she didn't move, "What you waiting for?"

"Sorry," she said, scrambling from the stool.

They began with 'Train Song'. Mom had written it in their traveling days. Zoe remembered Charley beating out the rhythm on her twelve-string as the sparks from the campfire blended with the stars.

"Four bar intro," said Riccardo's voice in her ears. "Country style, okay?"

Tom nodded. The guitarist huddled over his instrument, cradling it gently, and Zoe felt suddenly nervous.

"All good?" Tom said.

She swallowed, nodded. The red light above the window blinked on.

Four bar intro, thud, thud on the drum, sounding like the wheels of the train. The country riff from the bass: *one, two, three, four; ONE-two-three-four*. Then the song kicked in, and Zoe sang from the heart and the gut, country style.

> *Red wheel turning*
> *Gray lines burning*
> *Roll across the desert*
> *All day long*
>
> *Red sun rising*
> *Warm wind coming*
> *Roll across the desert like a song*
> *And it's ...*
>
> *High ho silver and it's*
> *Hunky dory missus and it's*
> *Gun-slinger, gun-runner and it's*
> *Rumor and a wildness and a crazy daisy song*

Red wheels turn
Gray wheels burn
Roll across the desert
In a never-ending song

The sax picked up the melody and played it back to her; she sang with it, and the drum beat fast, Tom's sticks blurring, and pushed the rhythm forward, forward, forward, like the train rolling onward through the desert. For a moment, the song felt like a living thing.

The silence at the end was a letdown.

"Okay," said Riccardo. He cleared his throat. "Right. I want a slide on the bass leading into the chorus. Take the tempo up, rock it a little."

He didn't sound happy or anything; he sounded normal. Zoe wanted to shout at him, did you *hear* that? Did you just hear what happened? But Tom nodded in agreement, like this was expected.

Riccardo cleared his throat. "And punch it more on the down-beat, okay? Just the first verse. When you're ready."

Tom nodded again. "Count-off, one-two-three-four ..."

When they finished the play-through, Riccardo nodded. "Yeah, that's good. Playback?"

"Yes, please," said Tom.

In her headphones, Zoe heard her own voice singing, and blinked in amazement. Something about those musicians ...

"Like it?" Tom asked.

She nodded slowly.

He grinned at her. "We're just getting started. Wait until the boys are warmed up."

"Zoe," Riccardo said abruptly, after the third play-through. "Take five. Rest your voice."

She went into the other room to grab her bag, and stepping into the corridor, dialed Jubilee. *Pick up, pick up.*

A man's voice answered. "Hello?"

"Jubilee?"

"This is Whittaker," said the voice. "Who's this?"

"It's Zoe."

"Zoe? Heck. Look, he's out. He, um, shouldn't be long."

"Is he okay?"

Whittaker's voice was guarded. "Sure. Yeah, he's okay."

"It's just, he was pretty upset."

"So I heard." A sigh. "Don't worry, he'll be fine."

"You sure?"

A pause. "I'll get him to call you, okay? When he gets in."

"I'm recording. I don't know if I can pick it up."

"I'll get him to leave you a message. He'll be back soon enough." He stopped, then added, "Leastways, he darn well better be."

"Okay, can you just tell him I called?"

"Sure."

"And can you say, I'm sorry?"

"Sorry?" said Whittaker. "From what I hear, you ain't got nothing to be sorry about. Your sister, she was pretty clear about that."

"You talked to Belinda?"

"Pretty girl. Dark hair."

"Chrissie?'

"Yeah. She said you'd had a real strange day; real strange week. Worried it might have all gotten too much for our boy. I said I was sure he'd be okay. Much like I'm telling you now."

"Wait – you mean you haven't actually seen him?"

"Look, Johnson ain't made of marshmallow. He's been in active combat, more'n once, and walked out of it okay. Probably he's just gone for a run. Loves his exercise, Johnson does."

"You're his friend, right? You got him this job."

"Yeah, that's right. Your dad, he was looking for a guard for you. But I was busy, yeah? I thought Johnson would be better anyway, I mean, he's closer in age to you an' all. Although," he added, "likely he'd do a better job if he was actually present. Darn it all, where can he have gone?"

"Zoe," Riccardo called. "We're waiting for you."

She covered the receiver. "Just a minute," she called, then added to Whittaker. "I've got to go. Can you try and find him, okay? It's important."

"How? He hasn't got his cell. I'm not the cops; I can't issue an APB."

"There's a store in Venice," she said quickly. "They might know where he is."

"Zoe!" Riccardo shouted.

"A store?" he said blankly.

"It's called Scheherazade Dreaming."

"Sch– what?"

"Look it up," she said. "They've got a website."

"ZOE!"

"I've got to go. Just, please? It could be important."

Whittaker sighed, but she cut the connection before he could say anything.

"About time," said Riccardo, looking annoyed.

"Sorry," Zoe muttered and stuffed her phone into her back pocket.

He shook his head at her, held out his hand. "No phones in here."

"You're kidding," she said.

"Tom," asked Riccardo, through the microphone. "Tell her. Am I kidding?"

Tom shook his head.

"A phone can ruin a take faster than a bung note," Riccardo said, and set the phone on a high shelf, out of her reach. "In you go, sweetie. And sing your pretty heart out."

✣ 44 ✣

JUBILEE IS FIRED

THE KNOCK on the door woke him. Jubilee sat up, yawned, glanced at the clock. Ten a.m. What the hell? Who was coming visiting at this hour? He thrust his feet into slippers and his arms into a bright yellow bathrobe, as half asleep, he stumbled to the door, slid the locks back.

"Mr. Johnson," said Val, perky-blonde on the stoop. "May I come in?"

He blinked at her, rubbed his hair. "Um."

"Thank you," she said, and stepped inside. "Goodness."

"Sorry," he said, clearing up the clothes from where he'd dropped them last night.

Last night! He stopped. He'd had the weirdest dream: something about a lake, and a house, and New Zealand. And then – he frowned. Glanced at the bathrobe. Hadn't that been in his dream too?

"Mr. Johnson? Are you all right?"

Jubilee, realizing he was standing stock-still in the middle of his sitting room, flushed. "I'll be with you in a minute." He gathered up the rest of his clothing, threw it into the bedroom, and made sure his robe was belted tight. "Right. Sorry, you woke me."

"So I see."

She'd pushed back the curtains, and the light (so bright) flooded into the white room. The effect was dazzling. She sat neatly on a sofa, one long leg crossed over the other. Her white t-shirt and jeans were almost the same color as the leather, so for a strange moment she appeared more like a disembodied head than a person.

"Um, can I get you anything?"

She shook her head, ponytail bouncing. "I'm fine, thank you." Uncrossed her legs, shuffled herself forward to the edge of the sofa. "I'm sorry to tell you, Mr. Johnson, that Mr. King no longer requires your services."

"What?"

"You're being let go."

"Why?"

"He's paying you – no, he *was* paying you – to provide a service. And that service does not mean being in a relationship with his daughter."

He flushed. "Look–"

She held up a hand. "I get it. Consenting adults and so forth." Glancing up at him, she smiled faintly. "I understand, believe me. If I were Zoe, well ..." She sighed. "I might just do the same."

He stared. Was she coming onto him?

"But, in point of fact you were expected to keep your hands to yourself. So," she stood up, "you'll have to leave."

"Leave?" he said blankly. "Go where?"

"That," she said, returning to the door – click click went her high heels – "is not Mr. King's problem."

"Does Zoe know?"

"Zoe?" She shook her head. "Not yet."

"Let me talk to her."

"She's busy. Anyway, it's better you don't. It might just upset her." She glanced at her watch. "I want you out of here by close of business."

"Close of business?" he repeated blankly. What the hell did that mean?

"Five o'clock," she said with a sigh. She glanced over at his bedroom, the rumpled sheets and the pile of clothes in the corner. "Look. I'm sorry, I really am. But it's better you leave quickly, and without any fuss."

He felt ridiculous in this bathrobe. "You can't do this."

"You really should read your contract," she said calmly. "I can."

He followed her to the door. "Look, Zoe and me, we kissed. I get that he's annoyed. But, honestly. That's all it was."

"I'm sorry," she said. "But it's enough."

"But Zoe's in danger."

"From you?"

"Of course not," he said. "What do you mean, from me?" His anger was rising now, and he swallowed it back, hard as he could, but he could feel it there, simmering. Keep calm, Johnson, calm. "Someone's after her."

"Who?"

He shook his head. "I don't know. Look, it's complicated. But Riccardo, Mr. King – he knows."

Val hesitated. "You have proof?"

Nothing that I can show you, no. I mean, nothing physical."

"So you have nothing," she said. "I'm sorry, Mr. Johnson, but Riccardo was very clear. You need to be out of here by five."

"Wait," he said.

Val opened the door, and stepped into the bright morning. "Five o'clock," she said and walked away, her white jeans disappearing into the morning haze.

He stood on the stoop, staring after her. "Shit!" he said finally.

His hands balled into fists, and for a moment he was tempted to set off after her. No. Better take it out on a punching bag. Yeah. He'd go down to the poolside gym, clear his head. May as well make use of the amenities, after all. Then he'd decide what to do.

Jubilee jogged lightly along the drive, hurdled the low hedge, and nearly stood on the gardener.

✦ 45 ✦

CAT ATTACK

BY TWELVE THEY'D finished 'Train Song', and Zoe was exhausted. She'd lost track of how many times she'd sung it and was starting to hate the lyrics; she certainly hated the tune.

"Time," said Riccardo, hands in a T. "Lunch. Val's organized food. Remember where the kitchen is, boys?"

"Always remember the food, Ricky," said Tom, and put his arm around Riccardo's shoulders. "Lead the way, Sir."

Riccardo opened the door, ushered them into the hallway. "You go first, I just want to have a word with Zoe."

"Sure, sure," Tom said. "No problem."

Riccardo put his hands on Zoe's shoulders. "How are you holding up, sweetie?"

"Okay," said Zoe. Riccardo felt way, way too close, and there was a look in his eyes that made her deeply uncomfortable. "I'm sorry," she said, "I have to ..."

She was trying to think of an excuse, when there came a shriek from the corridor. It was Tom. "Get it off, get it off me!"

"What the hell?" Riccardo snapped.

Over his shoulder, Zoe saw her cat clinging to the Irishman's shoulder, claws digging in deep.

"Helen!" she shouted. "Let him go!"

The cat gave Zoe an annoyed glance.

Tom flailed at the animal. "Get off!" He lifted his hands, tried to shield his face from the furious cat.

Zoe couldn't move. The man's eyes had changed; for a moment they'd seemed as golden as the cats'.

"Get out of here! Scram!" Riccardo shouted.

Helen hissed, jumped from Tom's shoulder, and darted down the corridor, toward the kitchen. Tom sank to his knees, holding his head.

"Are you okay?" Riccardo said, kneeling beside the stricken drummer. "Tom, are you all right?"

Through Tom's fingers, blood oozed. His voice was muffled. "I'm okay. I think. Yeah, okay."

He removed his hand; blinked, blinked again. His eyes seemed to flicker, and then they were normal; gray, just as they'd been before. "Why the hell did you get an animal like that, Ricky?"

"She's not mine," said Riccardo, helping him to his feet. "She's Zoe's."

"Ah," Tom said, dabbing at the claw marks with a handkerchief. "Is she now?"

"I'm sorry," Zoe said. "Really."

"Think nothing of it." Tom waved his handkerchief in a lordly gesture. "Unpredictable beasts, cats."

Riccardo put a hand in the small of her back, a proprietary action that made her stiffen. "Come on, sweetie. Let's have some lunch." He pushed open the kitchen door. "Ah, Val. Very good. Food?"

"In the dining room, Mr. King. I thought I heard a noise?"

"Cat attack," said Tom.

"Oh," said Val, staring. "Goodness! I'm so sorry. Can I get you a bandage? Some disinfectant, maybe?"

"You're a queen, my sweetheart," Tom said, and placing a hand over his heart, bowed deeply. "Ricky you dog, where do you find these lovelies?"

Val flushed. "Mr. King, do you have a moment?"

Riccardo sighed. "More work, Val?"

"It won't take long."

"Go get something to eat, Tom," said Riccardo. "I'll do my paperwork, and Val here will find you a bandage." He eyed Zoe. "And you, you'd better eat something," he said. "You're looking a bit peaky."

"I should go find Helen."

"Your cat won't be needing you, little human," said Tom. "Take my arm, Princess. Lead me to the banquet."

❧ 46 ❧

JUBILEE IN CAMO

"Soldier, you come, stay with me," said Juan.

"But if Riccardo finds out – won't that make things difficult for you?"

Juan shrugged. "Perhaps; perhaps not. But if you keep from sight, say nothing to Miss Richards, then Senor King will not know. I think you very good at keeping from sight, yes?"

For a moment, Jubilee was tempted to shake his head, say he had no idea what the little man was talking about. The Camo-tech terrified him. Sometimes the real world was hard enough to handle – but the unreal, fantastical place of the Camo seemed governed by rules he could not understand. And the dangers of the Camo were impossible to predict.

Actually, he thought, remembering endless, countless night patrols – danger is always unpredictable. Perhaps I need to learn to live with that, and get on with life.

Jubilee sighed. What the hell. "Sure. I can try."

"So you will stay with me, keep girls safe?"

"Sure. I guess."

After getting rid of Whittaker, Jubilee packed his bags – one thing the army taught you was how to pack – and carried them to the front gate where Juan was clipping the trees at the entrance. Jubilee deposited his rucksack in the man's wheelbarrow, just as the gardener cut a palm leaf that fell neatly onto the bag, hiding it from view. With a wink to Jubilee the little man wheeled the barrow toward another group of palms.

"I'm glad you saw sense," said Val, coming down the driveway. She held out a hand. "No hard feelings?"

Jubilee, wearing Camo beneath his jeans and hoodie, tried to smile. Sweat ran down his back as he took her proffered hand.

Val smiled brightly, insincerely, back at him. "Goodbye. All the best."

She waited for him to step out the gate. As he set off down the sidewalk, he heard it begin to close. He stopped, waited, then turned to see Val walking briskly back to the house.

Juan appeared at the bars of the gate. "Soldier!" he whispered. "Come!"

Jubilee quickly pulled off his jeans and hoodie and pushed them through the gate. Juan stashed them inside his barrow, and activated the gate control. As it slid back open, Jubilee took a deep breath and activated the Camo. As the world faded into gray, he tugged the mask over his face and slipped through the gate, just as it closed.

"Here," said Juan. "For you." Reaching into his pocket, he pulled out a spring-controlled knife.

"Where did you get this?" Jubilee asked. He pushed the button and the blade snapped into position. Turned it, feeling the balance. "Nice."

"E-Bay," said Juan. "You go to girls. Keep them safe."

Jubilee snapped the blade closed, pushed the thing deep into his pocket, then took off, running lightly through the Camo-world, toward the house.

As he drew nearer to the buildings, the Camo-gray thickened, darkening like ink-stained fog, until he could no longer see. He slowed, groping his way forward like a blind man.

"*Meow*," said a small voice. There, near his ankles, a pair of golden eyes gazed up at him, and as he squinted through the gloom, he saw a pelt of silver-gray fur.

"Helen," he said in relief.

The cat set off, running lightly through the murky darkness. Then she paused, glancing over her shoulder, as though waiting for him.

"I'm coming," he said, stepping forward warily.

"Meow!" said Helen imperatively. *Hurry!*

Now she scampered faster, until Jubilee was running to keep up. Sweat stung his eyes; he wiped it away. By his calculations they should have run straight up against the house by now. Jubilee paused. The cat was barely visible, just a dim gray shape in a wide gray world. If she vanished, he'd be alone, lost. Desperately, he sprinted after her.

And stopped.

In front of Jubilee lay a dark barrier that flowed and drifted like smoke. The animal passed through it, but when he tried to follow, dank wetness blocked his way. He pushed harder; the barrier moved sluggishly, enfolding him, so for a heart-stopping moment he was trapped inside. He shoved with all his weight until finally it broke, bursting like a bubble, and he was free.

He stood, breathing deeply, letting the panic subside. He was in a dark room, lit only by a sliver of light from a mirror. He was not alone: beside him were five long-haired, unkempt musicians bent over their instruments. Jubilee crept softly, watching their pale faces. Their long, claw-like fingers moved slowly as they played. Caught in this shadowed half-world of silence, Jubilee couldn't make out the tune.

Gradually, the Camo began to fade. As the black fog thinned and cleared, the musicians changed, morphing into men in jeans and t-shirts. And now, in the middle of the group stood Zoe, singing into a microphone as though her heart would break. He closed his eyes, listening, for her voice was beautiful, warm and fresh. He wanted to reach over, to touch her, but he didn't dare.

> *Oh I'll miss you when you go,*
> *So forgive me if I cry,*
> *Though I know we'll be together,*
> *By and by.*

> *Somehow I'm sure we'll be together,*
> *By and by.*

> *Why have wings if you won't fly?*
> *Why stand staring up at the sky?*
> *Lift your arms, soar up high,*
> *That's how we'll be together, by and by.*

Zoe's skin shone with sweat; she looked vulnerable, dwarfed by the looming figures of the musicians. Caught between Camo and Real, Jubilee felt like a ghost. Possibly, should anyone glance his way, that is how he would appear.

> *Oh, you know how much I'll miss you,*
> *But you know my love is true,*
> *So you know we'll be together,*
> *By and by,*

> *Yeah, I know we'll be together,*
> *By and by.*

Jubilee drifted through the wall and into the next room. This was a sound studio, containing a mixing desk large as an airline console, and flickering computer screens. At the desk sat Riccardo, left hand pressed against his headphones. The room was silent, but Riccardo's lips moved like he was singing to the music.

The song ended. In the studio next door, Zoe sat back on her stool and the musicians stirred, all of them glancing through the window into the sound studio. Jubilee ducked quickly under the recording desk, just in case.

Riccardo cleared his throat. "Okay. We need to go through the bridge again. Tom, I think we need to be punchier on the drums. Can you do that? Bang bang bang and ..."

"Sure," said a deep voice.

"And Zoe, rest your voice. Actually guys, take five. I need a break." Riccardo slipped his headphones off, stretched and sighed.

Jubilee slid back, into the shadows. Riccardo was clearly upset. Tears trickled down his face.

"Taking a piss," Riccardo said, his voice muffled as he stepped into the corridor.

He stood there for a moment, shoulders shaking, and didn't seem to notice Helen sneaking like a shadow through the open door behind him. The animal pranced over to Jubilee. *Go away*, he thought, resisting an urge to kick her.

Helen glanced up at him with golden eyes, almost like she'd heard his thoughts, as Riccardo returned to the room. He was breathing heavily, like a man who'd been running, and his eyes were red.

"All right. You can come out," he said angrily.

Is he talking to me? Jubilee held his breath. Then – *What's that!* A shadow on the wall stirred, and Jubilee froze. The flicker grew stronger; the clamminess of the Camo whispered. Slowly, in the far corner of the room, a dark shape emerged.

Awkwardly, Jubilee crawled back beneath the desk. Helen made a choking noise like a laugh as he settled his back against the wood of the desk, knees bent up about his ears. He felt like a kid in a spooky game of hide and seek.

A gruff voice spoke. "... not yours to make."

"But you've got one," Riccardo said, whiningly. Gone was the arrogant producer; now he sounded desperate.

"You made a bargain," said the darkness.

"And I kept it."

"Huh! Kept it, you say?" It hawked and spat. "*That* for your promises."

Jubilee wriggled about until he found a narrow gap. Now he could see the far corner of the studio, and Riccardo, crouched in his seat at the mixing desk, staring at a black shadow. On his face was a mixture of fear and wild amazement. The shadow moved, until it stood directly in front of the wide mixing desk.

"The boys say this is where you work your magic," said the voice.

Riccardo shrugged modestly. "I try."

"You try?" The shadow shot out a hand like a burned stick, and pocked Riccardo in the chest. "Way the boys say it, you do more than try. You use our magic, Riccardo King, and you twist it, and make it yours. And what do you do with that magic then? You make money with it! Money! That magic of ours makes you rich."

"It's not ..." He shook his head. "That's not why I ..."

"Folk like you, Riccardo King, it's only about money," said the shadow. "You want to get rich, and so you make a bargain. What was the bargain? Shall I remind you?"

"Look," Riccardo said, "I can explain."

"Riccardo?" Zoe's voice was through the microphone. "Are you okay?"

"I'm fine," said Riccardo. "Fine."

"Ha! No, you're not, King. You're talking to yourself. That's what she thinks; that's what she sees. Zoe don't see me here, calling in your debts. If you bargain with the devil, Riccardo, better make sure you pay."

"But I *did* pay," Riccardo said desperately. "I did!" There was a bang on the desk, like a fist thumping, and Jubilee tensed. "You took her! You took my daughter!"

"Sure, we did. But the wrong one."

"I gave you the oldest. As promised."

"Uh-huh," said the shadow. "See now Ricky, that's where you're wrong. Alice wasn't the oldest. That girl in there, she's the one you should have given us."

"You can't take her," Riccardo said, sulkily. "At least, not yet."

"Oh cheer up, we'll let you finish the recording. We're good like that. What do you say, Ricky? Can't say that's not fair?" The claw-like hand poked Riccardo again, and he shuddered. "Don't go all silent on me. I know that's why you've got the lads in. Good idea, really. She's got a great voice. Could listen to it all day."

Click went a switch, and the song filled the room, sung in Zoe's rich voice. *Miss you when you go ...*

"Listen to them," said the gritty voice. "They could be on a record."

"Of course they could be on a record," said Riccardo. "That's what I'm doing."

"Careful, Ricky. Be polite."

"Sorry," he muttered.

"That's okay. No hard feelings. And because we're generous and all, you can have the other back." The shadow moved, jumping like a dark mass onto the desk beside the mixer.

"Do you have to take her?" said Riccardo. He looked like he was about to cry.

"Now, don't be like that. A bargain's a bargain, after all."

Craning his head, Jubilee could make out a finger, like a blade, pushed into the base of Riccardo's neck. "Or would you rather we took you, hey? Mr. King, come to live with us? Yeah, that would be a solution."

Riccardo swallowed, pushed his head away.

"You don't like that, do you?" said the darkness. "Then you'd better give us the girl. What's her name? Zoe?"

"I need more time," Riccardo whined. "We've only done three songs."

"Three? What have you been up to? You've had months!"

"It's Evan's fault," he said sulkily. "He keeps dragging them out dancing, and she's too tired to sing."

"Had to inspect the goods, didn't we? Needed to see if the new one would fit in. And in case she didn't, we wanted to check the others. You've got four daughters, haven't you, unless there are any others we need to know about? You got any other daughters, Ricky?"

Riccardo shook his head. "No. No more daughters. Please, I need more time."

"One day. Got until sundown. So what are you waiting for? Better focus on the recording, Mr. King."

47

JUBILEE TAKES AWAY THE LIGHT

THE CAT JUMPED to her feet, ears pricked as though she'd heard something.

"What is it?" Jubilee whispered as the animal slid slowly around the edge of the room and out the door. "Hey! Come back!"

But she was gone.

Riccardo was still talking. "So if I do this thing, you'll return Alice?"

"Good as new," said the greasy voice. "You have our–" It stopped, and there was the sound of sniffing.

"What is it?" Riccardo asked.

"I can smell ..."

The thing jumped from the desk, landing on the floor with a thud. Jubilee held his breath. Through the narrow gap he could see it: a short, imp-like monster, just like the one in the tree outside Belinda's studio. Its eyes glowed red as it peered into the shadows. Jubilee held his breath, closed his eyes. Again, he heard the sniffing.

"What are you doing?" Riccardo asked.

It held up a gnarled finger. "Quiet!"

Carefully, silently, Jubilee drew his knife. The creature stopped, alert.

"There's nothing," Riccardo said. "You're paranoid."

Metal, Jubilee thought. It's metal they hate. He flicked the blade open.

"Poison," the dark voice said. "I smell poison!"

It crouched, then in one move bounded into the corner behind Jubilee, still under the desk. "Ha! I can smell you, soldier."

It pounced, tearing at his leg; he kicked it in the face. It backed away, hissing, and he scrambled out from his hiding place, knife at the ready. The creature leaped at him, teeth bared, reaching for his head, his neck. A confused impression of red eyes and sharp, sharp teeth. Something ripped, and tore, and there was pain, so sudden and intense that he cried out.

Riccardo shouted. "What's going on? Hey!"

Jubilee stabbed again and again, but it was like stabbing smoke. The creature crouched in front of him, ugly as sin: eyes red, mouth agape. It looked like a gargoyle; like a creature from a nightmare. Jubilee's throat burned. *That smell!*

"Oh, I sees you now," it croaked. "I see you."

Jubilee circled it slowly, looking for an opening. Knife at the ready, watching, waiting. *Only get one chance. Don't screw it up, soldier.*

It licked its lips. "What a scrumptious little meal you'll make."

Jubilee stepped in; his blade stabbed up. But the monster ducked away.

"Think we're easy to kill? Think we're stupid?" It hissed, then jumped, vaulting like an insect; impossibly high. "Huh! We're not like you. We ain't *human*."

"Stop it! I command it! Stop this now!" Riccardo shouted.

But neither Jubilee nor his opponent was listening. The creature fell on Jubilee. Its yellow teeth were knife-sharp and its breath stank of decay. With a grunt, Jubilee stabbed up, and drove the blade hard into the chest, aiming for the heart. It screamed once, before it fell. Blood oozed, black and sticky and smelling like wet tar.

Jubilee stood panting, staring at the creature he had just killed. Dimly, above the pounding of his blood, he heard someone shouting. Putting a foot against the thing's shoulder, he tugged the knife free.

The creature beneath him moved. "We see you now, soldier."

Jubilee stabbed the knife, hard, into its left eye and the monster stopped, frozen.

"Not anymore," Jubilee muttered. "Not seeing anything now."

He wiped the blade on its arm. The gray skin blistered at the blade's touch.

Jubilee peeled back the hood of his suit. He stood in the Real, in the mixing room of a recording studio. The room was in chaos: computer screens had fallen on the floor, a chair spun wildly, and the huge mixing desk was cracked. Where the creature had been, a dark stain was growing. Riccardo sat, crouched beneath the desk, face pale.

Someone thumped a fist on the window to the recording studio: it was the drummer. His mouth moved like he was yelling something, but the soundproofing held. Then the man's eyes, meeting Jubilee's, flickered gold-red, and his lips moved in a sneering curse. He pointed two fingers at his eyes, then at Jubilee: *I see you!*

The drummer began to change: his hair shortened, his frame grew taller, spindlier, his face growing taller, thinner until there, in the recording studio, stood Evan: fae-ruler, child-stealer. Zoe screamed and backed away, but Jubilee couldn't move. Evan smiled, a nasty stretching of his lips that didn't reach his eyes but showed his teeth, and seized Zoe by the hair. She shouted, eyes screwed up in pain.

Jubilee pounded on the window. "Don't you hurt her! You let her go!"

The headphone cable flew from the wall as Evan dragged Zoe across the recording room. She tried to pull away. Guitars fell, music stands toppled and, as Jubilee flung the door open, the cymbals fell with a crash.

Zoe grabbed Evan's hands, tried to get free, but Evan set a long, pointed, razor-sharp fingernail at her throat. "One more move, and there'll be no more music from you, princess." He glanced at Riccardo, half-hidden beneath his desk. "You should have taken the opportunity when you had it."

Riccardo licked his lips. "Evan," he whispered. "I can explain."

"Can you?" Evan asked. "Good."

Zoe made a startled noise, more like a choke than a scream, as blood dripped down her neck. Wide-eyed, she stared at Jubilee, and mouthed, *No*.

"Let go the knife," Evan said.

Jubilee lifted his hands, palm out, and the knife fell with a clatter to the floor.

"Kick it to me."

Jubilee did so, watching, waiting, for the moment that Evan would bend to pick it up, but he just smiled and pressed his hand a little harder against Zoe's throat. His other hand was buried in her black curls, tipping her head back.

"Jubilee," she groaned.

"Zoe," said Jubilee. "Hang on, baby. I'll get you out of this. I promise."

"How sweet. The princess and the soldier are in love," Evan said. He glanced at the chaotic recording studio, at the stained floor and the shattered computer screens and shook his head in mock regret. "Dearie me, Ricky. I really think you need a new cleaner. Now, in light of current events, the terms have changed."

Riccardo swallowed. "Terms?"

"Our agreement. I said you could have her until sundown?" Evan shook Zoe hard, so her head wobbled. "I've changed my mind. She's coming with me. Now."

Zoe's fear-filled eyes stared into Jubilee's, but he couldn't move, not with Evan's hand on her throat.

"You can't," Riccardo panted. His sweating face was pale. "I need her. Got to finish the album."

"Your album? What does that matter? She's your *daughter*, for chrissakes," Jubilee said.

"Exactly," purred Evan. "She is his daughter. His oldest daughter. And she belongs to me." He kissed Zoe on the cheek. She tried to turn away but his hand, still caught in her hair, held her tight. "And what do you know? I think she likes me."

"You leave her alone!" Jubilee shouted.

"Too late," said Evan. "I have her now. But I'm generous, and unlike Riccardo" – he aimed a kick at King, who yelped and shuffled back under the desk – "I'm a man of my word. So he can have the other one back."

"Other one?" Jubilee said blankly.

"Alice. Soldier, *do* try and keep up. It's really not that complicated. Look, I get this one," he shook Zoe slightly, "and he" – another kick at Riccardo – "gets his daughter back."

"But I don't want Alice," Riccardo whined. "I don't even know her. I want Zoe."

"Why? Do you love her?" Evan asked.

"Love?" Riccardo asked blankly. "What are you talking about? That girl," he gestured at Zoe, "has the voice of an angel. A fucking *angel*, man. You know how rare that is?" He scrambled out from under the desk, and got to his feet.

"Of course I do," said Evan, grinning. "And this way, we've got the perfect happy ending!" He whispered into Zoe's ear. "They're the best sort, you know."

"What do you mean, 'happy'?" Riccardo asked. "I'm not happy."

"Sure you are. Alice returns to her loving family, and I" – he stared intently into Zoe's eyes, and whispered – "Oh, I will have music. Every day."

Zoe turned her eyes away; tears rolled down her cheeks.

"Now don't cry honey-bun," said Evan. "After you've gotten to know me, I promise you'll have a wonderful time. You and I, we'll make sweet, sweet songs."

Jubilee's hands balled into fists. Surely there was something he could do? Perhaps if he faded into Camo, he might be able to grab her before Evan could prevent it. But Evan's frowning eyes met his, as though he could tell what Jubilee was thinking.

"I wouldn't," Evan said softly. "Not if I were you." He pushed the fingernail into Zoe's neck, so the skin dimpled with pressure; more red blood trickled down her throat. Evan bent to suck it up.

Jubilee started forward. "You let her go!"

"That's enough!" snapped a woman's voice.

In the door stood Chrissie, and behind her sat Belinda, half-hidden in shadows, and behind them ... Helen, now a silver-haired woman, stepped into the studio.

"Evan," she said. "What are you doing?"

"She's mine," Evan said sulkily. "I was promised the firstborn. Ricky owes me."

"Zoe has no quarrel with you."

"Oh, and I suppose you'd have me let Alice go, too."

Helen walked over to the mixing desk, ran a finger lightly along the crack in its frame. Belinda wheeled into the room behind her.

"Son, you have a right. I acknowledge this."

Evan nodded tightly.

Jubilee was watching Evan closely, waiting for his guard to slip. Because everyone slips, eventually. But Evan glanced in his direction, a clear warning in his eyes. "Don't you try it, soldier. Do not push me."

The guitarist and the keyboardist had been so quiet that Jubilee had nearly forgotten them. But now, glancing their way, he saw – they too had changed. Like Evan, they'd grown taller, and sported the all-too-familiar golden eyes. They were watching Jubilee intently, like they were ready for him should he try anything. But they'd be slowed by the doorway. Perhaps he might have a chance. If he could reach the knife in time.

Helen glanced in his direction, her eyes hard, *Keep still!* as Belinda slid from her wheelchair and landed on the floor behind Evan's feet. In her right hand was a can of spray paint.

"Ah, the cripple," said Evan. "What, you offer yourself in exchange?"

Belinda shook the can once, twice, and sprayed a black circle on the carpet in front of Evan. The smell was bitter and chemical and made Jubilee want to cough.

Riccardo got to his feet. "What the hell! Belinda! That's my carpet."

She ignored him, and filled in the circle with more paint until it was solid black. The paint gleamed wetly in the lights of the studio but its odor had changed, becoming mustier; damper.

That's Camo, Jubilee thought. *I smell the Camo.*

Belinda began painting swirls around and around the wet, black circle, making a little whirlpool; a vortex of black.

"Belinda," Riccardo said, "Stop! Or–"

But before he could say anything else, Helen pushed him on the chest.

He stepped back in surprise. "What the hell?"

She pushed him again, harder.

He backed away from her. "Stop it!"

But she pushed him again. Already off-balance, Riccardo staggered. Tried to regain his footing. Arms whirling, he spun clumsily. Then he tumbled to the floor, landing in the center of Belinda's black circle. But instead of sprawling inelegantly, Riccardo tumbled, screaming *into* the hole; passing through it and away, into the dark. Legs kicking, hands groping for balance, he plummeted down, down, down.

Jubilee swallowed and quickly shuffled back from the painted circle. Tried not to watch as all the while Riccardo disappeared, falling deeper into the Camo.

"You made a bargain, Son," Helen said to Evan. "The daughter for the father. I've given you the father. So your bargain has been fulfilled."

Evan gazed into the hole with a look of disgust. "I don't want him. I wanted *her*."

"Nevertheless," said Helen. She lifted Evan's hand off Zoe's neck and smiled at his irritated face. "What? You think you'll always get what you want?"

"Well yes. Of course," he said.

Zoe stumbled forward. Jubilee grabbed her in case she too might vanish down that hole. He held her close, arms about her. She was trembling.

"It's okay," he murmured. "I've got you. You're safe."

She clung to him, and her tears wet his face, and he never ever wanted to let her go.

Riccardo, no larger than a speck, was still falling.

Evan made a face. "And he's not even pretty."

"But he can teach you how to make your own music. You've got plenty of talent," Helen said, gesturing at the band members who stood in the doorway, just watching. They ducked their heads, seemingly reluctant to meet her gaze. "You only need the inspiration."

Evan heaved a philosophic sigh. "And Alice? Can't I keep her? Please, just one?"

Helen shook her head. "No. I have plans for Alice."

"All right, all right," said Evan. He glanced at Jubilee, still embracing Zoe, and his gaze hardened. "You!"

"That's enough." Helen interposed herself between them.

"Mother! He killed my man."

"It was self-defense," Helen said.

Jubilee nodded. "He was coming for me. I had no choice." In his arms, Zoe quivered, and he kissed the top of her head. "It's okay; it's okay."

Evan was still looking longingly at Zoe.

Jubilee felt a rush of rage. "Don't you dare. You leave her alone." He let go of Zoe, and suddenly the knife was there, in his hand. "You come for me – I do the same."

"Is that a bargain?" asked Evan, his face brightening.

"I don't bargain."

"Ooh, a threat," Evan said, delightedly.

"Don't you get it?" Jubilee asked. He stepped forward, blade pressed hard against Evan's throat, all in one smooth action. "I don't bluff. I don't bargain. I tell you as it is."

Evan swallowed, then nodded, stepped back. His eyes never left Jubilee's as he raised his hands, palms up. Slowly, Jubilee lowered the knife.

On the floor, Belinda's spray can was empty. She shook it a few times, but there was only a sputtering hiss. She tossed it into the waste bin and held up a hand to Chrissie. "Help me up, will you?"

Once back in the chair, she raised an eyebrow at Evan. "What do you think of my art, fairyman?"

Evan gazed at her thoughtfully, eyes narrowed. "I had discounted you as an option. Seems I was wrong."

"An option? For your harem?"

Evan looked taken aback.

"Don't tell me – you discounted me because – why? I'm a cripple? I'm in a wheelchair?"

He nodded. "As I said: I was wrong."

"Ooh, I bet that's a first."

"Yes," he said seriously. "I am not often wrong."

"Big of you," she said. "Well, sorry to disappoint, but I'm not going with you."

"No-one is going with him," said Helen sharply. "The debt is paid."

Evan sighed mournfully. "I liked the other one too. What's her name? The little designer?"

"You can't have me," said Chrissie, from behind Belinda's chair.

"No-one's having anything," Helen said.

"That's a shame," said Belinda. "I kind of like the idea of getting me a bit of fairy." When Evan stared at her, she raised her hand. "It's okay. I'm just kidding."

He laughed. "Cripple-girl, I like you."

"She's not yours," Helen said.

"Nevertheless," Evan said, "there's no rule that says I can't offer them assistance. If they need help." He brightened. "And there is precedence."

"Precedence?" Helen asked suspiciously. "What are you talking about?"

"You should know, Mother. Being one yourself. A fairy godmother." He snapped his fingers. "Yes! I'll be a fairy godmother. No. Not a godmother. A god*father*." He smiled brightly. "Evan, the fairy godfather."

Belinda laughed.

"What's so funny?" Evan asked suspiciously.

"Makes you sound like mafia," Belinda said. "*Gay* mafia."

The dank, metallic smell of Camo had faded slightly, but Jubilee could still feel it, close by. Helen took Evan by the shoulders, turned him around. "You'll leave them be. They already have fairy godmothers. They don't need anyone else."

Evan snorted. "What? You?"

"No. Not just me." She leaned closer, whispered into his ear.

"So, if you're tempted to get close to them again, just remember, Son – it's not just me that's watching."

"Who?"

"Inge," she said, and he swallowed, and went a little pale. "Yes, exactly. So don't you mess it up, son. Be content with little Riccardo and his music, hey?"

He shrugged nonchalantly. "Still. I'm allowed to look. I won't hurt them." Evan turned to the girls, Belinda in her chair, Chrissie behind her and Zoe, resting in Jubilee's arms. "Ladies," he said with a bow, "If you ever need anything, just let me know."

"And what will we have to give you in exchange?" said Belinda. "Our firstborn?"

"I'm a reasonable person," said Evan defensively. "I'm happy to negotiate."

"That's enough," said Helen. "You're not having anything from any of them."

"Yet," said Evan, and stepped into the hole.

Unlike Riccardo, he didn't fall. Instead, he sank slowly, until his shoulders were level with the floor. It was the weirdest thing, Jubilee thought. He felt a moment's thrill. This was real magic, and he was here to see it.

"When you see my brother, say hello," said Evan to Helen. "When's he coming to visit me?"

"It might be a while," Helen said. "Fatima's not up to traveling now."

Evan glanced sharply at her. "Oh-ho. Like that, is it?"

"And don't you go offering them anything, either," said Helen sharply. "I'm not having my first grandchild beholden to its uncle."

"Mother," he said mockingly. "I never dreamed." He tipped his head sideways to the rest of the band. "You coming?"

"What about him?" said the lead guitarist, speaking the first words anyone had heard him say. He nodded at the dark stain on the floor, where the creature lay. "Can't just leave him."

"Oh. Yeah, yeah. Sure. Push him in."

They tugged and heaved at empty space, but Jubilee knew this was the body of the monster, and with a grunt tipped it into the hole. Evan watched his soldier fall with a glum expression.

"I'm sorry for that," said Jubilee.

Evan's eyes were hard, but he shrugged. "Got plenty more."

The band members jumped into the hole and disappeared head first, falling into the dark. Evan waved at them, disappeared, then bobbed upward like an apple, head reappearing.

"Forgot to say," he said to Zoe. "You've got a great voice, kid. A pleasure playing with you. Any trouble getting a record deal, you let me know."

Helen stamped her foot. "Evan!"

"Okay, okay," he said, holding up his hands. "I'm going; I'm going."

And there was a blink, and he was gone. Zoe knelt beside the hole and ran a hand across its surface. She smiled, held up her hand. Her palm was covered in black paint.

❧ 48 ❧

A RETURN

"Meow," said a small voice.

The sisters glanced at each other and laughed. Zoe picked up her cat and rubbed her face into its silver-gray fur.

"There you are," Zoe said. "I've missed you."

Helen struggled out from her arms and dropped to the floor, and they followed her into the corridor. Faintly, they heard the doorbell ring. Through the window they could see, on the front doorstep, a slim girl standing alone. Well, not exactly alone. She seemed to be surrounded by a flickering, glistening cloud of butterflies. Behind her stood Juan, smiling.

Val opened the door. "Hello. Can I help you?"

"Sorry to bother you," said the girl.

"Alice!" Zoe shouted, and took off at a run. "It's Alice!"

❧ III ❧
AFTER

✄ 49 ✄

IN WHICH THERE IS A HAPPY
ENDING

ZOE HAD NEVER ASKED a guy if he'd like to move in with her, so she wasn't sure of the etiquette. In the end she asked it, directly, just like that. At first Jubilee said nothing, just lay staring at her.

"I mean," she said nervously, picking at the sheet, "if you want to?"

"Want to?" He kissed her, hard. "Girl, that would be ..." He paused. "Look, you sure you want this?"

She nodded. "Definitely." She crossed her fingers for luck, because she did, oh she did.

"Then yeah. Of course."

She couldn't stop smiling, but it faded as Jubilee raised a finger. "I've one condition."

She swallowed. "What? What is it?"

He indicated the mattress they were lying on. "Please, can't we have a bed? No more sleeping on the floor?"

She laughed and nodded. And later they went shopping for a bed.

Zoe didn't care that the apartment was small. After all, she'd been raised in a camper, and anyway, better by far to live in a small place with someone who made her happy than in a mansion with a father who barely knew her. Besides, outside lay the sand and the sea and the beach was plenty big enough for the two of them.

Over the next few months they settled in. Zoe bought house plants and bed linen and filled the two-roomed apartment with color. Juan helped Jubilee build a potted garden on the roof terrace, and they grew tomatoes and squash and fragrant herbs. Zoe started studying recipes and taught herself to cook. Surprisingly, she found she loved making food. Jubilee enjoyed it too, although he complained she was making him fat.

After a lot of thought, Zoe simply called the album *Charley*. After selling the Mercedes, she had enough funds for Val to manage the remaining production on the album and Val, who seemed to be relishing the chance to use her business degree, was cautiously optimistic about its future. But secretly Zoe hoped it wouldn't be too much of a hit. She wasn't ready for the attention that went with success, and anyway, there was the whole thing about wanting to be her own artist. But for Mom's sake she wanted it to do well, so there she was, torn.

Belinda had told her to chill, that she should focus on making art for art's sake, but that was easy for Belinda to say. It wasn't Belinda's voice that people listened to.

"Let's have the girls over," she said, after they'd been together for three or four months. It was fall, so the days were getting shorter, but the weather was still California-warm.

Jubilee raised a lazy eyebrow. "You think there's room for your sisters?"

"We could get some folding chairs."

He yawned. "Sure. Let's have them over."

"I'll make pasta." She planned to make the dough from raw ingredients: eggs and flour.

"And I'll order takeout," Jubilee said.

"*Takeout!*" she squealed, and threw her book at him.

He grinned. "Never hurts to have a back-up."

"You," she warned, "are on washing-up duty."

Zoe bought sunflowers for her sisters and set them in an old Mexican vase. The light from the open window fell onto the petals and made the room glow.

"Looks good," said Jubilee from behind her.

He put his arms about her waist, and she leaned back on his broad chest. They stayed that way for a moment, savoring each other's presence. She could hear the soft thud-thud of his heart and feel the gentle rise and fall of his chest. At night she'd lie with her head on his chest, and fall asleep that way.

"You don't think it's too much? I don't want them to think I'm trying too hard, you know?"

He laughed. "A bunch of sunflowers isn't trying too hard. Anyway, are you doing it for you, or for them?"

"For me," she said.

"Oh that's nice," he said. "Real nice. What about for me, eh?" He tickled her in the ribs. "Not very thoughtful."

"Stop it," she said, laughing, and twisted away, nearly tripping over the cat.

Jubilee kissed her mouth, then her neck, and slid his hands around her waist. "You taste nice," he mumbled into her lips. She swayed toward him, and there was a moment of silence in the bright little apartment, until the pot on the stove boiled, spilling tomato-scented sauce onto the floor, and they had to wipe up the mess.

In the afternoon she concentrated on kneading the pasta dough, while Jubilee beat eggs for the cake.

"I heard from Whittaker today," he said, frowning at the whisk. "Offered me a job."

She wiped hair from her eyes. "Doing what?"

"Personal security. He's picked up a contract with a studio."

"You interested?"

"I don't know. What do you think?" he asked, glancing at her. "You've got flour on your face." He tapped her nose. "Cute."

"Personal security? So, is it dangerous?"

He shook head. "I doubt it. Whittaker says it's a matter of standing about and looking intimidating."

"You want this?"

"I think so, yeah. Will be good to have a regular job again."

"So long as you don't fall in love with one of those actresses."

He set the whisk down, put an arm about her shoulder and kissed her softly. "Hey, no danger there. I promise you that."

She kissed him back, and they took a cooking break.

"How's Whittaker?" she asked, much later. Funny, how she'd got into the habit of calling his friend by his surname.

"He's good, yeah. Stopped drinking. Guess Teena helped him see sense."

"This job – it's a change for you," she said seriously.

Jubilee had never been one for settling down. Somehow, she thought he'd be as likely to drift out of her life as he'd drifted into it. She'd dreaded the day. Now, she felt a weight lifting from her shoulders at the thought he might stick around.

He knew what she was getting at, of course. "Guess I've had enough of moving on," he said, and grinned at her. "Kind of nice, having roots."

"Yo!" It was Belinda, shouting loudly into the speaker. "You going to help me up these fucking stairs?"

Chrissie giggled. "Sorry about her language."

Jubilee went down to help and returned carrying Belinda in his arms. Chrissie, balancing a bottle of wine, her purse and a folded wheelchair, followed. She was dressed in a sundress with a flower pattern and her shiny dark hair was caught in a bun, high on the top of her head. She looked amazing.

"What you want to do, getting a house with stairs?" Belinda demanded.

"Blame Helen," said Zoe.

Chrissie set the bottle on the table, and unfolded the wheelchair. "Where is the cat, anyway?"

"Gone out," said Jubilee, depositing Belinda. "Just as well. Zoe nearly stood on her."

"Thanks, soldier-boy," Belinda said, rubbing his arm. She smiled wickedly at Zoe. "I can see why you like him – all those muscles."

"He's mine," she said. "Hands off."

Belinda laughed.

"You expecting someone else?" Chrissie asked, eyeing the vacant place setting.

"I thought Alice might turn up."

"You invited her?"

"I tried," said Zoe. "But she doesn't have a cellphone, right? And it's not like I can send her an email, or a letter. I kind of hoped Helen might tell her something, so," she lifted her hand, "fingers crossed. You two know how to reach her?"

"She stays over, sometimes. Sleeps in your old room," Chrissie said. "I hope you don't mind. Val thought it would be okay."

Val had leased the music studio out to labels and put the gatehouse onto Airbnb. She was threatening to lease the cars to Uber drivers; Zoe was glad she'd sold the Mercedes before Val had had *that* idea. Val's latest dream was to start a vineyard, but Juan was trying to talk her out of it. He had his own projects, too; he'd started a community garden, the talk of the area. Val was encouraging him to sell his produce into local cafes, but Juan wasn't interested. He just wanted to feed people.

"It's fine," said Zoe. That room had never felt like hers, anyway.

"Alice hangs out in the studio with me sometimes," said Belinda, seizing a carrot stick and heaping hummus on it. "She comes out to the project with me too."

"Project?" Jubilee asked.

"You know. The old factory," Zoe said, and Jubilee nodded.

"So, are we going to eat?" Belinda asked eagerly. "I'm starving."

"Oh, yeah. I forgot," said Zoe, and turned on the stove.

"You only starting cooking *now*? Isn't that, like, leaving it a bit late?"

"It's pasta," Zoe said. "Best cooked fresh."

"Pasta? Isn't that full of carbs?" Chrissie asked.

"Oh, chill out," said Belinda, and threw a carrot stick at her. "Anyone would think you lived in *Beverly Hills*."

While the water heated, Zoe carefully fed the dough through the pasta maker. She felt ridiculously relieved when the tortellini came out perfectly. Chrissie and Belinda watched, fascinated. Good thing she'd practiced in advance.

Chrissie picked up one of the tortellini strands. "What's in this?"

"Eggs, flour, salt."

"That's it?"

"Yup."

"Wow," she said. "It looks amazing. So easy!"

Jubilee winked at Zoe. "Real easy." He'd eaten the many failures.

"And *voila*," said Zoe, and dropped the tortellini into the boiling water.

"It's like magic," said Chrissie, as the noodles whitened.

"It's just cooking," said Zoe, lifting the pasta into a sieve. She drained them quickly and deposited them in a bowl just as the door buzzed.

Jubilee pushed the speaker button. "Hello?"

Static on the speaker. He frowned at it.

"Jubilee?" Zoe asked. "Is it okay?"

"I'll go and check," he said.

"What if ..." She bit back the words: What if it's Riccardo? What if it's *Evan*?

"Take this," said Belinda, peeling off the iron-studded leather band from around her wrist.

"Thanks," he said, and headed downstairs, slipping it over his wrist as he went. Zoe heard the door open, and a low murmur of voices.

"Helen tell you anything? About Evan?" Chrissie asked softly.

Zoe shook her head. "She's been on cat time."

"What about Fatima?"

Zoe shook her head. "I don't like to ask. She's so huge now."

"Look who I found," Jubilee said, pushing the door open.

"Hey!" Belinda said. "It's Alice!"

A butterfly drifted past, fluttering into the room, as though checking it out. Then Alice smiled and stepped inside and Jubilee closed the door.

Belinda wiped a finger around her bowl. "This is really good. Oh hey, have I told you? I'm going to Australia." She licked pasta sauce from her finger.

How would Belinda cope with travel from a wheelchair? Then Zoe smiled at herself: probably there were people in wheelchairs overseas. And Belinda would manage just fine. "Are you meeting your mother?"

"Perhaps," Belinda replied. "But that's not why I'm going – I just want to see the world a bit, you know? I thought I'd go to Australia, then onto New Zealand. I liked what we saw of it, that time."

"I'll miss you," said Chrissie sadly.

"I know, honey, but you'll be fine," said Belinda, taking her hand. "You've got your work. And there's Val. And Juan."

"And me," said Alice, softly.

"I know," Chrissie replied. "But it's not the same."

"You must be careful," said Alice to Belinda. "You create ..." Alice frowned, as though searching for the right words. "Doorways. Yes. Things can pass either way, through a door."

"You think I might let something in?" Belinda said. "Do you mean Riccardo?"

Alice paused, eyes distant, as though thinking. "I do not think he will ever return. Unless Evan gives him leave. And I doubt he will do that."

"Is that how you reached us?" Zoe asked. "Coming through her doors?"

"Hers and others. But I could only journey in small, tiny pieces. I slipped into the world slowly, one piece at a time. That way Evan did not notice."

"You mean the butterflies?"

Alice nodded. "Although now I can come and go as I wish. You could say – I make my own door."

"What about Camo," asked Jubilee. "Does that make a – a doorway?"

Alice looked puzzled. "Camo? What is that?"

"I have a special ..." he paused, "cloak. Yeah, like a cloak. It makes me ... invisible, I guess."

"Ah." She nodded, then laughed. "So, that was how you did it? You made him very angry."

"Do you miss Evan? His world?" Zoe asked, then bit her lip. She was prying. "I'm sorry, I have no right to ask ..."

"I don't mind. Do I miss him? No. Not at all."

"I thought I'd miss Dad – Riccardo – but I don't," said Chrissie.

"It's a relief he's gone," said Belinda.

Chrissie nodded. "Riccardo, he wasn't always ... kind."

Belinda snorted. "That's for sure."

"But you will take care?" Alice asked Belinda.

She shrugged. "I guess."

Jubilee got to his feet. "Right. Anyone for dessert?"

Belinda's eyes lit up. "Dessert!"

"Jubilee made it," Zoe warned. "Just so you know."

"Gee, thank you so very much," said Jubilee.

Zoe laughed. "Don't worry, I'm sure it's fine." She stage-whispered behind her hand, "I checked it before he put it in the oven."

Belinda and Chrissie laughed, and Alice smiled brightly. Butterflies drifted around the room like golden snowflakes.

"This is nice," said Belinda, glancing around the table. "I like this. Being a family, I mean." She raised her wine glass. "How about a toast? To families."

They lifted their glasses. "To families."

ALSO BY R. L. STEDMAN

The SoulNecklace Stories:

A Necklace of Souls

A Skillful Warrior

A Memory of Fire

A Long, Long Life (A Novella)

The SoulNecklace Stories - Box Set

Stand-Alone:

Inner Fire

The Prankster and the Ghost

Short Story Collection:

Upon A Time

The Dancing Princesses:

Alice - A Short Story

Ghostly Melodies

Pictures in Time

Threads of Enchantment

ABOUT THE AUTHOR

My name is Rachel Stedman, and I write as R. L. Stedman. I live in the wild and windy place of Dunedin, New Zealand, with my husband and sons.

In 2012 I won the Tessa Duder Award for an unpublished YA work and my first novel, *A Necklace of Souls,* was published by HarperCollins in 2013. *A Necklace of Souls* was awarded Best First Book at the 2014 New Zealand Post Book Awards.

If you enjoyed this book, please do leave a review, as reviews help other readers discover great stories.

Find me at:
www.RLStedman.com

ACKNOWLEDGMENTS

Writing a book is an enormous amount of work, and I couldn't have finished *Ghostly Melodies* without help.

Heartfelt thanks to my patient husband and sons, who seem to cope with my mental lapses when I'm working my way through plot tangles.

My workmates, who only occasionally worry that they'll make their way into a book. I couldn't write that story, guys, because no-one would ever believe it.

My editor, Sue Copsey, who's always encouraging and the many, many writers who've offered assistance on this journey.

Thank you to the many and varied recording artists who have shared their craft so generously. The world is a better place because of you.

My reader, Stephen, who donated his name to a character in return for providing the title of the book. Thank you so much, Stephen. And a runner up, Myla – you also made it into the story, as I was very taken by your suggested title: '*The Voice of Magic.*'

And finally, a very special thanks to you, my readers, for

reaching the end of this book! Please keep reading – there's a couple of extra bonuses right at the end.

ALICE

A SHORT STORY

If you want to learn more about Fatima, Helen and the mysterious store, then you might enjoy *Alice, A Short Story*.

More information on *Alice* is available on my website: www.rlstedman.com

🎼

"There was a sign on the door (hand written in black ink copperplate script). Going closer, she read: 'Open until Closed'. With a mental shrug, Fatima turned the handle. Somewhere in the dim recesses of the store a bell jangled, and jangled again, when she closed the door behind her against the cold.

Inside felt delightfully cozy. Glass lamps, inlaid in rich colors, hung from the ceiling. Two old, cracked leather chairs were set against an overfull bookcase, and more books were piled in the windowsill, pressing against another lamp, the golden lettering on their spines reflecting the light.

The place was quiet, save for a fire crackling happily on the hearth. Fatima held out her hands to its warmth. The place smelt of musk and mystery and appeared more a library than a store. Or perhaps it was a bookstore ... "

WANT MORE?

GRAB A FREE STORY COLLECTION

Do you love fairytales? Then escape into enchantment in *Welcome to Faery*, my FREE story collection.

Just copy and paste this link into your browser:
https://bookhip.com/VHJFPS

www.ingramcontent.com/pod-product-compliance
Lightning Source LLC
Chambersburg PA
CBHW031437240626
47154CB00001B/303

* 9 7 8 0 4 7 3 4 5 6 5 0 4 *